# Prince
# of Snakes

### By
### Tom Towslee

PublishAmerica

Baltimore

First printing

ISBN: 1-59286-286-1
PUBLISHED BY PUBLISHAMERICA BOOK PUBLISHERS
www.publishamerica.com
Baltimore

Printed in the United States of America

*This book is dedicated to Jerry and Eileen.*
*God bless you both.*

# ACKNOWLEDGMENTS

Thanks to everyone who gave me support and advice in writing this book. Especially Nancy, Rob, Marla and Jeff for reading endless and ever-changing drafts. To Debra, who made me believe that writing is its own reward. To Jerry Baron, who introduced me to the giants of mystery writing and taught me to never be afraid to write. To the late Vince Kohler, who made me believe that I could get a book published. To my agents, who believed in this book and never gave up.

# Chapter 1

Proctor Scofield turned his attention from the dull-brown landscape twenty-thousand feet below to his secretary. Her child-like mannerisms, flat chest, and Shirley Temple hair fascinated him. Even from ten feet away, she smelled like talcum powder and bubble bath. Her high-pitched voice and tendency to use phrases like "oopsy-daisy" and "itsy-bitsy" only heightened his interest.

He'd hired her six months earlier, even though she didn't know how to use a personal computer, send a fax, or forward a telephone call. She was probably a virgin, he thought, tight as she was stupid, not that it mattered. Scofield figured she'd be ready after one more business trip to Paris or Rome. His tried-but-true plan of slowly winning trust by buying harmless little gifts and acting interested in such things as clothes or makeup would pay off again. With the seduction complete, she'd be conquered like the others. Then, he'd hustle her off to a comfortable job with one of his subsidiaries and the search for her replacement would begin. She would have given up her virginity for an office job in Bangkok and never know what happened or why.

When she turned to look at him, Scofield gave her a soft, noncommittal smile before looking away. Yes, he thought, she's coming along nicely. Gone were the looks of apprehension that haunted her pale, oval face for the first weeks after he hired her. In their place were long gazes filled with awe and trust. The hunt was nearing its end. After finding and tracking her, he felt oddly disappointed as he contemplated the conquest. The older he got, the more fun the hunt became, the less satisfying the trophy.

Scofield looked out the window again, the scene below familiar after countless plane trips along the same route. They were somewhere over Idaho. Ahead lay the Snake River that marked the Oregon-Idaho border.

At one time he'd gazed down from the coach section of cramped commercial airliners heading east, then back west again. When the office supply business he'd started in the late 1960s boomed during the formative years of the high-tech industry, he eagerly moved up to first class. After that came chartered jets. But for the last ten years, he'd traveled the world in a succession of increasingly expensive and well-appointed Lears, Gulfstreams, and finally the Citation X. The fifteen-million-dollar price tag paled when compared to the thirty-million dollars on the Global Express by Bombardier or the Gulfstream V, but he still preferred the Citation X with its intimacy and speed.

Along the way, what eventually became Scofield Industries had grown, diversified, gone public, and prospered beyond his wildest dreams in the most robust economy of his lifetime. There were homes, cars, office buildings, employees, businesses, and subsidiaries of businesses. The company that started in a storefront on the east side of Portland now ranked in the top fifty of the Fortune 500. His personal net worth put him somewhere near the top of the Forbes 400. There was so much, he didn't even think about it anymore. Anything he wanted was his.

Scofield fidgeted in his seat, anxious to end the week-long trip with its stops in Mexico, Brazil, and Miami. The flights were becoming more tedious. Viewing the world from four miles up was never that exciting, but had become tortuous at seventy years of age. Unlike most men his age, who had abandoned work for golf, Proctor Scofield could never imagine himself sitting around a country club playing gin and trading stories about monster putts and unlikely pars. While his hair turned white long ago, he still had most of it. A low-fat diet and a little exercise seemed sufficient to avoid the flab accumulated by his peers. Not that weight had ever been a problem. He'd been thin all his life; frail actually, which meant that as a young man he compensated for his lack of size by pouring all his energy into learning about business and how people accumulate wealth. It had paid off nicely. Still, he could stand to lose a few more pounds, but that would mean quitting drinking. He wasn't ready for that yet.

Lately, however, the quest for power and wealth that once consumed him was fading. His reputation as the predatory mystery man of high-tech lingered more as myth than reality. A small team of discreet and efficient vice presidents, accountants, and executive assistants did most of the real work. His role had become little more than telling them what he wanted, then showing up in the corporate jet at the end to shake hands and sign the papers. He rarely got off the plane. If he did, it was disguised as a pilot so he could indulge himself in local pleasures arranged by the same discreet and efficient people. There were no speeches, cover stories in national business magazines or testimony before Congress. Since he didn't meet the press on the way up, he wouldn't have to deal with them on the way down. He liked it that way.

He thought again of his secretary, who was moving down the aisle looking for a magazine. The details of leveraged buyouts and hostile takeovers had been replaced by fantasies about her and others like her. Wealth granted him unfettered access to people and places. The promise of intimate nights with a succession of younger and younger women was quickly becoming the sole motivation for each wearisome flight. Memories of nights in Hong Kong or Paris made him stir in his seat. He glanced back at his secretary, now diligently working on some useless document. So hot with promise compared to the icy predictability that awaited him at home.

It didn't take long for his thoughts to turn to his daughter. It amazed him how often and under what circumstances he thought of her even after twenty years. Getting out of the shower or reading the paper, her face would suddenly appear in his mind's eye.

He shook her image out of his head.

The secretary tapped him gently on the shoulder.

"This fax just arrived," she said, looking directly into his eyes.

She let her delicate fingers linger on the soft skin above his open shirt collar. Scofield ignored the gesture, but sucked in the scent of her baby powder.

The fax was as straightforward as the person who wrote it. "Mission accomplished. May have a problem. M."

The message jarred Scofield, making his temples start pounding out the familiar beat of an approaching headache. He didn't like problems. No one on his staff knew that better than the man who sent the message. "I'll call him from home," he said, folding the fax in half and laying it down on the seat next to him. The secretary paused as if waiting for an invitation to join him for the rest of flight. She quickly left when he turned his attention to the window again.

The fax cut to the heart of a subject that had always held a morbid fascination for Scofield. Politics came with the territory. He initially abhorred the idea of squandering even the smallest amount of his wealth on politicians, but gradually he'd come to relish the role of back-room power broker almost as much as the patient stalker of young women.

His initial observations of what motivated politicians had held up over the years. They fell into two general categories. First were those who clamber for the limelight and notoriety to feed some deep, inner need. Second were those who had some narrow agenda rooted in either the Bible or some insane economic notion about how best to force the rich to help the poor. The third group who actually believed in the nobility of public service were too few to be taken seriously.

But whatever drove people to run for public office, it made men like him indispensable. There wasn't a politician alive who didn't want access to his fortune and his connections. The way they coveted even the smallest of campaign contributions made treating them like rats in a maze with his money as cheese all that more enjoyable. Just wait until they see what I've really been up to, he thought. Not that anyone will ever know.

Scofield settled back into the soft leather seat. The gentle vibration of the powerful jet engine took the edge off his impatience to get back on solid ground. The plane moved northwest toward the Columbia River. From there it would head downstream into Portland International Airport. Below, cottony clouds covered and uncovered concentric circles of green farmland interspersed with vast expanses of brown wheat land. To the west, the clouds looked thick and dark, which meant the arrival in Portland would be greeted with rain. His Rolex said noon, West Coast time. In a plane with a top speed of six hundred miles per hour, that meant another thirty minutes or so to the hangar at Flightcraft and then another twenty home in the limousine. Whatever the problem mentioned in the fax, it could wait until then.

He slid down in the seat and tried to imagine what could've gone wrong with a simple and easy assignment. That was one of the problems with politics. Too many important things were left to people singularly unsuited to the task at hand.

He drained the rest of his drink before setting the crystal glass on the napkin with the Scofield Industries logo: two snakes intertwined with the letters SI to form a demonic crest. When he'd unveiled it years earlier at a stockholders' meeting the reaction was palpable. He'd worked closely with a graphic designer to get exactly what he wanted. Once he had it, he made it clear that there was nothing further to discuss.

"Another club soda, Mr. Scofield?" The secretary had suddenly reappeared at his seat.

"No, I think a vodka on the rocks this time," he said, "and please join me."

"Okey dokey." Her voice produced a familiar shiver that started in his thighs and ended in the hair on the back of his neck.

He glanced again at the logo on the napkin and thought of the rivals that he'd left broken and broke. Most of them eagerly accepted mergers or buy outs that made them modest fortunes, but nothing near what they could've made by holding on to their dreams. By the time they figured it out, the deal was done and he controlled everything.

Scofield took pride in knowing that the vanquished openly referred to him as "Hissssss Highness, the Prince of Snakes."

"If they only knew the half of it," he said to himself just as the secretary, clutching two drinks, bounced into the seat next to him with a giggle.

# Chapter 2

I caught the telephone in mid ring just to stop the noise, thought about throwing it out the window, but mumbled an angry "Hello" instead.

"Dead body. Portable toilet. State fairgrounds. Could be a great story."

The voice had a grating, Brooklyn accent that sounded tamed by a few years west of The Rockies.

I blinked to get my bearings, while grabbing the pen and reporter's notebook next to the phone. Cradling the receiver against my shoulder, I flipped to the first blank page and sat poised to take notes, then realized where I was and how I'd got there.

Shit.

I was sitting naked in the leather chair in front of the window. The temperature in the dull gray room hung in the low seventies, which put it about twenty degrees cooler than when I'd finally fallen asleep. I looked down at my stomach and legs. Not even a goose bump, let alone a shiver. My coal-pile beard felt harsh against hands that had done nothing more rigorous than type words into a computer.

"Who *is* this?" I said, still not sure if I was awake.

"It's Alfie Gitchell, John. Guess I woke ya. Sorry, but I ran across something you might be interested in. It's pretty bizarre. Might be worth a few bucks if you're still writing for those tabloids."

The clock on the wooden milk crate that served as an end table proclaimed with digital precision that it was a little after four in the morning. I fumbled a cigarette out of the crushed pack on the arm of the chair and looked around for a match.

"Give me the short version," I said, throwing the notebook and pen hard on the floor under the window.

"I just did. Dead body. Portable toilet. State fairgrounds. Whadda ya say?"

"And you're thinking tabloid, right?"

"You're the word man, Standard," Gitchell said. "I'm just trying to help."

I hadn't seen Salem Police Lieutenant Alfred Gitchell in the three months since the jury found me innocent of two counts of manslaughter. With no real friends in court that day, I found myself looking toward the back of the room at Gitchell after the judge read the verdict. The detective approved the decision with a slight nod of his bald head before being swept out the door by the first wave of reporters.

Giving the clock another glance, I leaned forward toward the window to get a better look at the sky. The cityglow of downtown Portland illuminated the underside of a thin layer of low clouds just visible above the airshaft. Clouds. Clouds meant rain. Rain meant relief from a week of ninety-degree temperatures, unseasonable for mid-July. An Oregonian praying for rain. Pretty bad, I thought. It's like a camel praying for sand.

"Body still there?" I asked Gitchell.

"For a couple more hours," he said, hacking a sharp cigarette cough into my ear. "Get down here. I'll fill you in and pop for breakfast."

I hung up and slumped back into the chair. "Salem," I said, dreading the forty-five-minute drive down the freeway to the state capital, but needing the money the story might bring.

I stared up at the ceiling where the paint peeled like onion skin. The stain on the wallpaper above the make-shift bookcase looked like a sleeping fruit bat. Thirty-eight years old and living hand to mouth like a college student again, I thought. Jesus. Can things get any worse? I conceded that they probably could.

A radio turned low in one of the apartments further down the air shaft played Credence Clearwater Revival's "Born on the Bayou." The swamp-rock beat matched the weather and the slow rumble of heavy trucks on nearby Interstate 405. I groped another cigarette from the pack, lighting it with a kitchen match scraped angrily along the milk crate's metal edge. The thin curtains fluttered with a breeze that turned deliciously cool as it whispered across the film of sweat that covered my body.

I got up and stumbled across the small living room, turning on the oscillating fan on the way to begin rearranging the dust balls. In the kitchen, I found a jelly glass amid the perpetual clutter of dirty dishes in the sink. Standing in front of the open refrigerator, I poured a glass of ice water from a plastic pitcher and drank until the cold made my fillings hurt. I rested my arms on the top of the refrigerator and let the cold air wrap around me until the smell of old milk made me slam the door shut hard enough to rattle the last two clean plates in the cupboard. It wasn't my fault I lived here. They should've stood by me.

Commitment without purpose; purpose without direction; direction without leadership; leadership without commitment. An endless circle. What happened to wisdom, compassion, and common sense? What happened to work hard and do the right thing? It had all been shattered in a millisecond of ill fate. Now, everything around me made me hate even more what had happened. Maybe hate wasn't the right word. It was more like a deep, festering resentment that made living each day like climbing Everest without oxygen.

I was in mid-tirade when the lights in the apartment across the way came on.

Vanessa the Undresser was home.

Vanessa was a stripper, probably at one of the clubs on the east side. Like so many nights before, I stood in the dark, watching as she dropped her oversized gym bag on the couch and wiggled out of her jeans and baggy T-shirt. She wore no bra or panties. From the twenty feet across the airshaft from her apartment to mine I could easily see the sweat glisten on her brown skin with no tan lines. Blonde hair, usually worn loose to her shoulders, sat perched in a pile on top of her head so the back of her neck could catch the same breeze coveted by everyone else in the city without air conditioning. She was well into her thirties with breasts that sagged a bit toward a stomach that had begun to pooch. In the few months that we'd been neighbors I'd grown accustomed to her turned-up nose, wide smile, perfect teeth and wrinkles in the corner of her dark brown eyes and along her graceful neck.

In the three months since moving in, I'd sat in the dark watching as she refined her various acts in front of a mirror on the back of the bathroom door. The first night I saw her she was a nurse. That was followed a month later by a cowgirl, then a cheerleader. I'd sit smoking in the shadows of my apartment while she unknowingly entertained me with stethoscopes, lassoes, and pom-poms. Each act ended with Vanessa totally naked and staring at herself in the mirror, her face sad and quizzical. While most men in my place would be beating down Vanessa's door, I could do little more than watch in sweaty fascination. I felt no shame or embarrassment, only a sadness that matched the life my imagination had created for Vanessa.

I named her Vanessa the Undresser after Mrs. Prentiss Simpson, the character played by Rita Hayworth in the movie version of *Pal Joey*. She was "V. Michaels" on the smeared label next to the mail box outside the front door of the apartment building.

Someday, if I ever decided to take an interest in my fellow cell mates, I might make an effort to get to know Vanessa better, assuming she wanted to know me. I couldn't blame her if she didn't. Events of the last year had left me gaunt and pale, my nose more pointed and hawk-like, and my thick, black hair an unruly mop that curled around my ears and bunched up on the back of my neck. Hiding behind wire-rimmed glasses were the red-rimmed eyes of someone who'd left their contacts in three days longer than recommended. I even *felt* smaller, as if bad times had eaten away at my six-foot frame and taken off the extra twenty pounds I'd always wanted to lose.

I watched Vanessa check herself in the mirror. After pushing her breasts up and pulling her stomach in, she visibly sighed, let everything fall back into the place nature insisted it be, and disappeared into the small bathroom.

I stared at the closed door for a few seconds feeling that Vanessa and I had a certain bond that would be shattered if I ever learned that she was nothing like I imagined her.

Instead of getting dressed for the drive to Salem, I poured another glass of ice water and stood in the open window, my hand clenched hard around the glass as if wanting it to shatter and slash my wrist. I imagined myself bleeding to death as I calmly watched Vanessa emerge from the bathroom, slip between the cool sheets next to her stuffed giraffe, and prop a cheap novel on her knees.

When I hurled the glass out the window into the inky darkness of the air shaft it seemed to float on the heat and humidity until sinking out of sight to shatter with a sharp pop amid the soiled mattresses and rusting shopping carts at the bottom.

Was I ever going to get the chance to make things right again, to square myself with the forces that stranded me in this hell hole? My life had become like the bottom of a dry well, nothing but hard-packed sand littered with the bleached bones of small animals that fell in and couldn't get out. I'll probably never learn that when your at the bottom stop digging.

"I want my *fucking* job back," I said between tight lips and clenched teeth. "I want my fucking *life* back."

13

# Chapter 3

The clouds kept their promise. Huge rain drops beat a determined rhythm on the hood of my battered Jeep Cherokee as I pulled into a visitor's space near the main entrance to the fairgrounds. I turned off the key and let the smell of water on a hot radiator fill the car with a rubberized humidity.

After rummaging around in the back of the car for a faded barn coat and a water repellent baseball hat with the words "Catch and Release" on the front, I went off in search of Alfie Gitchell.

On the way down the freeway, I had decided that Gitchell's call was the detective's way of getting together again; a payback for giving him a prominent place in a story I'd done on the arrest of a serial arsonist. While working on the story, Gitchell gave me free access to everything about the investigation, even though I was awaiting trial and free on bail. Long hours in the car and over bottomless cups of bad coffee, Gitchell became an unlikely friend when I needed one the most.

A patrolman in an ankle-length plastic slicker stopped me as I approached the main entrance to one of the exhibit halls.

"My name is John Standard," I said, then explained the call from Gitchell.

The patrolman checked my driver's license then directed me to a remote corner of the grounds near an equestrian area that had once been a horse-racing track.

"Thanks," I said and splashed my way through the puddles that dotted the steaming asphalt.

The state fairgrounds occupied almost two-hundred acres of prime inner city real estate. The land, with its vast parking lots, exhibition halls, and low-slung animal barns, dominated the surrounding neighborhood of older homes and thriving canneries. The state fair itself was an annual, eleven-day event that started at the end of August and ended on Labor Day. The rest of the year, the fair's buildings were used for RV shows, home shows, concerts, and a wine festival.

I had been to the fairgrounds two days earlier getting a close look at a gun show for a gun control article I was doing for a Philadelphia magazine. I'd spent several hours talking NRA issues with those who bought, sold, and traded shotguns, deer rifles, semi-automatic weapons, and the occasional Uzi. It had been an enlightening afternoon full of colorful quotes about the evils of big government and interesting theories from high school dropouts about the true meaning of the Second Amendment.

I found Alfie Gitchell standing with two uniformed officers and a woman wearing a plastic jacket with "Crime Lab" stenciled on the back. They were gathered around a portable outhouse parked on a narrow stretch of soggy, brown grass between two livestock barns. High-powered lights had been brought in during the night and left on under the dark morning skies. The din of squawking police radios mixed with the hum of generators.

A second soaked patrolman barely turned his head as I ducked under the yellow crime scene tape. I elbowed my way through them until I found myself standing in front of the outhouse.

If I had anything more than coffee for breakfast I would have lost it right there

Inside, sitting on the toilet, was a man with his pants around his ankles, a piano wire noose around his neck, and a tongue the size of a tennis ball sticking out of his gaping mouth. The scene resembled a vulgar exhibit at a low-rent carnival House of Horrors. I backed away, sucking in mouthfuls of rain-soaked air.

"Quite a sight, isn't he?"

The voice came from my right. It was Alfie Gitchell.

"You live in a sick world, Alfie."

"Tell me about it."

Gitchell told everyone else to get back and pulled me forward until we stood side by side directly in front of the outhouse.

"Name's Krychek. Ivan Krychek. A security guard. He's been sitting on that crapper for about forty-eight hours, which means he was killed sometime during the gun show Saturday. We'll know more after the autopsy. The cause of death seems pretty obvious, though, wouldn't ya say?"

All I could do was nod.

The rain had soaked the detective's raincoat. His felt hat drooped on both sides so the water ran off in a steady stream on to his stooped shoulders. He delivered the information between drags on a soggy cigarette and with the detachment of someone describing the rules of badminton.

"That's a long time to be taking a dump," I said.

Gitchell emitted a laugh that sounded like a duck call.

"It's get better," he said, handing me a surgical mask. When we had slipped the masks on, Gitchell motioned me to stick my head in the outhouse door. Harsh lights shining through the thin walls and translucent roof gave the outhouse the look and feel of being inside an aquarium. Flies buzzed around the body and beat against the outhouse walls. Despite the mask, the cloying smell of disinfectant burned the inside of my nose.

I couldn't avoid looking at the guard's distorted and bloated face. He appeared to be in his mid-twenties with a short, wiry build, thin light-brown hair, a patchy red beard, and ruddy complexion. Behind horned-rimmed glasses were a pair of bulging eyes with a sickly yellow hue that went nicely with the purple of the inflated tongue. Dried blood caked the collar of his brown uniform and around the piano wire embedded in his neck. A patch on the uniform's left shoulder read "Prestige Security" and matched the cheap silver badge on the left breast pocket of his shirt. A second patch above the other shirt pocket read "Krychek." The pants piled around his ankles were the same color as his shirt. Attached to his wide, black belt were a set of keys, a nightstick, and a hand-held radio. I noticed that the switch on top of the radio was turned to the "off" position.

"Look at this," Gitchell said, pointing at the ceiling.

He was yelling to be heard over the rain beating against the plastic roof. The cop's fat finger pointed to the back wall of the outhouse. The piano-wire noose around the guard's neck was tied to a thin, nylon cord that ran up the back wall, through two eye hooks screwed into the translucent ceiling, then attached to the inside of the outhouse door.

"I figure the killer set him up to look like some kind of puppet," Gitchell said. "Every time someone opened the door the cord would make the body sit straight up. The movement would startle whoever opened the door. Then, they'd close it real fast with an embarrassed 'excuse me' and move on to one of the other toilets. Can't say I've ever seen anything quite like it."

We pulled our heads out of the door and removed the surgical masks. After nodding to the woman from the crime lab, Gitchell led me around the corner into the shelter of the empty livestock barn.

"I'll say it again Aflie, you live in a sick world."

"Yeah, but this pretty much takes the cake."

"Who found him?"

"A guy who works for the company that rents these outhouses to the fair." Gitchell pointed toward the far end of the building. "We're getting his statement now. That's him over there."

A slender middle-aged man wearing a pair of overalls stained with substances that I didn't want to know about stood next to a red tank truck with "Here's Johnny" emblazoned on the door. Anger and impatience were etched on a tired face. He was nose to nose with an overweight man stuffed into a rain-spattered suit. Their angry voices echoed through the empty barn and off the wooden sides of the stalls.

"Who's that with him?" I said.

"Harry Butcher. One of our investigators."

Gitchell excused himself and trudged toward the two men. I watched while Gitchell spoke to both of them for a few minutes, then came back, shaking his head.

"Butcher's new to Robbery-Homicide. A good cop, but he has a unique ability to piss off just about everyone he talks to. I don't think it's intentional. It's just the way he is."

I looked again at Butcher. The detective's face had faded from purple to red. The angry voices had been replaced by Butcher's gestures with a small notebook and pen. His attempts at sudden patience and diplomacy looked forced. The man from "Here's Johnny" stood with arms crossed in defiance. Butcher finally walked away, kicking at sawdust with street-worn shoes.

Gitchell and I smoked cigarettes while I pretended to jot down notes on the back of an envelope.

Gitchell was short, dumpy, and even the rain couldn't wash away the smell of a lifetime addiction to Camel straights. What hair he had left lay plastered across a pink, pear-shaped skull. A dimpled golf-ball nose dominated a round, cherubic face with dark blue blood vessels scattered across fat cheeks. Sad, brown eyes hidden under thick salt-and-pepper eye brows had taken dead aim on the retirement that was just a few years away.

"This is a pretty good story, huh?" Gitchell said, giving me an expectant look.

"It is for today," I said, not wanting to explain what little value there is in a one-day dose of the bizarre and unusual. "Did you know I was here Saturday working on another story?"

Gitchell shrugged. "One of the patrolman said something about seeing you, but I'd forgotten about it until now. Sorry to bring you back down here again so soon."

"It's okay. So, what can you tell me about Krychek?" Before Gitchell could answer, one of the uniformed officers came in out of the rain to tell Gitchell that the technicians from the crime lab were finished. He asked permission to remove the guard's body. Gitchell nodded, then said he wanted the port-a-potty seized as evidence.

"You want it cleaned out first, right?" the officer asked.

"No. Leave it the way it is. Just get it downtown somehow. I'll be out in a minute."

The officer left with a queasy look.

Gitchell recited chapter and verse on Ivan Krychek. He was a twenty-five-year-old graduate student at Delaney College, a private college in Salem. He'd started working part-time five weeks earlier for Prestige Security.

"It's an outfit out of Portland. The owner said Krychek got married a couple of months ago and wanted to earn a little extra money to help make ends meet. The owner's name is Mather, Buck Mather. A real sweetheart. Militia type. Hates the ATF and the UN. Calls Oklahoma City a plot to discredit true patriots."

Gitchell explained that security companies were popping up all the time to feed the growing demand for protection. Most of the guards weren't trained to handle weapons and police were too busy handling real crime to worry about background checks on rent-a-cops.

"Anyone can start one of these agencies, and anyone can work for 'em," Gitchell said. "Training's optional, so it attracts a fairly weird crowd. Mostly it's people who just walk in off the street looking for work. There's some kind of certification process, but there's no time to deal with it. Hell, the state of Washington executed some guy a few years ago for molesting and killing children. Turns out the guy was one of these rent-a-cops. Incredible, ain't it?"

"What about Krychek's wife?" I asked, slipping comfortably back into the reporter mode again.

"Name's Anna. Here's the address. It's in Beaverton." Gitchell tore a rain-spattered page from a small notebook and handed it to me. "I know this ain't exactly down your alley, John," Gitchell added, "and I appreciate you coming down here, especially on a day like this. But before you blow this off, I want you to know that this is no garden variety murder. I've done a ton of homicides and after a while you get a feeling about these things. This one is weird. Don't let this outhouse stuff fool ya. This ain't no prank. There's something else going on here."

I stared at Gitchell's face. The look I got back said the detective was serious.

"Does his wife know?"

I had a picture in my mind of a grief-stricken, doe-like woman living in a cramped apartment and facing life without the paltry income her student-husband earned patrolling places like the state fairgrounds.

"Yeah. Someone's up there right now." Gitchell said, pausing for a moment to look awkwardly around the huge barn. "Listen, John, I've been meaning to call you and tell you how relieved I was about that verdict. You shouldn't have been prosecuted at all, but with the media attention you got, the DA didn't have much choice. There's an election year coming up, ya know. Anyway, I think she was as relieved as you were about the verdict."

"I doubt that," I said, remembering the district attorney with her pinched face, permed hair and pink blouses with little bows, "but thanks for the thought. I'm just glad it's over."

"But it's not over, is it?"

I answered with a weak smile. "It'll never be over. The verdict didn't do anything to change that."

"Patience, John. Patience." Gitchell said, reaching in his pocket for another cigarette. "So, I'm about done here, and I promised you breakfast. What do you say?"

I glanced at the outhouse, then at the two men in blue jackets and white pants hoisting Krychek's corpse into a body bag. "How about a rain check?"

"No problem."

With another cigarette firmly planted in the corner of his mouth, Gitchell waddled back out into the rain to supervise the impounding of the outhouse.

# Chapter 4

I headed back to Portland after cadging a couple of photos of Ivan Krychek perched on his plastic throne from a police photographer. Instead of taking the freeway, I pointed the Cherokee east, caught Highway 99E, and followed it north through the rich farmland and bustling small towns that would be a welcome contrast to the grotesque scene at the fairgrounds. Sprinklers oblivious to the rain storm shot arcs of water over nursery stock. Fields of berries and hops glistened in the wet. I rolled down the window to let the last few drops of rain cleanse my mind and the inside of the stuffy car. The smell of wet cabbage wandered in and quickly left.

Traffic slowed, picked up, then slowed again through Woodburn, Hubbard, and Aurora. A few more miles north, near Oregon City, agriculture gave way to urban sprawl. Run-down farm houses surrendered to new, spacious country homes. Two lanes became four. Old became new. Slowly, I crept back to my existence.

I followed McLoughlin Boulevard through Gladstone and Milwaukie before crossing to the west side of the Willamette River on the Ross Island Bridge and into downtown. By the time I found a parking spot three blocks from the apartment, the sky had cleared. A significantly cooler sun slowly dried the wet sidewalks. Tramping through steam and the smell of damp concrete, I thought about Alfie Gitchell's warning that Krychek's murder was no prank. It was hard not to agree. Anyone who took pleasure in turning dead bodies into marionettes needed to be taken seriously.

I had left crime reporting behind years ago after lobbying the paper hard for a chance to stop covering the violence and to start covering the reasons behind it. It had worked well, and my last three years there had been the best I'd ever had.

Then I was fired.

After riding up in the elevator and avoiding my neighbors, I got a beer from the refrigerator, turned on the computer, and knocked out a quick five-hundred words on the death of Ivan Krychek. Satisfied that it was lurid enough to get someone's attention, I reached for the telephone and started working the trap-line of tabloids I'd built up in the last year. I met with little success until I threw in information from an unidentified and totally bogus police source that the murder may be connected to a satanic cult implicated in similar murders in South Australia. I even suggested a headline, "Devil worshippers terrorize Pacific Rim."

"Any chance we could work some alien angle into this?" asked the editor at the last tabloid on the list. "This Roswell thing is pretty big right now."

"I asked about that, but this guy seemed convinced that the satanic thing is real solid,"I said with as much enthusiasm as I could muster. The fan in the corner swung back and forth in sad disgust.

"Then I guess that's it," the editor said. "Get the pictures in the mail overnight along with the story on a disk. We'll cut a check when the story runs. I could get you a little more if you had a Roswell angle, but I'll do the best I can."

I hung up thinking that what the tabloids lacked in ethics they made up in generosity, then called *Inside Oregon*, an alternative weekly known for its gossipy news about city officials and its expansive personal ads. Eldon Mock, the paper's editor, answered on the second ring.

"John, I've been meaning to call you," Mock said in a booming voice filled with the energy needed to keep a weekly newspaper profitable. "I've got some work for you."

"No more restaurant reviews," I said. "I'm still recovering from that Ethiopian place you sent me to last month."

"I got something better. We're doing a special section on topless bars, except they're not topless anymore. They're topless *and* bottomless. Hell, I'm not even sure they wear shoes." Mock laughed at his own joke. "Did you know there's a place on the east side with a sign that says 'Topless plus.' Plus what? Plus nothing, that's what. No wonder they call Oregon the Beaver State. Anyway, I need four or five stories, a lead, and some features on owners, dancers, and customers. See what the cops and the DA have to say about all this. Maybe there's a Topless Dancers Anonymous. You know, the exploitation thing. I'm thinking out loud now, but bear with me. How about a first-person thing? Single guy makes the rounds of Portland's flesh pots. The ad people are drooling over this one, so I can pay you a pretty good chunk of change and we'll take care of the photos."

I glanced across the air shaft at Vanessa's apartment, while Mock rattled off another half-dozen story ideas.

"Let me think it over," I said, reluctant to turn down any assignment that generated needed income. "I've got something else you might be interested in."

I told Mock about Krychek's murder and what Gitchell said about it.

"I know it's not topless dancers, but I think it might make a offbeat feature. What do you think?"

"Write it and I'll look at it," Mock said, sounding disappointed that I didn't share his enthusiasm for topless dancing. "Who knows? It might be good copy. True crime is hot right now. Maybe there's a book in it for you. Anyway, if it doesn't pan out and you still want to work on that topless thing, let me know. I won't contact anyone else for a few days."

"Even if I don't, I appreciate you keeping me in mind."

"No problem. I'm still hanging in there for the day you write your version of the accident and what it was like to go from hunter to hunted. There's never been a reporter who found himself on the other side of cameras and microphones the way you did. That's a hell of a perspective."

I told Mock not to hold his breath, then hung up. I slipped the disk with the Krychek story on it and the photos for the tabloid into a manila envelope, addressed it, and left to catch a bus downtown to the central post office at Broadway and NW Hoyt. I got there just as it pulled up, climbed on and took a seat across from two women in their fifties discussing the success they'd found with Alcoholics Anonymous. Despite the heat, they wore long coats with mud stains around the bottom and hats with big silk flowers. A wino in a thread-bare overcoat and urine-stained slacks dozed peacefully a few seats away. In the back of the bus, a man in his twenties with pink hair and pierced nose, tongue, and eyebrow held a copy of *The Iliad* close to his face. He read with lips that moved and eyes that followed his finger across the page.

I glanced down at the envelope, wondering if its contents made me any different from my fellow riders. By the time I reached my stop, I'd decided that the answer really didn't matter. Different or not, I had become one of them. I'd crossed the line into a simpler world, one that didn't care about homeowner exemptions, touring Broadway musicals, or season tickets to the Trail Blazers.

After sending the envelope next-day mail, I decided to walk home. Heading up Broadway into the heart of downtown, I got a newspaper and a latte' at a Starbuck's near Pioneer Square. I took both to an empty table within earshot of the street preachers shouting their angry gospels to no one in particular. The story on the front page reminded me of the gun control article still languishing on my computer hard drive. It featured opposing photos of two state senators, Brad Roark and Kingsley Landis, the leading players in what had become entertaining political theater.

I had covered state politics fifteen years earlier as a rite of passage for all new reporters. After being reassigned, I remained an interested observer for the same reason most people watch auto racing: the accidents. But the spectacle of liberals and conservatives pandering to their respective special-interest groups and campaign contributors had lost its appeal amid the new, harsh realities of keeping body and soul together. Then Landis and Roark came along to renew my interest.

Ever since incumbent Governor Martin Sloane announced that health problems would prevent him from seeking re-election, Roark and Landis had been popping up at high-profile events all across the state. Since Easter, newspapers and television stations had devoted endless column inches and precious air time to the two rivals. Both were in their late thirties. Roark, the Democrat, emerged as the stereotypical liberal champion of the downtrodden. Landis, the Republican, assumed the button-down role of anti-government friend to big business. They'd played coy about their intentions to run for the state's highest office, but no one believed that either of them would expend that much effort not to run.

To the delight of the state's political press, the two wannabes had been fonts of catchy sound bites as they sniped at each other while spouting their own versions of the extremist philosophies that had become the hallmark of modern political debate. It all added up to an election that promised voters a clear choice. Moderates need not vote.

Most of the stories about the two were standard political fare and produced predictable headlines: "Landis, Roark clash on abortion," "Roark, Landis at odds over environment," "Rivals collide on welfare reform." What made the whole thing so remarkable was that the primary election was still a year away. As entertaining as they were, I shivered at the thought of another year of tepid, party-driven debate.

The story had a photo of Roark in shirtsleeves, his tie loose at the collar and slung over one shoulder. He looked disheveled and sweaty as he stood at a podium pointing across the page at Landis. In his photo, Landis stood at the same podium pointing toward Roark. He looked out of place and uncomfortable in a neatly pressed shirt with a button-down collar, no tie, a sport coat, and casual pants.

The story between the photos chronicled their appearance at a state labor union convention held the day before and included the predictable positions the two men had staked out on the gun control bill that would be debated during the waning days of the legislative session.

I got as far as the third paragraph before realizing the story contained nothing new about Landis, Roark, or gun control. I scanned the rest of the paper, but it was too early for any mention of Ivan Krychek.

I found something uniquely male about the way Krychek was killed and put on display. It made sense that a man would take perverse pleasure in standing inside a cramped, sweaty outhouse screwing eyebolts into the wall, running the wire through them, and tying it to the door. There must've been people around. Maybe the killer didn't leave immediately afterward, choosing instead to hang around for the reaction of those who opened the door, then quickly closed it after seeing a man inside with his pants around his ankles.

The possibility of a good story pulled at me until it finally dragged me into a phone booth where I looked up the address of Prestige Security.

# Chapter 5

"Tell me about this problem," Proctor Scofield said into the telephone.

He was alone in the vast house. Margaret wouldn't return from Europe for a day or two, so he'd given the staff the night off in order to enjoy a few hours of solitude. He slumped into the leather chair in the study and listened to the explanation while gazing around at the teak paneling, floor-to-ceiling shelves and thick carpet. A huge walnut desk filled the corner by the window. The oriental tapestry behind it was a gift from the Sultan of Brunei. The lingering scent of expensive cigars and cognac filled every niche. It was his favorite room, one designed by a man who liked his privacy.

"Our man got a little carried away with his mission," said Mitch Penroy, his voice sounding distant against the background noise of the car phone. "A little over-dramatic would be a good description."

"Define 'over dramatic' to me," Scofield said.

He sipped a gin and tonic and puffed on a cigar while listening to more of what was becoming a lengthy and somewhat defensive explanation. The faster-than-normal delivery made Scofield wonder if Penroy was using cocaine again or if he had gone beyond the recreational use that Scofield disapproved of but tolerated.

"How do you propose to deal with this?" Scofield asked, finally.

"Our man has been a tremendous help to us," Penroy said. "I think it would be a mistake to cut him loose. While he may be a little irrational at times, he is enough of a professional to cover his trail. I'm confident it won't happen again."

"Then you've talked to him."

"No, but I will. Soon."

"Is there a backup plan?"

"Yes. I have someone eager to replace him if it comes to that."

"Can I assume that we still have someone appropriate to take the blame for this?"

"Definitely. That part's been taken care of from the beginning."

"See that it stays that way," Scofield said, and hung up.

He settled back into the chair. A thin veil of blue cigar smoke lingered over his head. He blew a large plume at the empty brick fireplace, then watched it get sucked up the chimney, knowing that's exactly what would happen to twenty years of effort if things didn't go right in the next few days. Cocaine or nor, Scofield had great confidence in Penroy, but he didn't like things that were "over dramatic."

Scofield spent the next half hour letting the cigar burn down slowly while he decided whether to make things happen or let nature take its course. Hating to rely on people who didn't know shit from fat meat, he fell back on the one thing that he prided himself in most, his instincts. Knowing when to trust himself or others made him a success. He also knew not to move too quickly.

Patience, he told himself, and mixed another drink.

# Chapter 6

Mid-Valley Business Park was nothing more than a series of long one-story buildings hidden amid the car lots, fast-food franchises, and hookers that line NE 82nd Street on the east side of Portland. The address in the phone book didn't help much, so I had to drive through the complex twice, peering through the fogged windows of the Jeep before finding Prestige Security wedged between a computer software company and a bookkeeping service.

The blinds were pulled shut on the front door, but a plastic sign in the window said "Open." Next to it, a large decal read, "This property protected by Smith & Wesson." The mixed message made me pause before parking, getting out of the car, and going inside. Colorful brochures about personal security devices littered the Formica top of a waist-high counter. The single desk behind the counter was bare except for a touch-tone telephone and a black beret with a Special Forces logo on the crown. A seven-foot divider covered with military insignias, anti-government bumper stickers, and framed photos of young, stern-looking men in combat fatigues blocked the view into the back of the office. Several of the photos were taken against a jungle backdrop, which I assumed was Southeast Asia. The hot, silent room smelled like a gymnasium with too many old socks and too few windows. I said hello loud enough to be heard in the back.

"Be right there," replied a husky voice.

I scanned a brochure on pepper spray until the man attached to the voice walked around the partition. He was in his early fifties and large, but moved with a certain grace. A too-small, black T-shirt stretched across a massive chest and stomach. The combination of a jutting jaw and the hooked nose of a spawned-out salmon all but hid a small mouth with more gums than teeth. He was totally bald, but sported a dense, graying beard that started at his temples and wrapped around the weakest of his three chins. He looked to me like a professional wrestler who'd given up barbells for Taco Bells.

"Can I help you?" The cold and arrogant tone matched the military appearance.

"I'm looking for Buck Mather."

"You found him."

"I'd like to ask you a few questions about Ivan Krychek."

"You're not another one of those liberal faggots from the media elite are you?"

I resisted the urge to proclaim my status as a nonvoting heterosexual.

"I'm a freelance writer just trying to earn a living. I was hoping you could tell me something about Krychek."

Mather crossed tattooed arms so they rested on the top shelf of his stomach. The stance was defiant, threatening. The tattoos were mostly of skulls and mermaids with perfect breasts.

"I don't know anything about his murder, if that's what you're asking about. Krychek worked for me on and off for a few months, and someone killed him. Them's the breaks. That's all I know."

"Was he a good employee?"

"He showed up when I needed him. Did his job and went home. I really didn't use him that much."

"What did he do?"

"He was a security guard, for Christ's sake. He walked around. If there was trouble, he was supposed to stop it. Simple as that."

"What kind of trouble would there be at a gun show?"

"Thefts mostly," Mather said. He snapped the brochure from my hand and tossed it on the table next to the phone. "They're expensive and you don't look like the pepper spray type."

I pulled a pen from my pocket to give my hands something to do.

"Did Krychek work anywhere else?"

"A couple of days out at the dog track in Gresham."

"How did you happen to hire him?"

"You're just full of questions, ain't ya?"

"Sorry, it's part of the act. They teach it in Journalism 101."

"Let's hope it's a short act," Mather said. "I got work to do."

"I'll keep that in mind. Now, how did you hire Krychek?"

"He just walked in one day a few months ago, asking if I had any part-time work. I did, so I hired him."

Mather pulled a gray handkerchief from a hip pocket and ran it across his shaved head as if polishing the fender of a car. We stared at each for few moments until Mather looked away.

"Like I said, I really didn't use him that much. He wasn't trained all that well in security work. I figured if anything happened, he'd hightail it anyway. That would be the last I'd see of him. Happens all the time. The whole damn country is full of faggots."

I stayed silent. The GI Joe routine came off as cheap as the desk on which

Mather had parked one cheek of his huge butt.

"When was the last time you saw him?"

"Sunday at the gun show," Mather said. The heel of his polished combat boot tapped softly against the desk's thin steel side.

"So you were there the day he was killed?"

"I drove down to the fairgrounds to make sure he was there. I told him he could go home at five when the show closed and then left. He was alive and well the last time I saw him."

"Know any reason why someone would kill him?"

"No." Mather stepped around the counter and opened the front door. "Listen, it's been great chewing the fat with you, but like I said, I got work to do. Krychek was a nice kid who died in the line of duty. I feel sorry for him and for his family. Put that in your article."

"How long have you had this business?" I asked, glancing around at the stark surroundings. I didn't particularly care about the answer, but hoped the question would further annoy Mather.

"Couple of years. Bought it from a guy who retired."

"Are you the sole owner?"

"Me and the bank."

"Who are your clients?"

"None of your business." Mather eyed me for another moment, then said, "I think it's time you hit the road."

I took a flyer advertising a fool-proof home-security system from the counter and began slowly making notes on the back. Mather gave his boots an impatient shuffle across the gritty concrete floor.

"Those pictures look like Vietnam," I said, pointing to the photos on the divider behind the desk.

"Two tours."

"Ever killed anyone?"

"Plenty," Mather said.

The blinds on the front windows were turned down against the afternoon sun. I watched the shadow of a delivery truck driving through the parking lot move across the floor at my feet and wondered why Mather worked so hard at coming across as some battle-hardened patriot. In the end, he came off just slightly more threatening than a cop on a Schwinn three-speed.

"Ever kill anyone with piano wire?"

Mather stiffened. He squinted. His faced became small and tight. He reached down toward his boot and pulled out a commando knife that looked about a foot long. The razor-sharp edge glistened in the light coming in between the blinds. A skull and crossbones adorned the scrimshaw handle.

"I prefer this," Mather said.

He stuck the knife in the counter top, where it wobbled back and forth like a depraved tuning fork.

"Good choice," I said.

Mather opened the door. I eased around him and out onto the sidewalk. When the door closed, Mather flipped the plastic sign from "Open" to "Closed."

I sat in the Jeep for a few minutes then drove around to the back of the building. A white Ford van with tinted windows sat in front of a sign that read "Prestige Security. Deliveries Only." I parked five spaces down on the other side of three other cars. After a few minutes, Mather came out, locked the door behind him, and left in the van. I jotted down the license plate number as I watched it drive away.

With the van barely out of sight, I rummaged through my shirt pocket for the rain-spattered piece of paper with Ivan Krychek's address.

# Chapter 7

It took forty-five minutes to drive back across Portland and west out the Sunset Highway to Beaverton, then another fifteen minutes of U-turns in a confusing maze of cul-de-sacs before finding 2852 Baltusrol Way. The elegant, single-level brick home with a cedar-shake roof and brick accents overlooked the fifth tee of a private country club. Neatly trimmed shrubs accented the small, low-maintenance yard. Bright green grass bordered a wide walkway of interlocking red paving stones that led to the front door. The license plate holder on the new Honda Prelude sitting in front of the three-car garage said, "I'd rather be shopping at Nordstroms."

I had assumed that someone who had to work as a security guard in order to stay in school would be living in student housing or a rundown apartment house like my own. One look at Ivan Krychek's house made me check the address again, thinking Alfie Gitchell had written it down wrong or the rain had smeared the numbers. Satisfied the address was correct, I parked in the street and walked toward the house. After ringing the bell, I stepped back to admire the garish stained glass seascape that filled the top half of the oak front door. When no one answered, I leaned over the porch railing to peek in the front window.

Footsteps were followed by a sultry, "Who's there?"

The door opened as soon as I identified myself.

The woman standing in the doorway looked like an extra in a Robert Palmer video: Simply irresistible, with the air-brush perfection of a professional model, minus the sunken cheeks and bored expression. She had dark eyes, a long narrow nose, and liquid-red lips. Long, jet-black hair pulled tight into a ponytail hung between tanned shoulder blades. She was tall, maybe five-ten, and young, probably mid twenties. A white, knit sheath clung to a slender figure that came from genes rather than gyms.

I fumbled out an apology and said I must have the wrong address.

"I was looking for Anna Krychek."

"I'm Anna Krychek."

I couldn't stop staring at her.

"Have the police been here?" I asked, confused and dreading the possibility that she didn't know her husband had been murdered and I was stuck with the task of telling her.

"They left a couple of hours ago," she said, her voice carrying neither sadness nor joy.

I felt like I'd missed something.

"So you're Ivan Krychek's wife?"

"Yes," she said with a coquettish tilt of the head and a smile that could raise the dead.

"Then you know what happened to your husband?"

"Yes, I do," she said with a fleeting downturn of her perfect red lips. The sign of sorrow passed as quickly as a bird across a full moon.

I finally got around to telling her why I was there.

"I'm sorry to bother you at a time like this," I said, "but could we talk for a few minutes?"

Without a word, Anna Krychek turned and walked away with a pneumatic stride, leaving me to close the door and follow her.

The small entry inside the front door opened onto an airy, formal living room with pink leather furniture and glass-topped tables on chrome legs. Expensive area rugs covered hardwood floors. A half-dozen recent best-selling novels looked lost amid the enamel bookshelves that surrounded a marble-faced fireplace. The broad mantle was lined with photos of Anna Krychek, but none of Ivan.

I followed her into a more comfortable-looking great room with natural leather furniture and a second fireplace. Unlike the front room, it appeared to have actually been used once or twice. Jazz played softly on an unseen stereo system. We sat at a round oak table in front of the French doors that opened onto a patio overlooking the golf course. The house felt cool and smelled of French soap and furniture polish. A Persian cat curled up on a leather ottoman in the corner by the door woke up long enough to decide that I wasn't going to blow my nose on the curtains, then went back to sleep.

"You look familiar," Anna Krychek said. "I'm sure I've seen you somewhere before."

"A lot of people make that mistake. They say I look like a young Jack Nicholson, from the 'Easy Rider' days."

She looked confused for a second, then said, "No, that's not it. Are you a television reporter?"

"Just print."

She dropped the issue with a slight shrug of her shoulders and watched silently as I glanced around the room.

"Is anything wrong?" she asked.

"I just expected something different."

"You mean the house?"

"Yes, and you."

She gave me the same practiced smile I'd gotten at the front door.

"We were married a few weeks ago," she said. "The house belonged to my parents. They gave it to us as a wedding present when they retired and moved to Palm Desert."

"Your family is wealthy, then?"

"Yes, but not Ivan's family." She pronounced her late husband's name as Ee-von. "He was living in a small studio apartment when we met."

"That explains the house. But what about you?"

"We met at school."

I sat mesmerized as she explained that she'd been a student at Delaney College, and that Ee-von was a graduate assistant in the political science department. They met earlier in the year at a seminar on the new order of post-Communist Eastern Europe.

"He told me he was from Prague and I had just visited there last summer. We traded stories about restaurants and shops. Things sort of took off from there. Ivan was a brilliant man and a brilliant researcher. He was working on his doctorate, you know, when he was killed. He so wanted to be a professor."

She spoke in a monotone as if reading lines at the first rehearsal of a bad movie.

"It must be hard losing someone so soon after the wedding," I said, "but you seem to be taking your husband's death pretty well."

Anna coaxed a single tear from one eye. As it ran down her cheek bringing with it tiny bits of mascara, she reached across the table to gently lay a soft hand on my arm. I would've ignored it as a benign gesture had she not started drawing circles on the back of my hand with a long, perfect fingernail. Her touch reminded me how nice it was to be near a woman again, even one whose husband had just been murdered.

A second tear chased after the first.

"I loved my husband very much," she said, slowly pulling her hand away, "but it is not my nature to show grief in front of strangers. I will deal with Ivan's death in my own way and in private."

Cut. Next scene.

I joined in the rehearsal by nodding sheepishly on cue to give the impression of having been duly chastised for jumping to unfair conclusions.

"Sorry. Cynicism and suspicion come with the territory."

She pursed her lips and swung her head so the pony tail wrapped around one shoulder like a snake. It curled perfectly around her perfect breast. I marveled at how many perfect things there were in Ivan Krychek's world. Too perfect.

"And who is it you work for?" she said.

"I'm a freelancer. I sell stories to whoever will buy them. Newspapers and magazines mostly."

"And who will you sell this story to?"

"I'm not sure yet, probably someplace local."

I made a mental note to add *Cosmopolitan* to the list of prospects.

When Anna Krychek went to the kitchen to get something to drink, I asked to use the bathroom. She pointed down a hallway at the opposite end of the house.

On the way, I quickly opened two doors, but saw nothing that looked unusual. I found the bathroom, killed a few minutes checking the medicine cabinet and flushed the toilet. On the way back, I checked two more rooms, including the master bedroom. The king-size bed and headboard looked like a furniture store display. I closed the door thinking that the house had all the charm and personality of the best room at a Howard Johnson's.

Anna was back at the table when I returned. She sipped tonic and lime from a crystal tumbler, while looking out the window at two women driving by in a golf cart.

"It looks like a nice course," I said. "Do you play?"

"Play what? Oh, golf. No. I never seen the point of it."

Which explains why you live on golf course, I thought.

"If you come from a wealthy family, why was Ivan working as a security guard?"

"Ivan was a very proud man. He wanted to work and earn an income to support his new wife. He was so cute. It wasn't necessary, but it was important to him. Being a security guard allowed him to earn a little money each month. He worked pretty much when he wanted to so he could continue with his classes and his research."

Cut. Once again, Anna. This time with feeling.

"The police told me your husband had been dead since Sunday night," I said. "Why didn't you report him missing?

"I wasn't here. I've been visiting my parents in California. I got back around ten last night."

"Weren't you worried about him when he wasn't here?"

"No. Ivan was gone quite often, sometimes all night. It was his research, you know, or his work."

"What kind of research?"

"I'm not sure, exactly. I know that sounds funny, but Ivan was very secretive. He didn't talk much about his work other than he wanted to get his doctorate so he could be a professor at the college."

I felt as if she knew what the questions were before I asked them. I restrained the urge to interrupt her delivery by asking her to name the capital of Delaware. Instead, I kept feeding her lines and getting back the answers I expected.

"A professor in what?"

"Political science. That was how we met, remember? The seminar on Eastern Europe was put on by the political science department at Delaney College."

"Any idea why someone would want to kill him?"

"Of course not. Ivan had no enemies that I know of."

"But you didn't know him for very long."

"True, but when you're married to someone, no matter for how long, you get to know things about them." Anna Krychek tried her best to make her point by looking a little embarrassed at her vague reference to intimacy. "I can tell you that Ivan was not the type of person to have the kind of enemies that kill."

"Did the police have any theories?"

"None that they shared with me. They pretty much asked the same questions you have."

"Except they probably wanted to know where you were Sunday afternoon."

Disgust tickled the corners of her mouth.

"I guess they have to ask those kinds of questions. Still, it made me feel dirty."

"So what did you tell them?"

Anna Krychek scowled.

"I don't like feeling dirty twice in one day."

"Good answer." I smiled to break the moment. "Is there someone at the college I could talk to about your husband? I just need a few quotes to round out my story."

She shook her head. The pony tail whipped around the back of her neck to embrace the other breast.

"You were a student in the same department as your husband, and you don't know anyone there I could talk to about him?"

Anna Krychek looked flustered for a moment, then, as if remembering her line, said, "I guess you could talk to the dean of the department. I don't remember her name, but she was also Ivan's adviser."

Cut. That's a wrap.

While winding my way back through the upscale homes with perfect lawns searching for the elusive exit, I decided that Anna Krychek had come came across only slightly less convincing than Buck Mather's macho-man routine. Heading east into the city on the Sunset Highway, I pulled a notebook from the glove box. Driving with one hand, I made notes to myself with the other about what Anna Krychek and Mather had told me.

It felt good to care about something again.

# Chapter 8

Proctor Scofield stood on the deck of his beach house with the cellular telephone to his ear like a conch shell, listening to the all-too-familiar voice of Mitch Penroy.

"He's doing pretty much what we expected him to do," Penroy said.

"Then keep it that way, god damn it." The sharp pain caused by anger knifed through his head.

"Don't worry, there are ways to handle things if they don't go the way they should."

Scofield sighed, knowing he'd have to step in before things went that far.

"How did your bitch do - Anna, I believe you're calling her?"

"I talked to her this morning. He was there yesterday. She said it went all right. He asked all the questions we thought he would. Apparently he was a little surprised by the house and by her."

No surprise there, Scofield thought, he was always skeptical about that part.

"But he bought it, right?"

"Sounds like it."

A few feet above the deck that stretched across the front of the house, a lone seagull held itself into the stiff wind that came up every summer afternoon. The bird flapped its gray and white wings just hard enough to stay stationary. Without missing a beat, it shit on the sun-bleached wooden decking.

"My thoughts exactly," Scofield said to himself as the bird slowed its wings enough to allow the wind to send it soaring inland.

"And the visit with that asshole Mather?" Scofield said into the phone.

"Same story."

After giving instructions to keep him updated and to call immediately if anything significant happened, Scofield hung up. At least Penroy was talking slower this time, he thought as he went inside and shut the sliding glass door to silence the sound of waves crashing at the end of the point and pounding into the deep crevasse along the north side of the property. With the door closed, the view to the west became a living mural.

He tried to calculate the hours he'd spent in the house alone in the last few years. Not enough, he decided. The three of them used to spend long weekends here. Margaret sat on the deck reading, while their daughter played on the grass below. When the inquisitive little girl got too close to the cliffs, Margaret would drop her book and run down to pull her back to safety.

How many times had Margaret been here since their daughter's death? Twice? Three times? No more.

Spindrift splattered against the glass, drying instantly and leaving behind another smattering of small white spots of salt. Pouring a second vodka tonic, Scofield glanced at himself in the mirror behind the bar.

Where had the time gone? How much did he have left? He could answer the first, but didn't care to know the answer to the second.

Scofield remained bothered by Penroy's call, wondering if the plan he'd reluctantly agreed to was the right thing to do. It wasn't his nature to interfere in what he considered staff work, but the stakes were too high. He ran the plan through his mind one more time looking for the fatal flaw. It wasn't there. All the bases were covered, but he still didn't like anything that involved reporters. They were too unpredictable, too principled one moment and too devious the next. He was never sure where their allegiances lie. Were they really serious about this public right to know stuff or did they just get their jollies pulling people's pants down in public? The rule he'd lived by for thirty years was never deal with the reporters. Now, he'd violated that rule and it left him with a queasiness that wouldn't go away just because John Standard was a pariah in his own profession.

What little he knew of Standard left him with the impression that the former reporter was the most dangerous type of person alive: someone with nothing to lose. He'd read Penroy's report about Standard's work as a reporter, the accident, the trial, being abandoned by his wife. Someone who'd lost that much that fast can be erratic and unpredictable. If they have any kind of conscience at all, they're trying to find some way to get back into good graces with themselves and the world. His guess was that Standard had a conscience.

Scofield looked at his watch. Five o'clock. She could be here before dark if she left right away, sooner if he had the helicopter bring her over. Spending the night with her would get rid of his headache, and a lot more. He picked up the telephone after a few more minutes of thinking about the things he'd do to her. They talked for a few minutes, and she agreed to come.

"Toodle-oo to you, too," he said before hanging up.

# Chapter 9

I parked on SW Columbia and walked across the narrow park that divided SW Ninth Street and Park Avenue to the local deli. I ordered a roast beef sandwich to go from Cosmo, the one-eyed Greek immigrant who owned the place, and grabbed a six-pack of beer from the small cooler. Cosmo put the bill on my tab without asking for the money he knew I didn't have. I thanked him with a grateful nod and walked back across the park.

The apartment house lobby had taken on a musty smell in the humidity that followed the rain. I ate half the sandwich and drank one of the beers in the time it took the decrepit elevator to arrive from the fourth floor and deliver me to the seventh.

I'd left the windows open all day, so the apartment smelled slightly better than the lobby. I glanced across the air shaft to see Vanessa heading out the door. It was Monday, which meant the gym bag hanging from her shoulder contained the nurse costume with the little white hat, candy-stripper dress, and stethoscope.

I stood in the kitchen, my back against the counter, and ate the other half of the sandwich. When it was gone, I opened a second beer and then called Benny Orlando.

Benny was the apartment building's manager and the only other resident I knew or cared to know.

Three months earlier I had shown up on Benny's doorstep looking for a cheap place to live. Benny immediately recognized me from the stories in the paper and on television. In a random act of kindness, he rented the apartment to me without the usual first and last month's rent plus deposit. Over time and beers, Benny became the only person, other than the police, to hear the whole story of what happened the night of the accident.

"You got a minute?" I asked when Benny picked up the phone.

"Come on down," he said, "and bring the beer you bought at the deli."

"Still keeping on eye on who comes and goes, I see."

"Always."

Passing on the elevator, I took the stairs down to the second floor, knocked on Benny's door, then went in without waiting to be invited. The apartment was spacious compared to mine and sat atop the building's front entrance overlooking the South Park Blocks, which began at SW Market Street near

Portland State University and ended six blocks north at SW Salmon Street across from the Arlington Club. The blocks were patrolled regularly, but still served as a gathering spot for the homeless, who slept amid the pigeons and under what is reputed to be the oldest remaining stand of elms in the United States. From the kitchen window, Benny had a clear view of the daily parade of students, bums, and office workers who occupied the benches or sat on the thin grass in front of the First Christian Church.

I followed the din of calliope music down the narrow hall to the back of the apartment. Benny sat in front of one of his three computers, tiny feet on short, fat legs dangling from his custom-designed chair. Sausage fingers flew around the keyboard in seemingly random fashion, eyes never leaving the screen as he created electronic works of art for people he'd never met, who sell products he'd never buy. For reasons even Benny admitted he didn't understand, he had an affinity for computers and the software necessary to create internet web pages. His clients included several traveling circuses, two Las Vegas casinos, and theme parks in five southern states.

"How are things in cyberspace?" I yelled over the music.

I handed him one of the beers then walked across the room to turn down the stereo.

The windows in the room had been covered with aluminum foil. The only light came from two hanging lamps with soft-white bulbs and the green glow of the computers that were turned on all the time.

"It's abuzz with a possible merger between Dell and Gateway. Who cares? I'm a Mac man myself."

What Benny lacked in height he made up in density with a thick chest and square head set on a massive neck. Thick, black hair dangled around the edges of a round, boyish face. The dimly lit room created shadows that made his eyes look like unlit charcoal. He had to turn his whole body to nod toward the corner of the room at a girl painting her toenails with purple polish.

"John, meet Ivy. Ivy, say hello to John Standard."

The girl pushed goggle-shaped dark glasses up into a tangle of unevenly cut, multicolored hair. Vivid blue eyes darted between me and her big toe. She smiled with the passionate apathy of the twenty-something generation, then emitted a squeak I took as a hello. The metal stud in her tongue winked at me. When she quickly turned her attention back to her toenails, I looked at Benny, who met my gaze with wink.

"You here to pay rent? It's a week late, you know."

"I know. How about fronting me for a few days?" I gave a vague explanation about the Krychek story I'd sold to the tabloid. "The gun control article should be done this week. I just have to make one more trip down to Salem. After that I can get it to the magazine."

As much as I liked Benny, I hated having to explain another late rent check. Why couldn't I just tell him I'd he'd have the money next week?

"No problem," Benny said.

Ivy blew on her toes for a second, then pulled the tissue paper out from between them. After slipping into a pair of clunky sandals, she got up to leave. Her bare midriff revealed a navel pierced with two gold rings. A tattoo of a gecko peeked out above her low slung pants.

"I'll be back," she said with no enthusiasm. "Nice to meet you, John."

"A little young, isn't she?" I said when I heard the front door close.

"Yes, but we have a lot in common."

"You mean she used to be a circus clown, too?"

Benny had spent half his life dressed up as a baby in costume diapers chasing other clowns around the ring while brandishing an oversized plastic baseball bat.

"That's what you need, John. Someone like Ivy, with long legs and a short memory."

"Sure, just send me the ones you don't want."

Before Benny could answer, the phone rang. He picked it up, listened, hung up, dialed, and hung up again. When the phone rang immediately, Benny grabbed the receiver before the second ring. He turned away from me, talking quietly for a few minutes, and hung up.

"You seem to be in great demand," I said

Benny nodded. "It's nothing important. Too many people wanting too much at the same time."

"Must be tough knowing everyone in town."

"Not everyone," Benny said, "but close."

The air conditioner set into the window rattled and dripped water into a plastic bucket. It was there for the benefit of the terminals, processors, printers, and modems, but made the cramped room a respite from the heat.

"That look on your face says you got something to tell me," Benny said.

For the next half hour we sipped beer while I described the scene at the state fairgrounds and my visits with Buck Mather and Anna Krychek. Benny swung his stubby legs back and forth as I explained the odd feeling I'd gotten from the two interviews. The beer can looked like an oil barrel in Benny's tiny hands.

"You think one of them did it?" Benny asked.

"Spouses are always suspects, but her alibi should be easy enough to check out. The way Mather looks should be enough to get him on the list, if not for this crime then some other."

"But you think they're both bullshit?"

"Yeah, but that doesn't make them guilty of anything criminal. I'll keep poking around. See what happens."

Benny hopped out of the chair to turn the air conditioner up a notch. The rattle got louder and the drips came faster. One of the computers beeped with another e-mail message from Benny's world-wide network of circus freaks and hi-tech nerds.

"You better check that," I said. "The bearded lady might be opening an electrolysis business."

Benny coughed out a short laugh.

"So what are you going to do with this story, assuming there is one?" he said as he waddled over to the stereo. The soundtrack of *The Greatest Show on Earth* soon replaced the calliope music.

"Hell, I don't know. *Inside Oregon* seems mildly interested. Other than that, who knows. Write a book. Stick it in a sock and swing it around my head like a dead cat."

I sank low in the chair and rubbed the cold can against my cheek.

"Or use it to get your job back."

The possibility of using the Krychek murder as a way of getting back into the good graces of the editor who fired me had crossed my mind. The hope was still there, but as rickety as the bridges I'd burned.

After the paper's executive editor fired me, I basically destroyed her office, turning over her desk and file cabinets and throwing her computer terminal out of the fifth-floor window into the middle of SW Broadway. The window glass showered down onto the sidewalk, narrowly missing a group of third graders on a field trip to the press room.

"No way," I said. "I'm damaged goods. They'd never take me back. Reporters are a dime a dozen, Benny. Why hire me back when they can find someone in New Jersey with none of the baggage, less attitude, and a willingness to take a pay cut to move out west?"

Benny tapped idly on the keyboard of a turned-off computer. "There's other papers, other cities."

I didn't answer. We'd been over the same ground a hundred times, staying up late into the night drinking Corona and arguing over how long I was going to feel sorry for myself. Benny would pound the arm of his over-stuffed chair, demanding that I get on with my life. "What's so damned great about this place, anyway? It rains nine months a year. You're friends, if you can call them that, treat you like O.J. Simpson. You can't get a decent job. I mean it isn't like you could go into corporate P.R. What the fuck is going on in that cast-iron head of yours? Get out. Get out now."

The silence was all the answer Benny needed. "Okay. I'm sorry. I know we've been over this before, but one of these days you're going to level with me."

"Yeah, Benny. One of these days."

# Chapter 10

After wasting the next morning tinkering with the gun control story, I conceded that the final touches would have to wait until the issue came up before the legislature.

Gun control wasn't a subject for which I had any great passion, but I felt lucky to get the assignment from a magazine in Philadelphia that wanted the wild west perspective on the use of guns and efforts to control who owns them. I used the editor's beliefs that everyone in Oregon wore buckskins and ate venison to negotiate a nice fee for a ten-thousand-word article with photos. The whole package had to be in the mail by the start of the following week.

A call to the state capitol told me that debate on the gun-control bill was the next day in the state senate. Then I called Philadelphia to let the magazine's editor know he'd have everything ahead of schedule.

Reluctant to spend the rest of the day sitting in the apartment, I left the building through back stairs that opened into an alley. A homeless couple pulled their heads out of a dumpster long enough to ask for spare change. I gave each of them a quarter and got two looks of disappointment in return.

I walked down Tenth Street to Powell's Books on Burnside, stopping at Jake's Famous Crawfish, but left after one beer because there were too many affluent-looking people inside having fun. A hot dog and a cola from a street vendor suited both mood and budget. The rest of the afternoon was spent wandering through the endless maze of bookshelves that made Powell's a Portland landmark.

Somewhere in the stacks of new and used books were the answers to everything, from how to make an omelet to the best golf courses in Scotland. It was a perfect place to grab a few hours away from my new reality and the memories of my old one. I hadn't planned it, but I eventually found myself in the journalism section. My heroes stood before me in mock judgment, leaving me wondering what the icons of American journalism would think of their profession today. Would they cringe at what they saw? If they didn't, I would.

On the day of my arraignment, I faced a small army of photographers with still and video cameras as well as reporters with notebooks and tape recorders. The most frightening moment was the jostling back and forth as I tried to make my way from the Washington County Courthouse to my lawyer's car. Looking back on it, I couldn't decide who I felt more sorry for, myself or the journalism profession.

After a couple of hours of combing the stacks, I spent a few bucks on a used biography of Edward R. Murrow, then walked up Burnside toward Civic Stadium. Scanning the book over a beer in a tavern up from Powell's, I noticed two people sitting at the bar looking over their shoulders and whispering to each other.

I'd been through this before, so I drained his glass, then headed for the stadium to watch the Class AAA Portland Beavers play the visiting Iowa Corn Dogs of whatever they were named. I left in the fourth inning after the umpire ejected the organist for playing "Three Blind Mice" after two bad calls at second base.

A breeze and the shadows cast by the buildings made the long walk home a little cooler. Still, I covered the last three blocks thinking of a cold shower and an even colder beer.

Both ideas went down the drain when I saw the large man in the sweat-streaked, gray suit waving at me from a park bench across from the apartment building.

It took me a few moments to recognize Harry Butcher. Spread out across the tiny bench, he looked larger than in the expanse of the barn at the state fairgrounds. I sighed, walked between two cars and across the street.

"You're Alfie's partner, right?"

Butcher's huge head went up and down.

"Harry Butcher's my name, Sergeant Harry Butcher, Homicide. Sorry we didn't get a chance to meet to the other day. Things were a little hectic. Not every day something like that comes along."

"To say the least," I said. "I take it you're here to see me."

"I got a murder on my hands, son. I think you might be able to help me."

Butcher shoved a red swizzle stick into his mouth. He had a good-ole'-boy drawl that made me think he was there to offer me a really good deal on a horse.

"How long have you been here?"

"Who cares?"

Butcher hauled his bulk off the bench and turned full circle to survey the park. I thought of the dancing hippos in 'Fantasia.' Beads of sweat collected on his freckled forehead and ran down purple cheeks. Thin hair tinted orange to hide the gray hung in wet strands over the back of his shirt collar.

"Nice spot you got here," he said. "In the last half hour, I counted two drug deals, four homos, and a couple of dykes."

Gitchell was right, I thought. Butcher did have a way of pissing people off.

"Thanks," I said. "I'll pass it on to the mayor."

"Can we go somewhere?" Butcher stretched short, fat arms and yawned. "I ask questions better over a plate of food."

Butcher shrugged at my suggestion that we walk down the street to the Virginia Cafe. The detective tramped along like a grizzly on the way to the dump. His huge body tilted forward as he struggled to keep pace while panting and smoking a cigarette. His well-worn wing-tips beat the sidewalk with rhythmic thuds. Butcher's momentum made me wonder if I should try to stop him in front of the restaurant or just let him charge on down Park Avenue and into the Willamette River.

Fifteen minutes after leaving the park, we settled into a corner booth and ordered. The waitress was a pro, the kind who doesn't write down your order and remembers to bring the glass of milk you asked for. I waited for Butcher to catch his breath before telling him that I didn't know anything more about Ivan Krychek than the police.

"I know, but you used to be a big-time reporter. I thought you might have a theory about who killed him. I've always been told that reporters are smarter than everybody else."

Butcher winked, then shed his coat like a man getting out of a wet suit.

"My money is on a satanic cult or aliens," I said. "At least that's what I hear some tabloid is going to publish."

"I think maybe it was someone closer to home."

Fleshy cheeks made Butcher's eyes little more than slits. The wrinkle where his eyebrows and the bridge of his nose came together looked deep enough to grip a quarter.

"I wouldn't know, but you must be in big trouble if you're turning to a reporter for help this early."

"You mean *ex*-reporter," Butcher said.

"Whatever I am doesn't make you appear any less desperate."

Butcher was starting to get under my skin.

"You had a chance to get a look at Krychek's wife. Real piece of work, isn't she? Seems a little odd that a dipshit like Krychek would be humping an uptown twist like that, don't you think?"

"What are you getting at, Butcher?"

"Nothing. Everything. Just thinking out loud. Wondering if maybe you and Mrs. Krychek aren't . . . you know, playing hide the salami."

The only answer I could come up with a sad shake of my head.

"I guess maybe you're beyond desperate."

We sat in icy silence until the waitress showed up with a dinner salad and a bowl of chili for me and a large platter of steak and mushrooms for Butcher. The detective dove in, holding the fork in his fist and shoveling the food into his mouth like coal into a furnace. He ate with his mouth open so I had a clear view of the meal being ground up between yellow teeth and pushed around by a concrete gray tongue.

"I understand you were at the gun show at the fairgrounds the day Ivan Krychek was killed," Butcher said between mouthfuls.

Drops of dark gravy began gathering on the paper napkin Butcher had tucked into his shirt collar.

"I got there around two and left when it closed at five. Alfie knows that."

"Did you see Krychek while you were there?"

"No."

"You sure?"

Butcher didn't let talking interrupt his meal. The mashed potatoes were gone before I had a chance to shake pepper on my salad.

"I'm positive. Why?"

"No reason. It's just that with all those guns there it seemed odd that Krychek was strangled to death. Don't you find that odd?"

When I didn't answer, Butcher put his questions on hold, concentrating on the steak. He cut the meat into a half-dozen pieces, set the knife aside, and devoured each chunk as if they were about to run off the plate. Five minutes later, Butcher scraped the empty plate with a fork, pushed it aside and pulled a pack of cigarettes and a lighter from his shirt pocket.

Watching Butcher had taken the edge off my appetite, so I could do little more than stare holes into my chili.

Butcher leaned forward so both elbows were on the table. Beads of sweat seemed permanently attached to his large forehead, his breath coming in short gasps. A sharp cough followed each drag on the cigarette.

"How do you feel about guns?" Butcher asked.

"I'm no great fan."

"How about piano wire, or do you prefer cars?"

The question stunned me. That night on the highway from the coast had cost me a career, a wife, and all that went with it. I couldn't believe Butcher wanted to bring it up as part of a murder investigation.

"Enough bullshit, Butcher. What's this all about?"

"Just a fat cop trying to solve a murder. Where better to start than with someone who was at the scene and has already killed two people."

"You know damn well that was an accident. There was a trial. I was found innocent."

Butcher shrugged and pulled the napkin from his shirt collar.

"Yeah, right. Juries, my aching ass. You'd been drinking and two little Mexican kids are dead. In my book that's a crime. My book also says that once a killer, always a killer."

I was dining on disbelief instead of chili.

"This is joke, right? Somebody's paid you to do this. You're like those guys in gorilla costumes who bring singing telegrams to birthday parties."

A smile appeared on Butcher's greasy lips.

"Believe that if you want, but I prefer to think this is a chance to correct a mistake. I don't like people who get away with things because of who they are or what they do for a living. I'm funny that way. If some poor son of bitch who just got off work at a lumber mill had killed those two girls, he'd be in the state pen making furniture and taking it up the ass from some nigger body builder. But a yuppie reporter like you mows down the same two kids and all he ends up with is a shitty apartment in downtown Portland and a stack of lawyer bills."

I lit a cigarette to give myself time to respond.

"I don't suppose you have anything as exotic as a motive."

"Not yet. If I did you'd be under arrest, and we'd both be on the way back to Salem." Butcher dug another plastic swizzle stick from a shirt pocket and began digging at his back teeth. "I checked your prints against those found inside that outhouse. They didn't match, but that don't mean shit. You could've worn gloves."

"You know what scares me about you, Butcher? That you're too stupid to find out who really killed Krychek, which means a killer goes free while you waste time trying to make my life miserable."

"Nice speech, but what I'm doing is nothing compared to how miserable Krychek's wife or the parents of those two little girls must be."

"Fuck you," I said and slumped into the corner of the booth.

The waitress brought the check, which Butcher ignored.

"I'll get this," I said. "I don't mind being accused of murder, but I wouldn't want you to think I was a bad host."

Butcher leaned back. A belly the color of uncooked bacon fat peeked out between his straining shirt buttons.

"You're pretty smart aren't you, word man? You think Harry Butcher's just an old boy blowing smoke up his own ass. Well, I could pin this thing on you whether you did it or not. I could even haul your butt in for questioning and turn you over to a few of those boys we got locked up down there in Salem. You could have a whole different sexual orientation before your buddy Gitchell even found out you were in jail."

"It's been great talking to you, Butcher," I said, getting up to leave. "Let's get together again and do lunch. You can show me how to eat with my hands."

With surprising quickness, Butcher grabbed my arm. Pulling me back down into the seat rattled the dishes and silverware. A middle-aged couple sitting at a nearby table stared. They moved their chairs a few inches away, then looked around helplessly for the waitress. Butcher ignored them, his purple face within inches of mine.

"Listen, wise ass," Butcher hissed. His breath smelled like cigarettes and mushrooms. The swizzle stick snapped between his teeth. "I think you're a killer. I can't prove it yet, but I will. For now, I may settle for leaking your name to the press. I'll let those piranha tell the rest of the world about your latest victim."

"You're crazy," I said, trying to let anger hide fear.

The hand that had my arm pinned to the table tightened for a moment before easing enough for me to get free. I rubbed my wrist while watching the middle-aged couple gather up their plates and move to another table.

"We'll see who's crazy," Butcher said. "For your sake, you'd better hope it's me."


It took most of the night to fight back the panic.

It was the same panic as the day the police showed up at my house. Two men in identical uniforms thumbing through little notebooks filled with questions about my whereabouts the night two little girls were left dead along the side of a dark highway. By the time they showed me the two marks on the front bumper of my Jeep, I was fighting back the panic with a whip and a chair. The struggle lasted through a week of being hounded by reporters, Christine's departure, and the wait before being indicted by the grand jury. It turned to a war inside me as I sat through the trial and the agonizing two days before the jury came back.

Even though the panic brought on by Harry Butcher felt like I'd swallowed a live rat, things were different this time. I hadn't killed anyone. The panic of being accused of murder by a half-wit homicide detective felt tame compared to not knowing the consequences for ending two young lives. Still, things could get worse if I found myself once again in the cross hairs of my own profession.

I sat in the leather chair smoking, sipping at glasses of cheap bourbon, watching the dirty curtains flap in the soft breeze that wandered down the air shaft. An image of Butcher's face across the table at the Virginia Cafe hung just out of reach like a bothersome fly.

I was still sitting there when Vanessa came home a little before three a.m. She went through her routine: Drop the bag on the couch; take off her clothes; look at herself in the mirror; sigh.

It was Tuesday, which meant the bag contained the cowgirl outfit with the white hat, rhinestone vest, and tear-away chaps. She could've been a banker, a computer analyst, or anyone who got up each day, went to work, then did it all over again without complaint. Nothing went wrong or right in her life. Things stayed the same, day after day. She'd probably never killed anyone or even been accused of it. Her life looked boring, but I watched her with an odd sense of envy.

I couldn't understand Butcher's determination to blame me for Ivan Krychek's murder. It might be a personal thing. Maybe I looked like an easy target for a lazy detective with a deep dislike of defrocked newspaper reporters. He obviously resented the fact that I wasn't convicted of the manslaughter charges and wasn't satisfied that I had lost everything I had. He probably didn't believe in accidents or that people could fall asleep at the wheel and not realize what they'd done.

I had relived the events following the accident too many times to want to do it again at three in the morning. I went to bed after watching Vanessa slip between the covers next to her giraffe. Laying face up, the yellowed wallpaper and peeling ceiling closed in around me. The panic smoldered somewhere in my chest, ready to burst into an uncontrolled blaze.

# Chapter 11

Margaret Scofield arrived the same time as the gardeners, but with less fanfare.

Proctor Scofield stood at the open window of his study watching the crew of three Hispanics unload rakes, shovels, weed eaters, and blowers from an old pickup and descend in unison on the hedges that guarded the front of the house. They wore identical dark green uniforms and tan safari hats that looked ill-equipped to deal with the mid-morning heat. Scofield admired the way that each went about their appointed tasks, proudly wielding their respective tools and barely looking up when the limousine pulled past their wheelbarrows into the circular driveway.

The limo's trunk popped open as soon as the car stopped. Edward, the chauffeur, scurried out from behind the wheel and around to the passenger side of the car. When the door opened, Scofield found himself watching with odd detachment as the elegant woman in the perfectly tailored suit walked slowly toward the front door.

"I'll have your luggage inside in a few moments, ma'am," Edward said.

"That will be fine, Edward. Thank you."

It wasn't that Scofield didn't want to see his wife, he just didn't have the time. Despite a month-long separation, he wasn't in the mood to play the dutiful husband and endure tales of shopping sprees across Europe.

Sipping luke-warm coffee, he watched Edward pull the dozen suitcases from the trunk of the limo. He wondered if Margaret knew about his affairs. If she did, she'd never mentioned them because it probably didn't matter to her anymore. They had made their peace with each other years before. He even knew the precise moment.

It was twenty-two years ago when their daughter's death created a crack in their marriage that had grown into a fissure.

Thirty years of marriage had gone by too fast. He met her at exactly the same time his business had taken off. He'd left behind the cramped office on Portland's run-down east side. Orders were coming in faster than he could fill them, and he was beginning to grasp the unlimited applications of office computers. His self-confidence and bank account were growing neck-and-neck. A year earlier and she wouldn't have given him a second thought. A year later and he wouldn't have given *her* a second thought.

There had been no women before Margaret. As the first, she taught him things about love and passion that would eventually make him seek more than she was capable of or willing to give. Her patience with his honeymoon fumbling had made him see things about himself that he later realized had been there all along. Without knowing it, Margaret's gentle whispers of encouragement had coaxed the cork out of years of pent up curiosity he would later satisfy on business trips through Asia, Europe, and South America.

The telephone in the study rang just as Margaret disappeared in the front door. The sharp bark of Mum, their pet Pembroke Corgi, greeting her return echoed up the staircase.

Scofield picked up the phone.

"It's Penroy, Mr. Scofield."

"I hope the hell you're calling me to say you've found that manuscript," Scofield said.

"We're still looking. It's not in his house, but there are still a couple of places to check," Penroy replied.

"This won't be successful if that manuscript isn't found. Am I making myself clear?" Scofield found himself yelling, which meant another headache couldn't be too far behind.

"Very. I'll let you know when we have it."

Scofield refilled his cup and popped a crust of toast into his mouth.

"You'd better go now," he said to his secretary. She pouted over her oatmeal and *People* magazine. "Get dressed and go down the back way. Edward will drive you home."

# Chapter 12

Delaney College was a private school founded in the late 1800s by a long-forgotten religious order. Over the ensuing century, it had emerged as a small but highly acclaimed school willing to forego its saintly roots for the worldly pursuits of high-priced tuition and aggressive fundraising from wealthy alumni. The small campus on the edge of downtown Salem was a mixture of buildings that tracked the college's evolution from late Nineteenth Century to late Twentieth Century. Stately brick and ivy of the original structures mixed with the concrete and glass of new buildings. The combination produced a cloistered atmosphere filled with the trappings of higher learning, but devoid of the realities of living in the real world. In other words, a typical American college.

I wasted fifteen minutes wandering around the campus trying to find the Political Science Department. The clock on the front of a large, brick building announced in Roman numerals that it was a little after ten-thirty in the morning. Plenty of time to find out what I could about Krychek before going to the Capitol to listen to the gun control debate.

The previous night's panic had ebbed slightly, leaving behind the stark reality that I still wanted to do an article for *Inside Oregon* on the murder of Ivan Krychek. The added dimension was that Harry Butcher probably wasn't going to be adding any name other than mine to the list of suspects in the case. For no other reason than self-preservation, I had gotten up early and headed for Delaney College armed with little more than what I'd learned from Krychek's widow. Fruitless or not, it filled the time and was better than doing nothing at all. Butcher had that job sewn up.

I stopped two girls with backpacks and Birkenstocks, who said the Political Science Department resided in the basement of Mayfield Hall. They pointed to a three-story, ivy-encased structure with a steep set of stairs leading up to the main entrance. From a distance, the tower on top could be easily mistaken for a church steeple.

Inside, it smelled of chalk blackboards, erasers, and hardwood floors. A sign halfway down a long, narrow hallway read "Political Science Department, Dean Jasmine Grant, Ph.D." An arrow pointed down a set of stairs to the basement where I found a parallel universe, but with cramped offices instead of classrooms. Small, white cards on each door announced the occupants' names and office hours. Yellow police tape stretched across one door. The card on the door said "Ivan Krychek."

The door at one end of the hallway led outside to a stairwell under the steps to the building's main entrance. A few feet away, a janitor emerged from a small closet with a mop and bucket that squeaked and rattled against the linoleum floor. At the other end, a half-dozen people milled around outside a lecture hall.

I joined the group, slipping inside to stand against the back wall. Descending tiers of seats were arranged in a half circle around a small platform with a podium, library table, and portable blackboard. Scattered around the room were men and women ranging in age from late twenties to early sixties. They all stared solemnly at a woman standing at the podium. She was in her mid-thirties, Asian, and dressed in the casual clothes of summer term in academia -- sandals, a colorful print skirt, and a tie-dyed tank top. Whisps of silky, black hair escaped the large plastic clip on the back of her head to dangle around a face with soft, Asian features. She constantly brushed at the unruly strands with long, graceful fingers with no jewelry.

"Some of you will probably be questioned by the police, if you haven't been already," the woman at the podium said. "Please cooperate with them. Whoever is responsible for Ivan's death must be found."

Everyone started to get out of their seats and head for the door.

"And one more thing," she said over the din of squeaking chairs and shuffling feet. "Please keep Ivan and his family in your thoughts. He was a very special person, and we should do everything we can to keep his memory in our hearts."

I pressed against the back wall to let the twenty or so people get by. With the room empty, I walked down the center aisle toward the podium where the woman was gathering up papers from the library table. I told her my name and that I was a freelance writer doing a story on the murder of Ivan Krychek, but left out the part about being a suspect.

"Nice to meet you, Mr. Standard. I'm Jasmine Grant, but I'm afraid I can't help you," she said, continuing to gather up papers and stuff them into a well-used backpack. "I've told everything I know to the police. I'm sorry."

"Are you sure you can't spare a few minutes?"

She stopped fussing with her papers long enough to give me a pleading look. Taken individually, her unkempt hair, overbite, angular nose with the small bump on the bridge, and Haight-Asbury wardrobe were not attractive. Collectively, though, they created a raw beauty, a look of innocence and vulnerability out of sync with the times, if not the place. She had an authenticity that made her far more alluring than the well-rehearsed Anna Krychek. The absence of makeup meant there was nothing to smear or streak when the tears in half-almond eyes started flowing down her cheeks. Finally, I thought, someone willing to shed a real tear for the late Ivan Krychek.

"Forgive me," she said. "Ivan and I worked together for several years. He was my student and then my graduate assistant. He was also my close friend. I can't believe someone would kill him like that."

"It looks like you're busy right now. If you're willing to talk to me about Ivan, then perhaps we could do go somewhere for coffee or something to eat."

"No, that's okay," she said, avoiding my eyes. It was a smooth, tactful, and practiced rebuff. "I'm sorry if I seemed rude. How can I help you?"

I explained most of what I learned from Mather and Anna Krychek. The intent look on her face made me feel like a student trying to explain how my lava lamp burst and spilled thick oil over a term paper. "All I really wanted to get from you was an idea of what kind of person Krychek was and some insight into the research he was doing."

"The first part is easy," she said. "He was a remarkably dedicated and resourceful researcher with an unquenchable thirst for the truth. How's that? Is that a good sound bite?"

She harmlessly touched my arm as we shared a smile at the expense of journalism's shallow reputation. I needlessly scribbled notes.

"That's pretty good," I said, "but what about his research?"

"Ivan had been working on his doctoral dissertation. It had something to do with the polarization of American politics. The conservative right versus the liberal left. Talk radio meets public bradcasting. That sort of idea. He'd started work on it last year. Three months ago he became kind of secretive about the project. I asked him several times how things were going. He said everything was fine, but made it clear that I would just have to wait until he was finished."

When I said Anna Krychek described her husband the same way, Jasmine went suddenly quiet. It wasn't a question so there was no need for her to say anything.

"Isn't it kind of odd that the head of the Political Science Department wouldn't know what kind of research a graduate student was doing?" I asked.

"I suppose it sounds odd." She swatted again at the strands of hair that had eluded the clip. "Ivan and I were friends. I didn't feel a need to check up on him. Knowing the general nature of his research was good enough. It didn't concern me that I didn't know the specifics. I would find out sooner or later."

Jasmine Grant said she'd spent spring term on a sabbatical in Hong Kong, so she didn't know about Krychek's moonlighting as a security guard until she got back in early June.

"If Anna said he was doing it for a little extra cash, I have no reason to doubt her."

I caught a cold, catty edge to her voice when she referred to Anna Krychek as "her."

"Do you know Anna well?"

She shook her head. More hair escaped.

"They must've made a strange couple," I said. "She's so beautiful and he was ...."

"I really don't know anything about Ivan's personal life," she said. "He married her shortly after they met. It all happened very fast and unexpectedly. That's all I know. I won't tell you that I wasn't surprised, but I never inquired, and he never talked to me about it."

"Was there a wedding?"

"Not so you could tell. I learned when I got back from Hong Kong that he'd left for a week in May, and when he came back they were married."

"Do you know where they went?"

"No, but it must have been somewhere nice, because I heard he was sunburned when he returned."

Krychek's marriage was an obvious sore point, so I changed the subject so she'd talk some more.

"I see the police have been here to look at his office," I said. "Did they find anything?"

"I don't know. They took nothing with them when they left."

Jasmine resumed stuffing papers in her backpack. Finishing that, she began erasing the blackboard. Her delicate arms made angry arcs across the surface.

"I'll be honest with you, Dean Grant," I said. "There are some things about Krychek that don't add up. I don't know what the police told you about how he was killed or where, but someone went to a lot of trouble just to murder a lowly security guard. Not only that, the guy who runs the security company doesn't seem too upset about it and, for that matter, neither does the widow. I don't understand what he was doing working as a security guard in the first place. I don't think he needed the money. I don't buy his wife's explanation that it was a matter of pride. And if that isn't enough, then this princess-and-the-frog marriage they had looks as phony as a ten-dollar Rolex."

Jasmine kept her back to me, wiping the clean blackboard over and over. "That's all very fascinating, Mr. Standard. Now, I've told you everything I know. I have a full afternoon of classes. I need some time to get ready."

With that she snatched up her backpack and strode up the aisle toward the double doors. Her walk looked purposeful, bent slightly at the waist and pumping her right arm across her slender body as she negotiated the wide, low steps. The faint odor of patchouli oil hurried along behind her.

"Could I talk you into dinner tonight? I've got a few more questions," I asked before she reached the last row of seats. I just sort of blurted it out as if a force inside me wanted a date worse than I did. "There's an Italian place downtown. DaVinci's."

She stopped, turned around, and gave him a quizzical look. "I've heard of it. Is it nice?"

"I hear the people who go there sniff the wine before they drink it."

That brought a gentle smile.

"Then it must be nice. I'll meet you there at six."

# Chapter 13

I moved quickly across the Oregon State Capitol Building's vast, marble-floored foyer under the gaze of large murals depicting significant moments in Oregon's pioneer history. Stern men who looked like Gary Cooper and women who inspired Laura Ingalls Wilder looked down at me. Brass stands connected by the same red velvet ropes used in bank lobbies surrounded the ornate state seal embedded in the floor under the dome. To the left, a wide set of marble stairs led to the second floor lobby outside the senate chambers. Climbing them, I could hear the muted chatter of legislators and lobbyists.

Keeping my head down in the hope of avoiding recognition, I worked my way around a crowd of people standing in front a closed-circuit television that showed the proceedings on the senate floor. On the screen, a man stood at a small desk talking into a microphone.

At the table guarding the entrance to the senate chambers, a polite, elderly woman gave me a copy of that day's senate calendar. I glanced through it, easily remembering how to decipher the cryptic document that had once been the bible that dictated my daily activities when I covered state politics.

Debate on the gun control bill was on the agenda right after the usual business of reading newly introduced bills before referring them to the appropriate committees.

If everything worked out right, I'd be out of there in time to meet Jasmine Grant for dinner. It had been six years since I'd been on a date; five years of marriage to Christine and one year of not caring one way or the other. My decision to invite her to dinner had surprised me as much as Jasmine's acceptance. I wondered what made her say yes and hoped it didn't have anything to do with my infamous status.

The senate gallery on the third floor occupied three sides above the chamber like the balcony in an Elizabethan theater. Even someone sitting in the back of the ten rows of theater seats had a good view of the activities on floor below. Most of the seats were empty, except for a contingent of a dozen men dressed in paramilitary garb sitting in the front row of the center section. They were leaning over the brass railing like kids at a Saturday matinee. Their berets, camouflage shirts, and parachute pants left little doubt about where they stood on the issue of gun control.

I hunkered down in a front row seat in one of the smaller side galleries as far from the militia boys as possible. While the senators moved through the mundane business of the day, I watched members of the capitol press corps slowly migrate onto the floor. They looked bored and weary at the prospect of covering yet another debate on an issue that would not be resolved in their lifetime.

Brad Roark stood on the far side of the chamber holding forth with two wire service reporters. They were scribbling down every word. Ten feet to Roark's left, Kingsley Landis was doing the same thing with a television reporter. The two stars of the day's proceedings looked relaxed and ready for their latest moment in the limelight. Within a few hours their faces would be all over the evening news as the major combatants in a battle that in all likelihood would be billed as a preview of the up-coming gubernatorial race.

The routine business of the senate dragged on until the presiding officer, an elderly man with an ice cream suit and a cheap hairpiece, banged his gavel and announced in a country drawl that the time had come to begin debate on the gun-control bill. He droned through an official script before yielding to Brad Roark.

The television lights on the other side of the gallery switched on as Roark rose from behind his desk to speak into the microphone. He looked about the same as in his newspaper photo a few days earlier. Black, stylishly long hair was mussed in a way that looked more intentional than natural. He was coatless with a slightly wrinkled white button-down collar shirt. The sleeves were rolled up, the tie loose. Throw in the baggy khaki pants, and you had the carefully cultivated look of a liberal man of the people.

"Mr. President, I rise today on behalf of the thousands of innocent people who have been slaughtered in this state and this great country because of some people's overwhelming and all-consuming fascination with guns. The ease with which criminals and criminals-to-be obtain handguns, assault rifles, and other deadly weapons has left behind a legacy of lost hope, lost dreams, and lost lives. It's time, Mr. President, for this great state to do what it can to send a message across this nation of ours that the mayhem stops here, now, today." He paused for effect and a well-timed choke in his voice. "There is enough blood in the streets."

The two wire-service reporters walked off the Senate floor. They had the quotes they needed and would return when Landis took his turn at stoking the sound-bite machine.

I jotted an occasional note as Roark spent the next twenty minutes delivering a tedious array of statistics about rising crime rates and the increase in homicides involving guns.

"It is time to debunk the myth perpetuated by the anti-gun-control lobby that the Second Amendment of the Constitution guarantees the right to keep and bear arms. Thomas Jefferson and other framers of our constitution lived in an era of muzzle loaders. Today we live in a world of Uzis, Glocks, and other powerful assault weapons capable of killing and maiming dozens of people in a single burst lasting no longer than a heart beat. I believe as Jefferson did, that we need a well-armed, well-trained militia, but gangs are not militias. They are children armed with weapons Jefferson never contemplated. They are children with no understanding of life and death, of right and wrong. They are children desensitized by the violence they see every day on television, in the movies and in comic books. We're not talking about hunting deer or ducks anymore. Enough is enough, Mr. President. Stop the bloodshed."

The end of the speech brought hoots and catcalls from the boys in the military suits seated in the front row of the main gallery. They were immediately gaveled down by the man in the ice cream suit and admonished by two guards who had drawn that day's gallery duty. Their protests stopped, but not without their mugging for the television cameras and grumbling about government agents infringing on their right of free speech.

The ruckus had died down when I noticed the uniforms worn by the security guards. They looked familiar, but I didn't remember from where until one guard turned toward me.

The emblem over the shirt pocket read, "Prestige Security."

At precisely the same moment, the presiding officer recognized Kingsley Landis. The two wire-service reporters returned to the senate floor on cue to take their seats at the edge of the chamber.

"Thank you, Mr. President," Landis said, rising to the microphone at his desk across the center aisle from Roark. The two men were about the same age, but they couldn't be further apart in appearance. Landis looked as if he'd spent the morning locked in a Brooks Brothers store. Everything about him looked perfect: blond hair cut to perfection; red tie and charcoal gray three-piece suit ready-made for television; body turned slightly to face the television cameras directly as he spoke.

"No one in this great state abhors the violence that has been visited upon us more than I do, Mr. President. I have walked through the streets of our major cities, ridden in the cars with our courageous men in blue, and talked to the families whose lives have been torn asunder by senseless violence.

Everyone I have talked to -- from the officer on the beat to the mother in the street -- has told me the same thing: It's not the guns, it's the people who use them. Lock them up and throw away the key, they say. They're criminals who break the law, they say. They're right, and I say making guns illegal won't make criminals more honest."

The wire-service reporters left again.

When Landis launched into his childhood reminiscences about deer hunting with his father and other joys of responsible gun ownership, I glanced over at the center gallery. The militia boys were hanging on Landis's every word, nodding in silent agreement each time he made a point. I predicted that they would break into cheers when Landis finished, which would earn them an escorted exit at the hands of the two security guards hovering near by.

More intrigued by the company the guards worked for than what Landis thought about the Second Amendment, I left the gallery. I wandered through the maze of hallways that linked the senate side of the capitol with the house side. At the end of a dead-end hall I found a single door with "Security" painted on the opaque glass. I knocked, then tried the knob when no one answered. It was unlocked.

Inside the cramped office a bank of small, black-and-white monitors showed both the house and senate chambers, the first-floor foyer, and a half-dozen other places I vaguely recognized. The monitor in the senate showed Landis finishing his speech and another senator beginning to talk. The sound was off, so I couldn't hear what was being said. It probably didn't matter.

The Prestige Security guard sitting at the cluttered desk wore a set of headphones and flipped the pages of a magazine. He looked to be in his twenties, whip thin, acne, and a cold sore on his lip the size of a roasted marshmallow. Large ears were like bookends on a face that was a permanent mask of confusion and fear, like a puppy tied up outside a Korean restaurant. His pants were two sizes too big and a small inner tube would fit between his neck and the collar of his shirt. I was just about to reach out and tap him on the shoulder, when the guard jumped up, startled.

"Man, you scared me," the guard said, pulling the headphones off and tossing them on the desk. "Sorry, I can't hear a thing with these on. Anyway, can I help you with something?"

I introduced myself and apologized for startling him.

"I was just wondering how long Prestige has had the contract to provide security for the capitol building."

The patch above the guard's shirt pocket said "Parchman." He looked confused by the question, unsure whether to answer.

"I don't know," he said finally. "Since the first of the year, I think. At least that's how long I've been working here."

"So you work for Buck Mather?"

"Right."

"You don't happen to know Ivan Krychek by any chance?"

Parchman's confusion changed to sadness.

"Did you know Ivan was dead?"

I nodded.

"He and I were good friends," Parchman said. His tongue darted out over the cold sore. He winced and pulled a tube of lip balm from the desk drawer.

"So, you worked together at the fairgrounds."

"No. We worked right here, a couple of nights each week since March. Ivan was a smart guy. Too bad someone killed him."

"He worked here? Doing what?"

"He spent most of his time patrolling the wing of the building that houses the senators' offices. I worked the house wing. Our shift started at eleven at night and ended at six the next morning. That left plenty of time to drink coffee together and talk."

"Talk about what?"

"Ivan knew a lot about politics," Parchman said, his eyes moving between me and the bank of television monitors. A police band radio squawked in the corner. "He was a student of some kind over at Delaney College. He said he only worked here to help support his wife and to work on his research."

"He didn't happen to tell you what that research was?"

Parchman shook his head.

"Beats me. It had something to do with politics, though. That's why he took this job."

I sat in a molded plastic chair and lit a cigarette. The smoke settled over the television monitors and the "No Smoking" sign on Parchman's desk.

"Did you ever meet Ivan's wife?"

"No, but he showed me a picture of her. Boy, if I had a wife like that I wouldn't be hanging around here all night." He let out the sigh of someone who would settle for any kind of woman. "He didn't say much about her, either, other than she was kind of rich and they had a nice house up in Beaverton."

"Did you think it was odd that Ivan was working here?"

"Sure. I even asked him about it a couple of times. He just said he had his reasons and changed the subject. Why?"

"No reason," I said. "Mather ever come by here?"

"Sure, lots of times. Getting this contract was a big deal for him. He wanted everything done just right."

"He and Krychek get along all right?"

"Sure, I guess. Mr. Mather isn't exactly the kind of guy who gets named boss of the year, if you know what I mean."

I agreed with a nod and a smile.

"Any idea why someone would kill Ivan?"

"No, sir." Parchman said.

I wrote my name and telephone number on a yellow sticky from Parchman's desk.

"If you think of anything else that Ivan told you about his work, here's how to get in touch with me."

Parchman looked at the name and then at me. Recognition flickered, then went out.

"Ivan was my friend, Mr. Standard. I'll help anyway I can."

"To be on the safe side, I wouldn't tell your boss I was here," I said on the way out the door.

A political science student wanting to work in the capitol, even as a security guard, didn't sound all that unusual, I thought as I negotiated my way back along the marble halls to the senate gallery. Why then, didn't Mather tell me about it? Better yet, why didn't Anna Krychek?

The gun control bill passed by two votes, signaling either a victory over senseless violence or a mortal blow to the Constitution. I got a few angry quotes from the militia boys, who denounced the action as a loss of freedom that will make it easier for American citizens to be subdued by UN troops intent on creating a one-world government, then headed reluctantly downstairs to the press room in the basement.

I cringed at the thought of showing my face in the press room. I hoped the other reporters would be too new to remember me or too preoccupied to care why I was there. I stood at the back of the circle of reporters and tried to stay as inconspicuous as possible, which wasn't hard in a room filled with television cameras and microphones attached to tape recorders.

Two dozen reporters surrounded Brad Roark, firing questions at him about the effect the vote would have on his decision to run for governor and whether it would give him a leg up on his likely opponent. Roark was calm at first, then gradually began to look like a condemned man fielding questions from his own firing squad. The more uncomfortable he appeared, the more pointed the questions. The well-oiled figure I had seen on the senate floor had turned into a rusty tin man nervously giving vague and stumbling answers to pointed questions. Finally, he held up his hands to signal surrender and quickly left the room.

On his way out, he stopped for a few moments and talked to a man with salon hair and a Caribbean tan that made him look out of place amid the pallid basement dwellers of the capitol press corps. He wore gray slacks, a dark double-breasted blazer, and a bright-white shirt with a tab collar and striped tie. They spoke for a few seconds. Roark nodded reluctantly to whatever the man whispered to him, then headed out the door.

Kingsley Landis arrived just as Roark left. Reporters quickly hit him with a barrage of questions about whether his failure to stop the gun-control bill dealt a blow to his chances of becoming governor. Landis remained upbeat about the defeat, predicting the house would reject the bill. If that didn't work, he'd ask the governor to veto it. Landis appeared much more comfortable than Roark, at least for the first ten minutes. Then, he too, began to ramble and squirm. As he left the room, Landis stopped to talk to the same slick-looking man standing at the door.

"Who is that?" I asked the woman standing in front of me. "The guy who was talking to Landis."

"Mitch Penroy. Lobbyist for Scofield Industries," she said, rubbing her fingers together in the international sign for money.

"As in Proctor Scofield?"

She nodded.

I knew little about the reclusive billionaire except that he owned a complex web of companies that manufactured silicon wafers, flat-panel screens, and computer chips used in most of the world's personal computers. His enormous wealth and influence made Scofield a target for every politician in the state who sought to rise higher than county commissioner. No surprise, then, that both Roark and Landis stopped to kiss the ring of Scofield's lackey.

When Penroy left, I worked my way through the dispersing crowd of reporters and followed him out the door, catching up with him in the basement parking garage.

"I'm sorry, but I didn't catch your name or the news organization you represent?" Penroy said after I asked if he had a minute.

"John Standard. I'm a free-lancer. You seem to know both Landis and

Roark. I'm curious about your reaction to today's vote."

"I thought it was an excellent debate and a good example of democracy in action."

He delivered the line with the style and grace of a Nolan Ryan fast ball, then walked away.

"What kind of impact do you think this gun control issue will have on the governor's race? What are the politics of this issue?"

"This is no race for governor," Penroy said over his shoulder. "No one has announced and the election is more than a year away."

"What do you think Proctor Scofield's reaction to the vote will be?"

The lobbyist stopped, turned, and stared.

"I haven't the slightest idea. Why do you ask?"

"Just curious. Isn't your boss the biggest game around when it comes to politics. Doesn't his horse usually win?"

"I never thought about it."

"Maybe I could ask him myself."

"Mr. Scofield doesn't give interviews."

"So he is alive, then?"

Penroy pulled a pair of expensive dark glasses with small, round lenses from the breast pocket of his suit, and walked away again.

"Do you go by Mitch or Mitchell?" I asked. "It's for the article I'm working on."

"I go by 'political observer.'" He said it without looking back.

On silent shoes, Mitch Penroy walked across the concrete floor to a dark blue Lincoln Town car. When he backed out of the space, I could see the sign on the wall read "Legislators Only."

I left thinking maybe it wasn't money that corrupted politics, but the people who handed it out.

# Chapter 14

I arrived a little early. Jasmine a little late. At her request we got a table in the no-smoking section and by six-thirty had ordered dinner, drank half a glass of Chianti each while fumbling with the awkwardness of what I stubbornly insisted on considering a date.

In between the foccacia bread and the salad, I learned that Jasmine's mother came from Hong Kong and her father was an American businessman from San Francisco. She grew up in the Bay Area, attended the University of California at Berkeley, and lived in Hong Kong for five years after her father died. She returned to California to get a master's degree and then a doctorate in Political Science at the University of San Francisco. Delaney College hired her eight years earlier. She'd been dean of the Political Science Department for two years.

It took me roughly twenty minutes to get this little bit of information out of her, learning along the way that she was divorced with no children and there was no one who inspired enough interest to qualify as a boyfriend. I found myself asking questions just to watch her talk, finding her attitude toward life and politics a refreshing testimony to the possibility that someone can understand both and not be poisoned by either.

Jasmine Grant was nothing like Christine. My ex-wife had a ceramic personality that could shatter into a million pieces at a word or phrase said the wrong way or at the wrong time. Jasmine was playful and mischievous. Durable. At one point, I found her staring over my shoulder at a man sitting alone at a table against the back wall of the restaurant. He looked to be in his mid-fifties with dark glasses, a diamond ear ring, a silk shirt open at the neck, and thin black hair pulled tight into a greasy pony tail. When I asked if she knew him, Jasmine looked embarrassed.

"I'm sorry," she said, then giggled, leaned forward, and began to whisper. Her eyes were the color of new ivy. "I'm an unabashed people watcher. I can't help looking at people and making up stories about them. I've decided that guy probably owns a warehouse somewhere full of Dalkon Shields he's trying to ship to some third world country."

We ordered a second glass of wine and more bread. I was starting to feel more comfortable, less like my every gesture was being judged.

"Can I ask you something?" she said. I nodded, already knowing the question. "When you came into the classroom this morning, I thought you looked familiar. I didn't realize why until later. You're the reporter who was in that accident with the two little girls."

She had paused over the word accident as if unsure it was the right one. I fingered the linen napkin with one hand and twirled the wine glass with the other.

"I remember reading about it when it happened," she said almost as if I wasn't there. "It was like a Greek tragedy. A good man leading a good life commits a heinous act through no fault of his own. It forever changes the course of his life. And I was right. You were acquitted. Free, but not really free."

I marveled at how she had turned the whole event into an intellectual exercise, depersonalizing it right before my eyes without offending me or making me feel like she was prying into areas that I wanted sealed off and forgotten.

"You're in the minority," I said. "Conventional wisdom said I was drunk, ran them down in the dark of night, then scurried home to hide under the bed until the police came."

"But the jury didn't think that."

I shrugged and tried to think of a polite way to change the subject.

"What was your life like before it happened?"

"Like my name: typical, normal."

"And now?"

"Anything but."

"So it was terrible?" she said. "Afterwards, I mean."

"What's your definition of terrible?"

"The stories in the paper and on television. Cameramen in your yard. Satellite trucks. Talking to the police."

"Then it was terrible."

"Did you learn anything in all of this?"

I pondered the question for a few moments, silently reliving the past year.

"I learned that I don't have an addictive personality so I can't become an alcoholic, that mind-altering drugs are too expensive, and that pain killers are best taken on an empty stomach."

"That bad, huh?"

"More wine?" I asked with a smile that told her to slow down.

She got the message, and an awkward silence replaced the topic of my past. Over the main course of salmon-stuffed tortellini and more Chianti, I finally broached the subject of Ivan Krychek. The wine had taken the edge off her emotions. She didn't balk or turn sad when Krychek's name came up.

"I told you before that Ivan was a dedicated and talented researcher. That wasn't quite the truth. He was dedicated, all right, and liked to take things head on, but he wasn't particularly talented. Don't get me wrong. Ivan wasn't stupid. Just the opposite. It's that he had strong opinions. His tendency was to believe things that supported those opinions and ignore things that didn't. I tried to coach him, but in the end he always came up short. I knew when he started work on his doctorate that he'd already reached a conclusion about the evils of a politically polarized nation. I also knew that those conclusions would be seriously challenged when it came time to deliver his thesis."

"How long did you know him?"

"Five years. A little more. He came to Delaney as a freshman and stayed. He graduated in three years, got his master's a year later. He'd been working on his doctorate for about a year."

Krychek wanted to finish his thesis by next spring, she explained, hoping to get his doctorate in time to become a political science professor at Delaney the following fall.

"We used to talk about what it would be like to teach together. I'm not sure the college would have hired him, but I didn't say anything. He was so excited about his future."

With one long swallow, her wine disappeared. She didn't notice or didn't mind when I ordered another for her and coffee for myself. We concentrated on our meals for a few minutes until I asked about Anna.

"I didn't mean to sound catty earlier," Jasmine said. "I only met Anna once. She seemed very nice. It's just that running off and marrying someone like her was so out of character for Ivan. He always planned things so carefully. I guess I felt disappointed, a little betrayed maybe."

"What do mean by 'someone like her'?"

She looked sheepish.

"All right. That was unfair. I shouldn't put labels on people, but I take it you've seen her and you've seen Ivan.

"She is beautiful."

Jasmine shrugged as if to say beauty explains everything.

"Her looks just made me that much more disappointed in him. I felt like he had chosen style over substance. She was beautiful, but Ivan was always uncomfortable around women. He seldom dated and was silent and awkward when women were around."

"Except you."

"Ivan and I were never involved, if that's what you mean. We didn't have that kind of relationship. Anyway, I thought he'd end up with a stronger, more intelligent woman. Instead, he chose a Barbie doll, a mannequin."

"A wealthy mannequin, at that."

She raised her glass in a mock toast to beauty and money over strength and intelligence.

"So tell me. You've seen the Widow Krychek. What did you think of her?"

"Not my type," I said.

"How can you tell?"

"Too sophisticated. Too perfect. If she squealed during sex it would probably be because she broke a nail."

We split a chocolate mousse. Over coffee I asked about Krychek's part-time job at Prestige Security.

"That really baffled me," she said. "Ivan's family wasn't rich, but they had enough money to keep him at Delaney for five years, which is not cheap. He never worked before. I couldn't understand why he felt the need to work now. From the way Anna looked and acted, I doubted that he would ever work at all."

"Anna Krychek said he worked because he came from a poor family and wanted to support his new wife as a matter of pride."

"That sounds noble enough," she said, "but that isn't what Ivan led me to believe during the five years I knew him. No, that job had nothing to do with supporting Anna."

"What did it have to do with, then?"

"My only guess is that it had something to do with his research. Ivan could be fanatical about his work. I don't see what patrolling the state fairgrounds would have to do with a doctoral thesis on politics, but I do know that he didn't do anything that wasn't in some way related to that thesis and his desire to become a professor at Delaney."

"Except marry Anna."

She conceded the point.

"Did you know that he was working security at the state capitol?"

"No, but that doesn't surprise me. It had to have something to do with his research. That's the kind of thing Ivan would do." She finished her wine. "So, who do you think killed him?"

"Have you talked to the police?"

"A detective named Butcher questioned me and some of the other faculty. He was sort of belligerent. When he left, I felt like I was a suspect."

"I doubt it," I said, remembering my own status with Butcher. "As to who killed Krychek, I was hoping you could tell me."

"I've asked myself that a thousand times in the last few days. My only guess is that some depraved individual was determined to kill someone in that grotesque manner. Ivan just happened to be in the wrong place at the wrong time. I know it's sick, but what could he have been involved in that would've made someone kill him that way?"

She excused herself to go to the rest room. While she was gone, I paid the bill with my credit card and sipped coffee. When she returned, she walked to my side of the table, leaned close to my ear, and in soft voice that made my skin tingle said, "It's time to go."

Her mood had changed. A slight lustiness had emerged or my imagination was working overtime after a year in the deep freeze. But there was something in her voice, her eyes, and the way her hand gently brushed my shoulder when she moved away from me. I followed her out the door, unsure what to do next.

"One more question," I said when we were standing on the sidewalk outside the restaurant. "What made you change your mind about having dinner with me tonight?"

"I don't know. I guess I wanted to know more about Ivan and his wife." Then the mischievous grin returned and she moved a half step closer. "Maybe I wanted to know more about you."

Suddenly she kissed me on the cheek, thanked me for dinner, and walked toward her car at the opposite end of the street from mine. I stood watching her, the trail of patchouli tugging at me. Half way down the block she turned and walked backed.

"I have a meeting in Portland tomorrow morning," she said. "I'll be done by eleven. Perhaps we could have lunch."

I wrote my telephone number inside a matchbook cover and handed it to her.

"I'd like that very much. Call when you're ready."

# Chapter 15

I finished the gun control article a little before midnight. After running it through the spell-checker one more time, I copied it on to a disk, then packaged it up with the photos and a cover letter to the editor in Philadelphia. After two glasses of cheap chardonnay and a quick replay of my dinner with Jasmine Grant, I went to bed feeling disappointed that Vanessa had the night off. Something about Jasmine and the anticipation of lunch the next day had stirred something inside that made Vanessa's nightly act more interesting than usual.

I slept until ten, then showered, dressed and went downstairs to have coffee with Benny. Ivy rattled around in the kitchen trying to figure out the coffee maker. She looked exactly like she did the first time I saw her. I wondered if she'd spent the night with Benny and thought again about Jasmine.

Benny put down the newspaper so he could listen to me describe my new status as a murder suspect and my meeting with Jasmine Grant.

"You lead a pretty interesting life for a guy who's been doing everything possible to make himself invisible," Benny said, folding the paper and tossing it on a pile of others behind his chair. Useless things had a way of piling up around Benny.

"If you think being accused of murder meets the definition of an interesting life."

"I was thinking more about the professor," Benny said. "Dinner last night. Lunch today. Remember, technically you're still married."

Ivy plopped down on the arm of Benny's chair like a parrot, her pale arm snaking around and coming to rest on his shoulder. Benny watched my face and then started slyly humming Gene Autry's "Back in the Saddle Again."

When I refused to rise to the bait, Benny asked, "What are you going to do about this Butcher fellow?"

"I'll call Alfie Gitchell. He'll tell me what the hell is going on. Alfie got me into this by inviting me down to the fairgrounds. Maybe he can get me out by dragging someone else under Butcher's nose."

Two cups of coffee later, Benny disappeared into his computer room and Ivy went back to painting her toenails another shade of purple. I returned to my apartment to wait for Jasmine's call. It came a few minutes after eleven.

"I'm at Portland State," she said. "Where are you?"

"Not far. Pick me up in front of the Portland Art Museum. It's just a few blocks away on Ninth between Jefferson and Main."

Ten minutes later I was sitting in the air-conditioned comfort of her Volvo. The giant hair clip had been replaced by two large oriental needles that seemed to be doing a better job holding everything in place. Her clothes were the same as the day before, but with different designs. Her skirt was pulled up and tucked under her legs so I could see her thighs. The curve of her breast was just visible through the side of her sleeveless top. Blood pulsed in places I'd forgotten about.

"Where to?" she asked. Her smile made me feel five years younger. The patchouli had been replaced with gardenias.

I suggested the Dan and Louie Oyster Bar on SW Ankeny, but she insisted on someplace with outside seating, so I gave her directions to Papa Haydn's in Northwest Portland. We drove up Burnside and turned right on Twenty-third. After ten minutes of driving along residential streets, we found a place to park, and walked three blocks to the restaurant. We got a table on the street under the shade of a pinwheel-colored awning and ordered wine and sandwiches. By the time the tables on either side of us filled up, we had once again gotten past the awkward small talk.

"How come you didn't want me to pick you up where you live?" she asked. "You married or something?"

"The art museum was easier to find," I said, then thought about it for a minute. "And my place isn't exactly something out of *Town and Country*."

"And?"

"Separated. About a year."

Jasmine sipped her wine and delicately pulled a slice of bread from the half loaf wrapped in a calico napkin.

"When I got home last night, I searched the internet for some news articles about your accident," she said. "I found a few things, but nothing that told your side of the story. You didn't even testify, did you?"

I told her that the boy lawyer said there was no reason for me to take the stand.

"He said it was an accident, pure and simple, and that the jury was either going to convict me for an accident or they're weren't. My testimony wouldn't change anything. When I agreed, a sense of relief swept over me. I never wanted my day in court because I never wanted to *be* in court. Anyway, it wasn't much of a story. I fell asleep at the wheel. I thought all I did was wake up in time to keep the car from going in a ditch. Instead, I ran them down and never knew it."

I swirled the wine in my glass, wishing I'd ordered something stronger. "So you went home?"

"I spent two days never knowing it even happened. I mowed the lawn, trimmed the hedge, and took my wife out to a romantic dinner. Made love to her on the lawn in the backyard. Everything was great until the state police showed up. After that, I lost everything. Still got the car, though."

"How did they find you?"

"Someone saw a car like mine and called it in." She was leaning toward me, elbows on the table, ivy-green eyes focused on my face. "Why are you asking me this? You read all of this in the news clips about the trial."

"I just wanted to hear you say it. Watch your face while you talked about it."

"Is this some kind of class project?"

"Of course not." She leaned back and sipped her wine. "One of the stories had an interview with some of your jurors. They said what happened was terrible, but it wasn't a crime. It was an awful accident and that convicting you wasn't going to change anything."

I remembered the story and the sympathy notes I got from four of the jurors.

The food arrived. I ordered another glass of wine, after finding out from the waiter that Papa Hadyn's didn't serve hard liquor.

"So," Jasmine said. "How are you going to get over this? Even a political science professor from a podunk college can see that what happened that night is right under your skin. So, why not throw in the towel. Give up. Leave town."

"I almost did. After Christine left and the paper fired me, I didn't see much to fight for. Hell, it took me six months to get up the nerve to drive at night. I still don't like it."

"Christine is your wife?"

I nodded.

"Did you ever go to a psychiatrist?"

"The lawyer ordered an evaluation in case things got so bad I had to fall back on a mental incapacity defense or some other nonsense. Anyway, the outcome was deep depression with self-destructive tendencies."

"Suicidal," she said.

"More or less."

The awkward silence returned. I gazed over her shoulder at the stop-and-go traffic moving along Twenty-Third Street. Noon-hour shoppers strolled through the trendy clothing stores on the east side of the street. A block away, teenagers sat in front of a coffee shop smoking cigarettes.

"So what's your interest in Ivan?" she asked, appearing to sense the need to change the subject.

I started by telling her how my research on the gun control article had led me to the gun show at the state fairgrounds and the telephone call from Alfie Gitchell, but left out the part about seeing Krychek's body. She stopped eating when I described Mather and what he said, then stared in stony silence as I talked about my visit to Krychek's house. Her eyes turned dark and angry with the news that Mather and Anna Krychek had failed to tell me about Ivan's stint as a night watchman at the capitol building.

"You think they're involved in his death? That can't be," Jasmine said and accepted my shrug as explanation that anything's possible. "So, you're doing all this for an article for *Inside Oregon*?"

I tried not to look sheepish.

"Not exactly," I said and launched into an explanation about my status as numero uno on Harry Butcher's list of suspects.

"It's because of those two little girls, isn't it?" she said. "How ridiculous."

We ordered coffee and shared a slice of chocolate cheese cake. Jasmine insisted on paying the tab, despite my weak protest.

"You bought last night," she said.

We walked slowly back to the car, stopping in the off-beat stores along the street before going into the Nob Hill Bar and Grill and getting a table in the corner. We both ordered glasses of Black Butte Porter and glanced around at the Cubs-Giants game on the big-screen television in the corner near the front door.

"You know you didn't answer my question," Jasmine said. A thin mustache of dirty-white foam clung to her upper lip. "The one about how you're going to get over this. How you're going to forget what happened to you?"

I knew the answer. I'd kept it from Benny Orlando, but for some reason felt eager to share it with Jasmine Grant. Maybe it was the wine with lunch or the sleepy glow I was getting from the beer. Maybe it was Jasmine. Her air of calmness and confidence made me feel like I was the only person in the world and all I had to do to make things right again was tell her everything I felt inside. Maybe it was simpler than that. Maybe I was like a stray cat hanging around the back door of someone who showed even the slightest bit of affection. Whatever it was, it didn't make any difference. I believed what I wanted to believe because I couldn't keep anything inside anymore.

I let it all out at one time, afraid to stop for fear that I might not finish, grateful that Jasmine had the patience to listen and not interrupt. I told her about the huge debt I owed. Not in terms of money or legal bills, but more important than that. Two little girls were dead and no amount of money was going to make that any different. No jury could wipe the slate clean, no matter how strongly they felt that it was just an accident and not a crime. Somewhere, someplace, I needed to find a way to make good on what I did.

"This is bigger than just doing something for the parents of those little girls, isn't it?" Jasmine said when I finished.

"If that's all it was I could send them money or go to them and beg their forgiveness. Someday I probably will. But this is a debt against my soul, a debt I incurred by fate, by some force that put me and those two girls in the same place at the same time. It's going to have to be fate that allows me to repay the debt in full. Anything short of that is just a token payment, pennies in a beggar's tin cup."

"Are you familiar with the Tao Teh Ching?" she said.

The question caught me by surprise, then I recalled a distant memory of a college class on Chinese philosophy.

"Lao Tse. An older contemporary of Confucius. The Tao Teh Ching is one of the sources of a religion, Taoism, isn't it? The I Ching. Tai Chi. That sort of thing."

"Very good," she said, eyes gleaming with approval. "But Taoism is more than a religion. It's a way of life, really. Tao has been translated to mean the path, the way, Teh is virtue and Ching is laws. Tao Teh Ching is The Law of Virtue and its Way. In it, Lao Tse wrote that misery may yield happiness; happiness may conceal misery; who can say which will be for the best?"

She spoke in a slow whisper, letting the words wind around me, pulling me closer until our faces were inches apart over the table and I was answering her in the same intimate way that she talked to me.

"I'm not sure I'm miserable or happy," I said. "There are times when I can't get comfortable. Where ever I am, I want to be somewhere else. Whatever I'm doing, I want to be doing something else. I think it's because I never saw a chance to determine my own fate. It gnaws at me that I didn't see those two little kids and have the opportunity to jerk the wheel the other way in time to avoid them, even if it meant killing myself. That was fate, pure and simple, that put three people, me and those two girls, in the same place at the same time. After that, nothing was the same."

"And finding Ivan's killer is going to change that?"

"Who knows? All I want to do is break even."

"Do you remember what Lao Tse wrote about fate?" she said.

I shook my head without taking my eyes off her face.

"Fate does not contend, yet all things are conquered by it; it does not ask, yet all things answer to it; it does not call, yet all things come to it; it does not plan, yet all things are determined by it."

"So, there's a chance that fate will make things even again," I said, "put me in a place with two other people and the chance to make things right?"

She gave me a knowing smile. I drained my beer and motioned to the bartender with the empty glass.

"It will," I said, answering my own question. "I'll get that chance. I have to, but it must be something unequivocal. The only question is will I recognize it when the time comes."

Instead of answering, she moved around the table to sit next to me.

"Taoism supports the concept of non-action, yet nothing is left undone. Things will develop naturally. In other words, John Standard, patience."

She laughed when I looked lost and confused.

"Enough mysticism," she said. "But I do want you to know that if anything ever happened to me and I needed help, you'd be the first person I'd turn to."

I could only nod my appreciation.

"How about another beer?"

"I don't think so," she said, her voice a soft whisper. "I'm free the rest of the afternoon. How about we go someplace fun?"

"How about the zoo?"

"How about your apartment?"

She said it without hesitation, like a line she'd been thinking about all day. It didn't catch me totally by surprise, but the gentle squeeze she gave my crotch did.

"You're not one of those take-a-loser-to-bed freaks, are you?"

Her eyes turned a shade darker and slightly more exotic. Her breathe felt like a warm towel against my cheek.

"Would it matter?"

# Chapter 16

I hung around the apartment most of the next morning, hoping Jasmine would call and debating whether to call her. Her smell clung to my fingers. The taste of salt and gardenias lingered on my tongue. Memories of the previous night were fading too quickly. All I wanted was to hold them the way you'd hold a child about to fall off a cliff. When we were naked in bed she had asked what I liked.

"To forget for a while," I said.

It was all she needed to know.

She'd been both soft and passionate, playful and serious, exotic and conventional. When she lowered herself onto me the first time, my memories of the last year disappeared like smoke on the wind. By the third time, the sad surroundings of my bedroom had become a playroom full of dark, mysterious places to explore and hide from the world.

Just remembering each moment brought back the urge to call her, but I forced myself to wait. It had only been a few hours since we'd walked together to her car, and I'd watched her drive away, waving to me through the Volvo's sun roof as she disappeared into traffic.

I found the note when I got back to the apartment. It was attached to the bathroom mirror and written on a piece of toilet paper in perfect block letters:

"All that ever stays the same is change. And I Dream. I Wander." Lao Tse

I carefully folded the note and gently placed it in the top drawer of the bureau in the bedroom.

Then I forced myself to attend to business by giving the contents of the package for the Philadelphia magazine one final check before walking it down to the post office. On the way out the door, I checked in the mailbox and found a letter containing the check from the tabloid for the Ivan Krychek story.

Feeling happy and flush, I sent the package next-day mail, then walked over to the House of Louie for an early dim sum lunch over the morning paper. Roark and Landis were still on the front page as the featured acts in the aftermath of the gun-control debate. I read the story with a sense of relief that I was done with the topic for good.

Walking through the city cleared my head of everything except Jasmine and the lingering uneasiness about being a target of a murder investigation. After spending the night with Jasmine my status as Harry Butcher's prime suspect seemed more like a bad dream. Except it wasn't.

On the way back to the apartment, I found more interesting stores and restaurants tucked away in small corners of the city. I had lived in Portland for more than a dozen years. Still, I knew little about Portland. Christine preferred driving over to the upscale restaurants in the wealthy suburb of Lake Oswego with its ample parking to the hassle of going downtown for the same meal at half-again the price. Not caring one way or the other, I had acquiesced. As a result, I always felt like a guest in my own city. I owned a home there, paid taxes, drove on the streets, and shopped in the stores, but somehow kept the city at arm's length.

Since losing my job and moving into the apartment, I'd had time to explore, mostly on foot. After finding it full of interesting nooks and crannies, I came to the conclusion that Portland was an often-overlooked metropolitan area that badly wanted to have the same reputation for sophistication as Seattle to the north and San Francisco to the south. The collective whine of nearly a million people was, "Notice us, *please*."

I walked through Old Town, across Burnside, and up Fifth Street, cruising through Meier & Frank and Nordstroms, but resisting the urge to buy anything despite the deplorable condition of my so-called wardrobe. Patience, I told myself; wait until the check from Philadelphia shows up.

I got home a little after two and called Alfie Gitchell, who listened without comment to my description of dinner with Harry Butcher.

"I'll talk to him," Gitchell said, "but he's just doing his job. After all, you were *there* the day Krychek was killed."

"So were a thousand other people."

"Yeah, and they're suspects, too, but your reputation is not exactly on a par with Mother Theresa."

"Yeah. Yeah. Once a killer, always a killer. The gospel according to Butcher."

"Slow down, John, and listen for a second. I'd not defending Butcher, but he's had a hard time of it. His wife and only son were killed by a drunk driver a few years ago. The guy was a stockbroker. Got a good lawyer and walked on a technicality because of a police screw up. Harry's had a hard-on ever since for anyone he thinks is getting away with something. I've talked to him about it, but he's a hard man to reason with."

78

The sympathy I felt would've been more than a twinge if Butcher would take out his frustrations on someone else.

"What all this tells me is that you've got nothing in the way of evidence or motive," I said. "If you did, Butcher wouldn't be hanging around my apartment building."

"You're right. No motive. The rope, the hooks, and the piano wire found in the outhouse are all standard issue, if you'll pardon the pun, available in any hardware and music store."

"The wife's story check out?"

"All down the line. Airline and parents confirm everything. She was no where near Salem the night Krychek died."

"What about Mather?"

"Still checking it out, as far as I know."

I hung up still feeling uncomfortable about being a suspect.

With the gun-control article finished, I needed to keep beating the bushes for work. I called the Reuter's bureau in Seattle to see if the news agency needed anyone to cover the US Women's Open, which started in three weeks at a golf course west of Portland. The bureau chief sounded interested. He said to check into getting press credentials, then get back to him before the tournament started.

"By the way," the bureau chief said, "anything new on Bob Packwood or Tonya Harding?"

I hung up after mumbling something about looking into it.

I was thinking about calling Jasmine when Qwest escorted Christine back into my life.

All through our five years together, I wondered why I ever married Christine. Her deep beauty and thin skin kept me constantly on guard with her. My questionable skills as a husband were no substitute for the wealthy and protective family that treated me more like a guest than a son-in-law. We met at a party arranged by mutual friends who believed that no one could be single and happy at the same time. Her southwest beauty, blonde hair, and permanent tan made her easy to spot in a crowd. What started as a quiet conversation over wine about the best resorts in Mexico, turned into a whirlwind courtship that made me feel like the last guy in crack-the-whip. Within months we were living together. A year later we were married in a Scottsdale church in front of two hundred people of which I knew three, including Christine.

The last time I saw her, she was frozen in horrified silence while the police questioned me in the living room of our house. The look on her face said I had more to worry about than a hit-and-run charge. Within hours she was gone, back in Scottsdale with her parents. Since then, all communications had been through her lawyer.

"My attorney says I'm not supposed to talk to you," she said after a few minutes of icy small talk.

"I think that's excellent advice."

"Don't be snide, John."

"You called me, remember?"

"Can't you be civil for just a minute?"

"You leave me in the dark of night when I needed you most, and you want me to be civil."

The remark got exactly the effect I expected.

"Damn you! You ruined everything. I had everything I wanted. The man I wanted. The house I wanted. The job I wanted. You *ruined* it."

"You make it sound like I did it just to make your life miserable."

"I couldn't stand it. Those reporters kept taking pictures of me and asking questions. Some of them looked through our garbage. Our garbage, for Christ's sake! And those trucks with big satellite dishes parked up and down the street. It was humiliating. Your own profession turned on you, John. The hunter became the hunted. I remember how you used to stand there at cocktail parties glibly defending reporters, telling people there was no real difference between the *New York Times* and those TV tabloids. That it was only a short leap from William F. Buckley to Geraldo Rivera. Well, there *is* a difference, damn it. I saw what your profession had become, and it scared me."

"So, you did what every good wife does. You went immediately to the airport and flew home to mom and dad."

The silence at the end of the line told me that she knew I was right. It gave me no sense of satisfaction.

"I knew it was over," she said, finally. "I wanted out. It was never going to be the same again after that. We were going to lose everything."

"What you did was wrong, Christine. The first time our marriage was tested, you bolted."

"Don't give me that crap, John." The words came out like she expected the accusation and had rehearsed her answer. "I know what kind of person you are. It wasn't like you were going to let me help you. You were going to do what you always did, handle it yourself. Keep it all inside, wrapped up inside one of those moods you'd have that made me feel like I was living with a stranger. Then, you'd let me know later on what you did and why. You weren't going to ask me to help you. I was never going to be your partner. You never would've let me."

I shrank from the telephone. It was Christine's turn to be right. In a way, I was envious. She had gotten out, while I had to stay. While I gave up and passively accepted my fate, Christine simply left, taking the action that I was too afraid to take myself.

"Please, John, I don't want to talk about this anymore," she said. Her voice was quieter, calmer. She was crying, but I knew the tears were more for her loss than mine. "I only called to tell you that the divorce is final next month. The wedding is scheduled for the end of July."

I tried to think of Jasmine Grant so I wouldn't feel so alone and abandoned.

"Gee, that's great Christine. I'm living in a flea-bag apartment house, trying to pay the bills selling stories to the scum of the Earth, and my wife calls to tell me her wedding plans. Well, I hope you and Jasper are very happy together. Can I hang up now?"

"It's not Jasper. It's Jacob."

"Tell me, does Jacob make you scream?"

"No," she said after a long pause, "but he doesn't make me cry either."

The image of what life had been with Christine and the reality of a four-room apartment sent me out the door again to get lost in the city. Heading down Clay Street, I wondered if my suspicions about Anna Krychek had anything to do with how much she reminded me of Christine. That air of sophistication the two of them shared really consisted of nothing more than acting bored and pissed off at the world. They even seemed to share that same sense of privilege and entitlement that made them view the rest of the world with a distant, cold disdain. I really didn't miss Christine. It was just what her absence represented that made me feel like a pissed off orphan.

At Tom McCall Waterfront Park, I stood along the Willamette River and smoked. The cigarette felt harsh on the back of my throat, so I dropped it in the water with the other flotsam and jetsam that washed up against the rock seawall. The dinner ship *Spirit of Portland* went by, churning dark water as it headed upstream with another wedding or retirement party on board.

The sleek, white ship was well beyond the Marquam Bridge before I left to walk past the colorful tents going up for the Waterfront Blues Festival. I followed Yamhill Street into the heart of downtown again. At Pioneer

Square, the street preachers brought me and a small group of disinterested shoppers up to date on the latest from heaven and hell. I found an empty table in front of Starbuck's. It felt good to be lost in a crowd, to know that none of the women walking by with packages containing new shoes or a new blouse cared who I was or what I'd done.

I wondered how many of them would have done the same thing Christine did. Not many, I decided, then walked home. Somewhere along the way, I lost Christine again.

At nine that night I thought about calling Jasmine to find out where Krychek's parents lived, but knew it was a ruse to talk to her again. Instead, I decided that another trip to Salem was in order the next day to see if I could find out more about Krychek's research. At the same time, I would see if Jasmine was free for lunch. My hand was inches from the phone, when she called me.

"Sorry to bother you at home this late," she said. Her voice sounded strained and tense, not at all what I expected from someone I'd just spent the night with. "I got something in the mail today that I think you should see. It's from Ivan."

"And?"

Go ahead, I thought, invite me over so we can pick up where we left off and I can get lost inside you again.

"It's the first draft of his doctoral thesis."

"What does it say?"

"It's too complicated to tell over the phone. You'll have to read it for yourself."

"Is everything all right? You sound kind of odd."

"Fine," she said a little too quickly. "What should I do with this manuscript?"

"Have you called the police?"

"No, but maybe I will after you see it."

"I take it you want me to come down tonight?"

I tried to say it without sounding suggestive or eager.

"That would be fine," she said and gave me an address and some vague directions.

"I'll be there in an hour."

I grabbed the last bottle of good wine I owned, put on clean pants and a shirt, and headed out the door convinced that the call from Jasmine so soon after hearing from Christine was the first sign that my life was turning around.

# Chapter 17

Jasmine Grant's neighborhood was a collection of one- and two-story homes built in the early 1900s and considered Salem's historical district, which meant the owners got a tax break if they opened up their doors one day each year so strangers could come in and wander around for a while. Volvos, Saabs, and Ford Explorers were parked in the driveways and along the tree-lined streets. Jasmine's house was a one-story bungalow with baskets of fuchsia and ivy geraniums hanging from the large, country porch.

I parked at the curb and walked up the driveway. The lights in the house threw narrow squares of dim light onto the porch and the damp grass of the front lawn. Concrete stones crossed the lawn and up to the porch. The front door was open, but the screen pulled closed. Classical music - Ravel, I thought - drifted out into the night. My breath shortened. There had been some clumsy moments the night before. There would none tonight.

I knocked on the screen door, expecting to see her appear at any second, dressed in her flowered skirt, tie-dye top, and Birkenstocks.

"Jasmine?"

When no one answered, I knocked a little louder. Still nothing other than the music.

I took a few steps to the left to peer in the front window at a living room cluttered with nick-knacks and comfortable-looking furniture. Yellow light from a floor lamp set between an easy chair and an overstuffed couch reflected off bookcases that lined the far wall. Art fair posters and little paintings in ornate frames decorated the off-white walls. The music came from an upright stereo cabinet that occupied the corner near an unused fireplace. On the same wall as the bookcases was a door that I assumed went into either the dining room or the kitchen. The only sign of Jasmine Grant was a coffee cup on a low table next to the easy chair.

"Jasmine? It's me, John."

I opened the screen door and stepped inside. The hallway in front of me led to the back of the house. The sitting room to the right had been turned into an office, with a Macintosh and a printer on an expensive modular desk unit surrounded by more bookshelves. Sitting abandoned in the corner was one of those backless, ergonomically sound computer chairs.

I turned left and walked cautiously through the living room to the small dining room with a round glass-topped table with four spindle-backed chairs. Beyond, through an arched doorway, I could see the brightly lit kitchen with expensive gourmet cookware on a chef's rack suspended over a waist-high butcher's block. The refrigerator door was covered with cute, little magnets that held up recipes, photos, and a postcard that read, "Pittsburgh ... a Special Place."

Even though I'd explored every part of her body, I felt odd roaming through Jasmine's house. Everything was neat, clean, and in its place. I put the bottle of wine on the counter, hoping that I wasn't cluttering things up too much.

The house was still, as if the air had been compressed to mute the usual sounds of dripping faucets and creaking floor boards. The heavy smell of incense came from the potpourri on the gas range to mix with the faint scent of orchids and patchouli.

I pushed open the door on the far side of the kitchen. It led back into the main hallway. I looked down the hall to the right at the front door, then left through the screened back door to a small porch. No one.

It dawned on me that the invitation might have been a ruse. She might be waiting naked on a bed covered with rose petals. Champagne chilling in an ice bucket on the night stand. It's possible, I thought, remembering some of the more exotic moments from the previous night. We had nothing left to be shy about.

The door on the other side of the hall was ajar. I gently pushed it open and peered inside. My heart beat a little faster, then nearly stopped.

Jasmine Grant was in bed all right, and naked.

But her arms were tied to the brass bed frame crucifixion style, a piano wire noose around her neck. Blood from where it cut into her flesh ran down her chest and soaked the flowered sheets black. Her eyes were open, and her tongue hung out one side of her mouth, giving her the look of a little kid making a face over a plate of spinach. The swampy smell of blood, urine, and feces filled the room.

The body on the bed was a grotesque parody of the woman who the night before had opened herself up to me like a lotus flower. Blood covered the breasts where I'd laid my head and listened to the heart now silenced forever. I wanted to hold her one more time, but couldn't bring myself to do it. Would her skin be cold yet? It didn't matter. That wasn't the way I wanted to remember the last time I touched her.

Jasmine Grant had lived in a world of tea bags and macramé, term papers and tie-dye. The violence so foreign to that carefully crafted life had crept in and destroyed her. I searched for reasons to hold myself responsible for her death and came up with enough to make myself crazy.

Stomach roiling, I backed out of the door and across the hallway into the kitchen. Hands on either side of the sink, I waited to vomit. I turned on the faucet and splashed cold water on my face to try to keep down the bile.

Maybe it wasn't her. It was a mistake. The wrong house, perhaps.

No. It was her. But why?

After another face full of cold water, I tried to decide what to do. Calling the police made the most sense, until I remembered Harry Butcher and what he would think about finding me at another murder scene. I could leave, but what if someone had seen me or could identify my car? It wouldn't be the first time that had happened. That would give Butcher that much more reason to think I was a murderer.

I found myself not really caring what Butcher or anyone else thought. Finding Jasmine Grant was taking the fight out of me, the willingness to keep on going. What was the point?

I reached for the wall phone in the kitchen, then stopped. Where was the manuscript she'd call me about? I glanced around the countertops, then moved through the dining room and, living room, back tracking toward the front door. In the office next to the computer, I found a large manila envelope addressed to Jasmine and postmarked the previous Friday. It was empty. There was no return address. Careful not to leave fingerprints, I gently poked around in the drawers and along the bookshelves looking for something that resembled a manuscript. Finding nothing, I thought about going back into her room, but that would mean seeing her one more time. I couldn't do it. If the manuscript she wanted me to read was in there, then it would have to be the police who found it.

I went back to the phone in the kitchen and dialed Alfie Gitchell at home rather than using 911. Within minutes, the sound of sirens came like the howling of distant wolves.

# Chapter 18

The next two hours were pretty much what I expected. Patrol cars blocking the street. Red and white lights reflecting off houses and cars. Squawking police radios. Yellow tape strung between trees. Gawking neighbors in bathrobes. People wearing latex gloves scurrying in and out of Jasmine's house. Jasmine herself, reduced to an indistinguishable shape in a black body bag. Harry Butcher.

I had met the patrol cars in the front yard and was hustled into the garage by the first uniformed officer to arrive. The image of Jasmine's body haunted me as I stood amid the garbage cans and garden tools. Visions of what her last moments must've been like made me want to run outside and suck in lungs full of cool night air, but the officer blocked the door. I tried to recall what she looked like across the table at lunch or beneath me in bed, but her face seemed distant as if I were looking at her backward through binoculars. Thinking about what we were doing just twenty-four hours earlier only made things worse. In my head, I replayed our brief time together, concentrating hard on the way she talked and the inflections in her voice.

I tuned her voice in like a station on an old radio, then compared it to the way she sounded on the telephone just a few hours ago. The difference was too great. She should've been excited about seeing me again, her voice eager, playful, and full of promise. The last time I saw her, she happily waved at me through the sun roof of the car. We were like little kids. But on the phone that night telling me about the manuscript, she sounded hesitant and afraid.

Then it hit me. Jasmine Grant hadn't been alone when she called. Someone else had been there with her, making her say the things that would bring me to her. Someone who wanted two things: the manuscript and to frame me for her murder, for another murder.

"Well, well," Harry Butcher said, as he walked into the garage. A blue swizzle stick shaped like a pirate sword stuck out of one corner of his mouth. "Two murders, and you show up at both. Small world isn't it, word man." Butcher took out a small notebook. "Let's hear it."

Just seeing the bear-like detective made me feel that all hope of finding the killer or killers of Jasmine Grant and Ivan Krychek was lost.

"We had a date," I said. "I showed up, and she was dead."

Butcher's laugh was a kind of snort.

"Is that your wine on the kitchen counter?"

I nodded.

"How long you been fuckin' her?"

Butcher had the smug look of someone who didn't need facts to decide the truth.

Burying my fist in Butcher's face wouldn't help my cause, but I was already at the point of not caring. It wasn't just Jasmine's murder, but everything that had happened. During dinner at DaVinci's, she had compared me to a character in a Greek tragedy. I considered myself more like a figure out of Greek mythology who's forced into performing endless deeds by the bored and meddlesome gods of Olympus.

My life felt out of control and now Butcher wanted to push me one step farther. I fought back the anger for no other reason than I didn't want to give Butcher the satisfaction of seeing me lose my grip. My eyes desperately searched the garage for something to focus on that would help me deal with Butcher. A half-empty bag of steer manure in the far corner seemed to be the most appropriate.

"We met a couple of days ago at Delaney College," I said, finally in control of my emotions and looking the detective in the face.

Butcher sneered and flipped the swizzle stick to the other side of his mouth.

"That wasn't my question. Maybe you and Krychek and Grant were into some kind of kinky, three-way thing. Huh? Things got a little out of hand. Jealousy maybe? Let's say they were going to cut you out of the action, and you decided to kill them?"

A rumpled and cranky Alfie Gitchell, the ever-present cigarette wedged in the corner of his mouth, arrived just before I lost complete control. Gitchell's baggy jeans, grass-stained tennis shoes and a sun-bleached golf shirt made him look like he might have a life outside the police department.

Gitchell nodded at me, then took Butcher out into the driveway. Through the garage door, I could see the suddenly subservient Butcher reading his notes and looking back into the garage. Gitchell didn't say a word, listening intently as Butcher gestured with his swizzle stick in my direction. Gitchell finally nodded, and Butcher walked down the driveway toward the street.

"He's pretty convinced you're our killer," Gitchell said when he came back to the garage.

"Ignorance is invincible."

"Take it easy, John," Gitchell said, offering me a cigarette and taking one for himself. "There's more to this homicide stuff than circumstantial evidence. You're as much a suspect as anyone else who happened to be at both murder scenes."

"Is that supposed to be comforting?"

"Just tell me what were you doing here, and don't feed me a line of crap or I'll walk away and leave this whole thing in Butcher's hands."

We eyed each other for a few seconds. I blinked first, telling Gitchell everything – or almost everything. For reasons I wasn't sure about I left out anything to do with the manuscript. Telling Gitchell about the document would give the police a plausible motive for Jasmine's death. It might even get me off the hook, not that I should be on one anyway, and send Butcher charging after someone or something else. Still, I didn't do it. It would be safer to know what's in the manuscript before telling Gitchell or Butcher that it exists.

"She invited you down for a sleep-over, and when you got here she was dead. Is that your story?"

"That's it."

"Are we going to find your fingerprints all over the place in there?" Gitchell gestured with his cigarette toward the house.

"Probably, but not where they shouldn't be."

"Let's hope not." Gitchell glanced down at his little notebook. "So, you think that between the time she called you and the time you got here, someone just happened to break into her house and kill her for no reason."

"There must have been a reason, but I don't know what it is."

Gitchell glanced out the door. Butcher stood at the end of the driveway talking to a woman in a terry-cloth robe. Large curlers bounced as she gestured towards my Jeep and then at Jasmine's house. Standing in the background were three other women, all looking ready for bed, nodding their collective heads.

Gitchell gave me a skeptical look.

"Let me give you some advice. You better not be playing games here, because if you are, you're in over your head. It looks to me like the same person killed Krychek and your new squeeze. We don't know why, but if you know something you're not telling, you'd better be very careful."

"I'm not a part of this," I snapped.

"You better not be, because if you are, then you're going to see a lot of Harry Butcher, and take it from me, that's no bargain."

"Are you trying to scare me, Alfie?"

"Damn right. The guy who did this don't dance. He's one sick son of a bitch."

"So, you believe someone else killed her, not me?"

"This is Butcher's case, but I don't think it'll take much to convince him that a killer wouldn't hang around and call the police. I'm sorry about your friend, but you did the right thing tonight."

I stayed in the garage and smoked another cigarette, while Gitchell walked outside. His conversation with Butcher was short and animated.

When he returned to the garage, Gitchell said, "You can go now, but I'm warning you as a friend and as a police officer, be very, very careful."

I walked down the driveway to my car. The crowd in the street watched me, but nobody yelled "Killer." When I got to the Jeep, Butcher was leaning against the front fender. I ignored him and got behind the wheel. The engine had just started when the detective's wide face appeared in the driver's side window.

"I think you're a killer, word man," Butcher said in a hoarse whisper. "I still can't prove it, but I will. When I do, even your buddy Alfie won't be able to save your sorry ass."

I rolled up the window, backed out of the driveway and drove through the crowd of people. They stared at me like something stuck too long to the bottom of a trash can.

# Chapter 19

I drove around Salem for thirty minutes before stopping at a sports bar with a half-dozen television sets turned to three different channels, an equal number of video poker machines, and a bartender who could care less that a murder had been committed just a few blocks away. I ordered a bottle of Bud and took it out to the small, empty patio that was surrounded by a wood fence that did little to mute the noise of passing cars and trucks.

The body blows of anger and disappointment kept pounding at my insides. The beer sat untouched while I once again tried to remember every moment with Jasmine, every touch, every word. She told me that if anything ever happened to her, I would be the first person she'd turn to. How prophetic.

Despite the late hour, traffic swooshed by a few feet on the other side of the patio fence, headlights flickering through the gaps and sending long fingers of light dancing across the cracked concrete. The bartender poked his head outside, noticed my beer was still full, and disappeared back into the dark bar.

I lit a cigarette and drained half of the now-warm beer.

"Get a grip, John," I said, then looked around to make sure I was alone.

Finding Jasmine's killer was a foregone conclusion. I owed her that much. I owed myself that much. Knowing who killed her and why wouldn't bring her back anymore than a jury verdict would bring back two dead girls. It might, however, help chase away my own demons and square myself with the world.

The key was the manuscript. Jasmine had died for it, so its contents must be worth at least one life and probably two, if I counted Krychek. Where would a graduate student keep a document as important as a doctoral thesis? I ran through the possibilities, then stopped on the one that was last on the list. I looked out over the top of the fence at Salem's unimpressive skyline and the spire on Mayfield Hall that jutted upward from the campus of Delaney College four blocks away.


Delaney College looked different at night. The tree-lined paths that wound between the buildings and criss-crossed the emerald green lawns were empty of students. The scattered lights in the windows of the dormitories made the buildings look like a half-finished bingo card. Despite the quiet, I felt reluctant to move out of the small grove of madrone trees. The fifty yards to the front steps of the building that housed the Political Science Department seemed more like a mile.

After being accused of murder, breaking and entering didn't seem all that serious. At least that's how I rationalized it after leaving the tavern, finding an all night drug store, and buying a roll of masking tape and a box of rubber gloves, a pair of which were tucked inside my pants pocket. As incriminating as my purchases were, the woman behind the counter had barely looked up.

I had to find Krychek's manuscript, and I wasn't going do it hanging around my apartment or a bar feeling sorry for myself. The manuscript Krychek sent to Jasmine must have been a copy. There are no original manuscripts anymore. Everything exists in computer hard drives and on floppy disks. I hadn't seen a computer in Krychek's house, so there had to be one in his office at the college.

By two a.m. I was sitting in the Jeep in the school's visitors parking lot staring out at the late-night calm. I didn't have a plan, just the hope that the doors to the building were unlocked, that the tiny cubicle that passed for Krychek's office was open, and that a clearly labeled computer disk containing the manuscript was sitting on the desk waiting for me. I could just step in, pick it up, and leave. In and out in a matter of a few seconds.

If it wasn't, then the Jeep's tire iron would come in handy in furthering my reputation as a career criminal.

Another option would be to come back the next day with a simple request to see Krychek's office. At least then I might find out if Krychek even had a computer. That wouldn't work, though, because no one would leave me alone in the office. There had to be a computer, and I needed time to get into it.

I pulled the baseball cap down tight on my head and stared intently at the darkened building. The large, old-fashioned, ornate windows were hidden in shadows that made them look like the half-closed eyes of an old man. The ivy that clung to chiseled rock walls had the appearance of thin fingers stretching from the ground toward the back-lit spire that crowned the old building. I took a deep breath, walked out of the stand of madrones, and strode casually across the lawn toward the front steps of Mayfield Hall trying my best to look like I belonged there.

I could feel myself fade into the dim light of the grass expanse between the madrones and the building. After a few steps that seemed to take minutes instead of seconds, I re-emerged in a circle of light cast from a nearby street lamp. A few yards from the steep steps up to the front door, I moved around to the left side of the staircase. I knew from my first visit to the building that there had to be steps that led down to the basement level.

I was right. A narrow, damp stairwell lay hidden behind the bushes. I found the top step with my foot. Groping along the wall for the handrail, I carefully worked my way down a dozen steps slippery with water and moss. Reaching the bottom, I worked my hands into the rubber gloves, felt around for the door knob, and turned it slowly. Locked.

I put face to the glass to see if there were any lights inside. Seeing none, I pulled the roll of masking tape from my coat pocket. The window in the door was divided into six separate panes of glass, each about the size of a sheet of typing paper. I covered the one closest to the door knob with the tape and smashed the glass with my elbow. The tape kept all but a few small pieces of glass from crashing to the floor. I reached inside and opened the old, bolt-action lock.

So far, so good. I had violated the breaking-and-entering statutes without setting off an alarm. At least not one I could hear. Fireworks and sirens may be going off at the police department or at some security company, but peace and quiet reigned inside Mayfield Hall.

My own brazenness surprised me. The reluctance I felt standing in the shadows of the madrones disappeared, replaced by a sense that I had crossed a line into a recklessness that produced its own style of freedom. The shattering glass added a reality to what I was doing that didn't come with the benign act of buying gloves and tape at a drug store. Realizing I was totally and utterly alone, my heart beat seemed to slow and my breathing no longer came in short, sharp gasps. What could possibly happen to me that was any worse than what had already occurred?

The first squeak of my shoes on the hard linoleum floor sounded like gunshots as they echoed down the hallway . Before the echo died, I darted into an alcove near a porcelain water fountain. Reckless didn't mean stupid. Standing in the dark silence, I listened for any sound that would tell me I wasn't alone.

Hearing only the faint ticks and creaks of an aging building, I stepped back into the hallway and walked another thirty feet through the blackness. At the stairs leading up to the main floor, I crossed to the other side of the hall and felt my way past each door. One door. Two. Three. In the dim light, I could just make out the name "Ivan Krychek" on the white card in the thin, brass frame on the fourth door. The office was unlocked, so I slipped the tire iron down in the back of my pants where it poked against the small of my back. The light switch was inside on the wall to the right.

The office was little more than a closet with walls lined floor-to-ceiling with shelves filled with a jumble of books, magazines and three-ring binders with colorful spines. Of the dozens of binders, any one could be the manuscript. On one wall was a cluttered metal desk piled high with papers that nearly covered the small computer terminal and keyboard.

I started on the shelves immediately to the right, running my fingers along the books, stopping at each binder to read the title. Ten minutes of frenetic searching turned up nothing but a deeper understanding of the kind of material aspiring political science professors were required to read. There was no book, binder, or anything that resembled a thesis, let alone a title related to the polarization of American politics.

I turned on the computer. The hard drive whirred and buzzed until a black screen that read PROGRAM MANAGER popped up.

"I know this," I whispered.

I clicked on ACCESSORIES and went into FILE MANAGER. The mouse felt comfortable in the palm of my hand, despite the rubber gloves. A list of folders came up arranged like the tree of a rather linear and short-lived family. I ran the cursor down to one that said DOCTORATE. After double clicking on a file that read Thesis1.DOC, a document popped up with the title "The Right versus The Left: A Study of the Polarization of Politics in America."

"Bingo."

Shoving the small mountain of papers aside, I found an anemic printer that would take hours to pump out the entire document. Instead, I rummaged around until I found a package of computer disks on a shelf above the terminal. Slipping one into the processor, I watched as it quickly formatted, then copied Krychek's thesis onto the disk. When it finished, I ejected it, slipped the disk into my coat pocket, and deleted all the files from the hard drive. The life's work of Ivan Krychek, such as it was, had been reduced to a small, square computer disk.

I turned out the light, waited for my eyes to adjust to the dark, and opened the door. I retraced my steps down the hallway and past the stairs leading to the first floor. The alcove with the water fountain was just a few feet away when I heard the noise. It came from behind me, back down the hall toward Krychek's office. It resembled the faint squeak of new basketball shoes on a hardwood floor. There was only one sound. Nothing before. Nothing after.

But enough to tell me that I was no longer alone.

I ducked into the alcove and peered through the darkness back toward Krychek's office. As if on cue, the figure of a man appeared at the bottom of the stairs. He had no features, everything black from head to foot, a shadow against the dark gray background. He was large, both in height and weight, but moved with sure-footed quickness down the hall. His head moved back and forth in swift glances in both directions before gliding into the even darker shadows at the end of hall.

The man stopped at Krychek's office, but instead of testing the knob, he moved back a step and smashed the door open with a short, violent kick. Before the office light came on and the echo died on the plaster walls, I dashed out the basement door.

Standing frozen in the dampness of the stairwell, I fought the urge to run like hell. Dim light shining through the bushes cast lattice patterns on the wall. Water dripped from a leaky faucet near the top step.

Think, I told myself. Who was the man in Krychek's office? Why was he here? It had to be for the same reason I was there. I squeezed the small plastic disk in my pocket.

"Too late, asshole."

I moved two steps closer to the top of the stairs before deciding to stay. If it was the killer and I could identify him, then no more Harry Butcher. That made it worth the risk. And then there was Jasmine. How would I know if it was her killer? What would I do if I did know?

I took a deep breath, waited for my heart beat to slow, then went back down the dark stairwell. The light in Krychek's office still shown across the hallway's linoleum floor. I watched for a few more seconds, then grabbed the basement door. It was a moment of truth I could never get back.

"Who cares?" I said. "Do it."

I slammed the door shut as hard as I could. Glass from the broken window shattered into diamond-size pieces that slid across the waxed floor. The light in the office at the end of the hall went out long before the sound died away.

I sprinted up the stairs, tire iron in hand. A rock wall sat atop the descending stairwell, parallel to the front of the building. It was four-feet high and hidden from the open area in front of Mayfield Hall by a dense photenia hedge. I ducked into the space between the wall and the hedge. From the vantage point, I could see both the main entrance above me and, below me, the basement door I'd just slammed. Either way, I had the cover I needed when the man inside the building emerged.

I waited, ignoring the dampness of the dead leaves soaking through the knees of my pants as I concentrated on breathing normally and not letting the cobwebs in my hair and face bother me. A car drove by on the street adjacent to the building, the vehicle's head and tail lights visible through a line of Japanese plum trees. As if knowing something was about to happen, the car pulled away just as the basement door swung slowly open.

I heard the crunch of footsteps on broken glass, then ducked down and hunched tighter against the rock wall. All I could smell was damp dirt and rotting leaves. Shoes scraped against the thin grit on the steps. The man in black was probably less than two feet away, separated from me by the thickness of the rock wall. I listened for two more steps then slowly stood, hoping I had timed the move exactly. If I hadn't, all hell would break loose, and the chances I would get out of there alive would drop to zero.

But I had timed it perfectly. The man's head appeared on the other side of the wall at the same moment I stood up. The man was looking straight ahead, the same direction as the knife in his right hand. In one swift motion, I brought the tire iron down across the man's forearm with a sickening crunch. The man's scream was cut short when I backhanded the metal bar into his hooded face. The knife rattled on the steps. The man in black let out a groan before tumbling down the steps into a heap at the bottom.

Without thinking, I jumped the wall and ran down the steps. I stood over the dark figure, poised to give him another taste of the tire iron should he get up. Instead, he lay motionless except for the gentle rise and fall of his chest. One arm lay bent at an odd angle. The black mask looked damp and sticky.

I reached down and snatched off the man's hood. It slid off easily to let Buck Mather's shaved head drop back to the concrete with a soft thud.

# Chapter 20

The decision to head for the coast had been instinctive. I could've gone any direction; east into the Cascade Mountains or south toward California. North to Portland was never an option. It was too soon to go home. I wanted to disappear, to distance myself from Buck Mather lying at the bottom of the stairs and from the image of Jasmine Grant trussed up on her own bed.

I tried not to jump to conclusions about Mather and whether he'd killed Jasmine. But if Mather's hadn't, then what was he doing in Krychek's office? I didn't know whether to be angry with myself or relieved that I didn't do more to Mather than work him over with a tire iron. Could I have killed him? The answer was yes, but it was a question I never wanted to ask myself again.

I stopped at an all-night grocery store for gas, food, and something to eat. I settled for chips and two cans of beer, then ate and drank while waiting for the tank to fill. Ten miles down the road I popped the second can of beer and settled back into the seat to nurse it while driving into the darkness.

The car moved from fog bank to fog bank as if seeking cover. The thick patches of gray provided brief moments of safety before bursting into the open again. I rolled up the window to keep the dampness out.

Driving at night used to offer rare moments of solitude. Riding along in anonymity behind headlights, the radio tuned to a jazz station, alone with thoughts and feelings. But in the months following the accident, I did everything to avoid driving at night. Even at dusk, trying to get home before the street lights came on, I'd creep along at half the posted speed limit paying more attention to the sidewalks and curbs than what was ahead of me. Eventually, necessity made me get over it, but even now, a year later, I could remember how quickly it had happened and think of what might be ahead of me around the next corner. Maybe it was someone walking along the side of the road ready to be in the wrong place at the wrong time and send my life careening off in some new, detestable direction.

I slowed the Jeep down another five miles an hour and turned up the radio to make sure I stayed awake.

I toyed with idea of calling Alfie Gitchell. A call even this late to tell him about Buck Mather would put an end to my undeserved status as a murder suspect. But something about the encounter bothered me. Mather wasn't the political science type. Assuming he was the killer, why did he commit two murders over a manuscript by an opinionated graduate student at a backwater college?

I crossed the summit of the Coast Range and started down the other side where the curves became sharper as the road wound through the rain forest along the Salmon River. Fog banks became thicker, but less frequent. I felt like a feral cat moving from bush to bush in the middle of the night, invisible to anything that posed a threat.

Lincoln City was a ghost town at three-thirty in the morning, Highway 101 a darkened bowling alley. At the north end of the city, I turned off the highway and followed the wide residential street into the Roads End area of Lincoln County. Roads End was an artsy enclave wedged in between Lincoln City and a rocky point of land that stuck like a finger into the soft belly of the Pacific Ocean. Just past the Dory Cove, a seafood restaurant favored by tourists, was a small state park with a few parking spots, a restroom, and access to the sandy beach that fronted Roads End's modest-looking, but expensive homes.

I parked the Jeep a few spots away from two slumbering motor homes, turned off the engine, and sat with the window down listening to the waves crashing onto the sand. I thought about crawling in the back to sleep, but instead sat immobile smoking cigarettes and watching thin clouds drift slowly past a million stars.

I had every reason to be paranoid, to believe that somehow I had been followed and that I was going to pay the price for breaking into Krychek's office and sucker punching Buck Mather with a tire iron. Instead, I sat calmly with the window down, not caring who found me or why.

Eventually, I pulled my coat over me and fell asleep to the sound of the ocean and the smell of a salty breeze. It was the sleep of the dead. A sleep *for* the dead.


The next morning started with the rumble of the diesel engine of one of the motor homes. I jumped awake with the smell and noise, hitting my thighs on the bottom of the steering wheel. Still groggy, I watched an old man in baggy shorts, sandals and a golf shirt fuss around the outside of the huge motor home. When the RV finally drove away like a tramp steamer leaving the dock, I walked across the parking lot to the restrooms to wash up. The roughness of the paper towels erased the last bits of sleep.

I drove back to Highway 101, following it south until seeing a bank with an ATM machine. After taking out a hundred dollars, I kept heading south until I found a Kinko's in a strip mall. A clerk about half my age, but whose knowledge of computers put him on a different evolutionary track, slipped the disk from Krychek's office into one of the computers behind the counter. The thesis was written with a common word-processing software, so the clerk had it on the screen within seconds.

"Give me twenty minutes," the clerk said. "I got a couple of other projects and then I'll get to yours."

I got a cup of bad coffee from the convenience store next door, then fed fifty cents into the *Salem Statesman-Journal* box near the front door. The murder of Jasmine Grant had made the front page, complete with a photo of Harry Butcher standing in Jasmine's front yard surrounded by yellow police tape. I read the story carefully, relieved that Butcher hadn't leaked my name to reporters as a possible suspect. The article contained few details other than Butcher's comments connecting the murder to the death of Ivan Krychek. Butcher had, however, come up with a catchy name for the killer, the Piano Man. I folded the paper and left to pick up the manuscript.

Another thirty minutes south along the coast, I found a dockside cafe in Newport, ordered breakfast, and watched the fishing boats bob gently at their moorings. The eggs, bacon, and hash browns with sausage gravy came on a plate the size of a hub cap. I looked down at enough food to feed a class of third graders or one fisherman about to leave for three days of dragging for shrimp. I ate the eggs and bacon, but shied away from the hash browns.

With the plate gone and the coffee cup refilled, I started reading Krychek's doctoral thesis for clues to why it had cost two people their lives.

# Chapter 21

Proctor Scofield stared out the window, refusing to look at Mitch Penroy sitting on the other side of the desk talking in a tone that for some reason Scofield found irritating.

At one time, a street ran along the west side of the Willamette River in downtown Portland. Some time during the 1970s, it had been turned into a park named for the former Governor Tom McCall, with fountains, grass, and a seawall that paralleled the river's wide, dark waters. From the window of his office at Scofield Industries, Scofield could look down on the colorful tents that were going up on the grass between the seawall and Front Avenue. The tents were similar to the ones that had just been taken down at the end of the Rose Festival, which each year turned the park into a swamp from the inevitable rain. Scofield believed that the Rose Festival was the only reason it rained in June. Cancel it, he thought, and the rains would probably stop in May.

Even from twenty floors up, the city looked alive and vibrant, bustling with the commerce that made him and men like him rich and successful. Early-morning joggers, bikers, and people on their way to work filled the park. From his perch, he felt like he could see across the United States and gaze at the prosperity created by the strongest economy in his lifetime. New buildings going up; existing ones being remodeled; high wages and low interest rates fueling the explosion of new homes in the suburbs south and west of the city. Never had he felt more secure, more confident that what he'd built would last forever. Sure there were some economic problems, but nothing that wouldn't pass. The recession, he thought, only weeded out those people who weren't supposed to be rich anyway.

He just wished he could live to see how it all turns out.

It seemed that old age had just moved in and taken over. One day, agile and alert. The next, stiff and forgetful. Small things at first, but someday it would be important things. He shook the thoughts from his head. No use burying himself sooner than necessary. Still, he should go in for that physical his doctor demanded. The reluctance was fueled by fear of what he might hear, that his lifestyle had caught up with him and issued a death sentence he'd rather not know about. He'd taken precautions, but probably not enough.

"That's pretty much where we're at right now, Mr. Scofield," Penroy said.

"We'll have the manuscript tonight, but with a slight change in plans."

Scofield's face turned to stone. The phrase "change in plans" sent an electric shock through his head.

"Such as?" he asked.

"He wants a hundred-thousand dollars in exchange for the manuscript," Penroy said, refusing to look at Scofield. "Give him the money, and he says he'll disappear for good."

"We don't even know what the fucking manuscript says. Why would I give someone that kind of money without knowing what I'm buying?"

"I agree, but it may be worth it to get rid of him."

"Then pay him with your money. God knows I pay you enough."

Scofield turned his attention back to the window. The river shimmered between the rock and concrete that lined its banks. A shiver as cold as the gray water ran down his back.

"How do we know there aren't copies?"

"According to Mather, Krychek swore before he died that the Grant woman had the only one."

"What about that house we bought for him and that woman?"

Penroy paused before saying with conviction, "I'm positive there wasn't one in the house."

Scofield had heard that tone before, so he didn't press.

"The computer in his office?"

"Mather told me that he found nothing in the computer that resembled a manuscript," Penroy said. "All the files had been deleted. He thinks the police did it, probably by mistake."

Scofield whirled his chair around.

"Mitch, listen to me," he said, anger making his head throb. "This is the Twenty-First Century. The computer age. I know. That's why I'm rich! There are no more typewriters. No mimeograph machines. No fucking scribners with quills and bottles of ink. Krychek's thesis is a document in a computer. Documents in computers don't just disappear."

"I understand, sir, but Mather was in Krychek's office. He searched the computer. All the files had been deleted."

"They could've been copied on to a disk. Even the police could have figured that out."

"You're right," Penroy said, his voice contrite. "Let me check on that angle."

"Do that," Scofield said.

He sat back in the chair and pulled open the desk drawer. He rummaged for a bottle of aspirin, shook five tablets into his trembling hand, and swallowed them with a gulp of cold coffee. The act of taking the pills made him feel better.

"And no one got into the computer before him?"

"Other than police, Mather says no," Penroy said.

"And you believe him?" Scofield felt calmer, his voice less shrill.

Penroy paused for a moment, staring past Scofield out the window.

"Mather is nobody's bargain. He's made some mistakes, but I've never known him to lie."

Scofield was dubious, but Penroy's explanation made sense.

"And what about John Standard?"

"I really don't think he's going to be a problem," Penroy said. He let a thin smile dance across his face. "It seems the police have him pegged as a suspect in both murders."

Scofield nodded his approval.

"You say he's a writer. Is he writing something about this?"

Penroy shrugged. "No way of knowing, but it may not matter. The police are doing exactly what we planned."

"You put this deal together, Mitch, so I'll let you play it out. I just want you to know that I don't like screwing around with reporters. They're too unpredictable. Talking to them is like a woman dating a gang of bikers. Something bad is going to happen, you just don't what or how long it's going to last."

"They're bloodhounds," Penroy said. "They'll follow anything if you give them the right scent."

"And where does this scent lead?"

"Hopefully to jail on murder charges."

"No," Scofield snapped. "I want no trials. No witnesses. No evidence. No testimony. I just want to keep the cops busy until I get that damned manuscript. After that, I could care less what happens to Standard, Mather, or anyone else."

"That part is taken care of," Penroy said. "The cops have plenty to keep them busy and away from the manuscript."

Scofield turned his attention back to the view outside the window. A yellow and black tugboat pushed a barge slowly upstream, its blunt bow struggling against the current as it made its way between the Morrison Bridge and Hawthorne Bridge. The tug looked lonely and overworked.

Scofield said, "I believe there's another way to get the manuscript and assure ourselves that Mr. Mather will no longer be a problem."

The two men stared at each other in silence for several moments before Penroy nodded.

"I'll take care of it."

# Chapter 22

Ivan Krychek's thesis was a vision of hell to anyone who cared about representative democracy. He was convinced that the left and the right were moving farther apart and taking with them their respective political parties. He believed most Americans held moderate political views, but were faced more often than not with a choice between two evils, an arch-conservative from the Republican Party or a flaming liberal from the Democratic Party. While differing vastly on issues, both ends of the political spectrum engaged in the same type of politics.

The right, he wrote, remained as beholden to the National Rifle Association and the Christian Coalition as the left was to AFL-CIO and the American Trial Lawyers. For the foreseeable future, the political pendulum in both state and national politics would swing back and forth between these two extremist factions, as voters turned desperately to one side after becoming quickly disillusioned with the other.

Krychek's thesis predicted an era of pandering presidents trying to be all things to all people, when in reality they were either the lap dogs of certain special interests or the sworn enemy of others. He envisioned chaos caused by elected officials who sought quick solutions to complex problems in order to accomplish something in an era of term limits. He boldly predicted that real politics would soon die out, replaced by trivial skirmishes between rabid interest groups.

The thesis scoffed at the notion of campaign finance reform, describing instead a future in which each side sold their respective souls to lobbyists and foreign interests in order to amass huge amounts of money to heap on candidates who worshipped at the alter of their political philosophy. Those who got the money would be called upon to support the extremist agenda or be quickly cast aside and replaced by someone more accommodating.

This disparity of political choice, Krychek wrote, would create even more widespread voter cynicism, which would result in ever-decreasing voter turnout. No longer capable of meeting the needs of the people who looked to it for help, government would become irrelevant. The actions of legislatures and Congress would hold little interest to average Americans, who would turn their energies toward satisfying more personal needs rather than waiting for an inactive and inattentive government.

Newspaper coverage of politicians and issues would fall by the wayside, as a new generation of editors and reporters looked for topics that would interest readers, rather than earn their disdain and disinterest. Stories on politics and government would consist of real or imagined scandals, or be replaced altogether by celebrity journalism led by packs of paparazzi. The entire political process would be left open to manipulation. Anyone with the money and foresight to recognize the depth of the polarization would step into the void, triggering a corporate takeover of a weak, struggling political process. This person or persons, Krychek wrote, would more than likely hold an apolitical viewpoint. In other words, they wouldn't care which side won, because they had feet in both camps.

I didn't follow politics close enough to know if Krychek was a visionary or a crackpot. Probably neither; just a student trying to produce a paper worthy of a doctorate. In the end, Jasmine had been right. The zealousness of Krychek's opinions far outweighed the supporting evidence.

The waitress filled my coffee cup for a fourth time and brought the check. I looked around to see if someone was waiting for my table by the window, but the room was empty, except for the waitress and the cook sitting at the counter smoking cigarettes. I turned my attention back to the manuscript.

To illustrate his point, Krychek had delved into the background of the two candidates he felt best demonstrated the polarization of politics, at least in Oregon, which he conveniently deemed a microcosm of the national political stage. Krychek devoted more than twenty pages of this thesis to the rapid rise of Brad Roark and Kingsley Landis. The tale that emerged was of two men totally ill-equipped and unprepared for their roles as the poster children for their divergent political philosophies. Yet both stood on the verge of political careers that would make one of them governor and probably more. In Krychek's ivory-tower world, Roark and Landis were twin symbols of evil.

I lit another cigarette and read on.

Brad Roark and Kingsley Landis met on the first day of classes at the University of Oregon. They were freshmen drawn together by their similar upbringings, their overwhelming passion for the social side of college life, and their disdain for anything that smacked of education.

Roark had grown up in a wealthy suburb on Portland's west side, the youngest son of a successful car dealer, who used his money to keep his children in expensive automobiles and out of scrapes with the law. For his high school graduation, Brad Roark received a new Corvette and enough cash to spend the summer driving it around the United States.

Landis fared almost as well by his indulgent father, a corporate lawyer from up-scale Lake Oswego. Since his son already had a car, Landis's father bought him an expensive condominium two blocks off campus in Eugene. He furnished it for him, while Kingsley explored Europe at family expense.

The first known meeting of Roark and Landis came at a fraternity kegger on the weekend before classes started. Neither had any intention of joining a fraternity or going to classes on Monday morning. Instead, they spent the weekend exploring parties and coeds, finding plenty of both for the taking. By Sunday night, they had made an arrangement. Roark would live rent-free with Landis in his condo in exchange for unlimited use of the Corvette. By early October, Roark and Landis were the best known freshmen on campus to everyone except the faculty.

Despite their loyalty to the party life, the pair managed to scrape by their first year. They maintained grade points high enough to avoid flunking out, but low enough to guarantee them little to brag about should they ever graduate. There were rumors that they paid other students to take exams and write papers for them. At no time during their first year in college did either of them show the slightest interest in learning, let alone politics.

The genesis of their transformation appeared to be an allegation by a freshman girl who attended a party at the condo at the start of Roark's and Landis's sophomore year. She told police of being drugged and repeatedly raped by the two men. When she began screaming, Landis and Roark threw her, naked and hysterical, out the door and refused to let her back in. Her screams woke the rest of the condo residents, who stood on their balconies laughing at the naked, frightened girl in the middle of the parking lot. The police arrived to find her in a fetal position on the asphalt, covered in beer, wine, whiskey, and urine that had rained down on her from the floors above.

Landis and Roark were arrested the next day on rape, sodomy, and kidnapping charges. Three days later, the frightened and confused victim dropped the charges. Two weeks later she committed suicide by jumping off a freeway overpass into the path of an oncoming semi.

Immediately following the girl's death, the pair disappeared totally from the school's social scene and re-emerged as model students. They were in class every day and home studying every night. They entered campus politics, eventually mounting successful campaigns for student body president. Landis was elected first and Roark succeeded him, each acting as the other's campaign manager. They espoused political philosophies that were right for the times. They were likable, shrewd strategists and office holders, even though they shunned most opportunities to speak publicly.

Three years later, they graduated in the top ten percent of their class and were accepted at different law schools in the Midwest. Their law school years were undistinguished, marked neither by trouble nor stellar grades. Both graduated at the same time, returned to Oregon, and passed the bar the following summer.

Their political careers began after three years of obscurity in blue-blood Portland law firms. Roark's employer specialized in personal injury cases, priding itself in doing pro bono work for a group of environmentalists intent on saving old-growth forests. In contrast, Landis went to work at a conservative button-down firm that defended large corporations against lawsuits over rat droppings in breakfast food or cockroaches in soft drinks.

Both took on the politics of their respective firms. Roark began showing up at fund-raisers to save the whales, stop the fighting in Nicaragua, and boycott bananas. Landis, while less visible, became deeply involved in conservative causes, such as banning abortion and balancing the federal budget.

At almost exactly the same time, both left Oregon for Washington, DC. Roark became chief of staff for a California Democrat noted for his fiery diatribes against Pentagon spending and industrial polluters. Landis popped up in a similar position with a Florida Republican renowned as the champion of corporate welfare and who appeared to have never met a weapons system he didn't like. Throughout their Capitol years, the two kept in close contact with politicians, staffers, and lobbyists from Oregon. Their mutual desire to one day return home and seek elective office was an open secret.

Five years later they did just that. They bought homes in legislative districts that were ready and waiting for their respective political philosophies. Within eighteen months, both were freshmen members of the Oregon Legislature. Somewhere along the way, they picked up wives and the appropriate number of children.

Their time in the legislature included high-profile involvement in carefully selected issues. Roark took up causes that endeared him to the liberals who controlled the Democratic Party, while Landis took the same approach with the conservatives who controlled the GOP. They quickly attracted the attention of the state's political reporters and quietly encouraged speculation about higher office.

The seeds of that speculation bore fruit earlier in the year when Governor Martin Sloane announced he would not seek a second term because of health problems. Both Landis and Roark popped up immediately on the short list of likely successors.

The last few paragraphs of the unfinished thesis speculated that the two rising political stars were the product of a carefully orchestrated effort going back to their college days. According to Krychek, the transformation of Roark and Landis from party monsters to bookworms was the result of a deal struck between the boys' parents and the family of the girl they were accused of raping. The thesis said nothing about the girl's parents or the nature of the deal. It contained only her name, Amanda Bishop.

# Chapter 23

Highway 101 from Newport north to Lincoln City runs hard up against a shoreline that changes from long stretches of sandy beaches to rugged headlands jutting into the blue-gray ocean. Motels, fast food stops, and souvenir shops line both sides of the two-lane road with its occasional passing lane. The homes run the gamut from beach-front shanties huddled amid scrub pine to spectacular mansions with panoramic views of the Pacific.

I was through Lincoln City and near the small community of Neskowin before I could stop thinking about Ivan Krychek's manuscript. It had given me two things: an insight into the untidy past of Brad Roark and Kingsley Landis and a new name, Amanda Bishop.

Roark and Landis might be nothing more than receptacles into which an over-zealous college student had poured a conspiracy grown out of a cynical outlook on politics. They could also be murderers. Better yet, instead of murdering Jasmine and Krychek themselves, the two politicians had hired Buck Mather. That, at least, made sense. Roark and Landis might have something in common with the doctoral thesis on polarization in American politics. That's more than I could say for Mather.

The Jeep swayed through gentle turns as the highway turned inland past the dairy farms near Cloverdale and Hebo. I stopped at a gas station in the small town of Beaver to get rid of the gallon of coffee I drank that morning and to call Benny Orlando.

"Do me a favor," I said when Benny answered the phone. "Run upstairs to my apartment and make sure everything is all right."

"Why? What's going on? Where are you?"

"Relax. I'll explain later. I just need to know if anyone's been in there."

I gave Benny the pay phone number. I had just finished a cigarette when Benny called back.

"I'm in your apartment and everything looks fine, I guess," Benny said. "You're not exactly *Good Housekeeping* material, but if it's ransacking you're looking for, it didn't happen here."

I felt relieved. If Buck Mather had figured out that I had cold-cocked him and why, then he hadn't had time to do anything about it, such as search my apartment for the manuscript.

"You want to fill me in now?" Benny asked.

"Let's just say I poked a stick into the wrong beehive. I'll be back in a few hours. I'll tell you more then."

At Tillamook, I turned east onto Highway 6 to Portland and spent the next hour lost in thought.

My mind wandered back to Amanda Bishop. Exposing what happened to her would ruin the political aspirations of Roark and Landis. But why was the manuscript so damn important? If the revelations in Krychek's thesis were true, wouldn't they have come out eventually anyway once the two of them announced their candidacies for governor? I found it hard to believe that even Oregon's moribund political press could overlook something as obvious as a potential governor's involvement in the rape and suicide of a co-ed.

The path circled back again to why Krychek and Jasmine were murdered and by whom? Mather was the likely candidate, but Roark and Landis had a motive.

The only answer was that someone wanted Krychek dead before he found out more about Amanda Bishop's death. But who?

The content, tone, and writing style of the thesis only made me more convinced that Buck Mather was working for someone else. There was no evidence that Mather was the killer, but he was the one who tied everything together. Krychek, the manuscript, Jasmine Grant.

Going to Alfie Gitchell or Harry Butcher with a bag full of conspiracy theories was out of the question. It would mean telling them about the manuscript, and I wasn't ready to do that yet. Besides, Butcher would sneer and accuse me of trotting out some wild tale in order to save my own ass.

Of course, I thought, I couldn't blame him.

# Chapter 24

It was early afternoon when I cautiously entered my apartment. Not that I didn't believe Benny, but I wanted to make sure for myself that everything was safe. If Buck Mather was smart enough to figure out that Krychek's manuscript might be stored in a computer at Delaney College, then maybe he could figure out other things as well, such as who hit him with a tire iron.

After hiding the disk and the manuscript in separate places in the kitchen, I showered until the hot water ran out, shaved, and crawled into bed. In the middle of a dream about Jasmine Grant and a piano with teeth instead of keys, the telephone rang.

"Mr. Standard?" The voice was sultry and quickly recognizable, even to a man who'd been asleep for six hours. "I'm sorry to bother you at home."

"That's okay, Mrs. Krychek. There's no other place to bother me."

"I'm afraid I wasn't totally honest with you the other day when you came to see me," she said. "I know more about Ivan's death than I told you. So does Buck Mather."

I sensed what came next.

"And now you want to clear your conscience?"

"Yes." She said it too quickly, as if I had just answered a question on a quiz show. "Mr. Mather came to see me. We shared what we knew about Ivan and his research. We'd like to tell you about it. We think it will help find Ivan's killer."

Anna Krychek was delivering lines again, only they were less polished than the ones I'd heard a few days earlier.

"You and Mather? Together? Want to talk to me?"

"Yes."

"But why tell me? Why not go to the police?"

"We will, but we want to talk to you first."

"I'm flattered," I said, trying to give her the impression that I was buying what she was selling. "I assume you want to meet somewhere."

She paused. I heard the sound of a hand scraping across the receiver at her end.

"Yes," she said, finally. "Could you meet us at Mather's home later tonight? Maybe around ten."

I looked at my watch.

"I'll be there. Give me the address."

Buck Mather lived on Packer Lane in an area inside the Salem city limits where the last few acres of prime farm land were gradually giving way to urban sprawl. After the drive down Interstate 5, I went through downtown Salem, then southwest out of the city on River Road past Salem Golf Club toward the small town of Independence. Near a vacant building that once housed a small mom-and-pop grocery, I slowed, almost missing the small Packer Lane sign engulfed in a huge blackberry bramble that paralleled River Road and guarded both sides of the turnoff.

I turned and drove a short distance up Packer Lane, which was little more than a gravel track with barbed-wire fences on either side, and stopped a few feet past the blackberry bramble. A small, single-story house stood about a hundred yards to the right. It appeared harmless and pastoral with lights in the windows and a perfect plume of smoke curling out the chimney into the night sky. It looked like elves lived there.

To left of the road lay a nearly square, two-acre pasture. On the other side, diagonally across from where I stopped the Jeep, a dingy two-story farm house crouched in the gathering darkness. The front porch sagged at one end. Shingles missing from the roof looked like gaps in an old man's dentures. The upstairs windows were dark, but the downstairs lights shone through dirty panes of glass covered with thin curtains. Beyond the house a dilapidated barn leaned beside what remained of a corral. A driveway leading down to Packer Lane skirted along the far side of the property. Parked in the flood-lit gravel between the house and the barn was Mather's white van.

I slowly backed the Jeep through the overhanging vines and onto pavement, then drove fifty yards up River Road to a turnout that gave me an unobstructed view of the entrance to Packer Lane. It started to rain, a gentle sprinkle at first, but distant thunder promised hard drops were on the way. I checked my watch. Nine p.m. An hour early. Perfect. I dug a plastic rain coat out of the back seat, then waited in the dark to see who was helping Anna Krychek frame me.

# Chapter 25

At first, I didn't recognize the car that showed up twenty minutes later. I'd only seen it once before, but there weren't many makes like that cruising the bramble-infested back roads of Marion County.

As soon as the taillights disappeared into the blackberry tunnel, I got out of the car and followed on foot. By the time I was far enough up Packer Lane to see Mather's house, the car had parked behind the white van. Its lights were off, but I could hear the motor idling and see the exhaust from the tailpipe pumping out onto the gravel drive.

I vaulted the barbed-wire fence into Mather's pasture. Keeping close to the huge blackberry bramble, I sprinted the entire left edge of the soggy field, then worked my way across the pasture to the side of the house opposite the driveway. Harsh lights bathed the gravel parking area, back lighting the house and casting deep shadows that swallowed me as I moved toward the near end of the sagging porch.

Thirty feet from the house the skies cut loose. Rain came straight down onto the marshy ground with a deafening roar. Soaked and shivering, I ran to the porch, ducking underneath and putting my back against the cold, concrete foundation.

The storm lasted about ten minutes, and then ended as soon as it began. Angry voices from inside the house replaced the sound of pelting rain drops. Sitting amid the drips and dirt, I heard the words "money" and "manuscript." After a short pause, the old house shook as someone wearing heavy boots walked across the floor inside. The footsteps clomped toward me, stopped, then moved away. A chair scraped across the floor, followed by a muffled pop. A door slammed. Gravel crunched.

Down the full length of the front porch, I could see the first few feet of the driveway. I heard an engine accelerate. Loose pebbles clattered against metal. Headlights fanned across the pasture followed by taillights headed down the driveway. A few seconds later, the dark Lincoln that was parked behind Mather's van turned onto Packer Lane and disappeared into the gap between the blackberry bushes.

It was suddenly mausoleum quiet. Something was wrong.

Mather had to still be in the house, I thought. I was sure only one set of footsteps had crunched across the gravel to the Lincoln.

I crawled out from under the porch, wiping globs of mud off my jacket and pants as I moved along the end of the house toward the weed-infested back yard. At the end of a path of broken concrete blocks that ran along the rear of the house was a small porch with a screen door. Beyond that, I could see the barn and adjacent corral.

Three windows lined the back of the house. I moved around the corner to peer in the first window at the living room, which had a television set, a threadbare couch, a couple of worn-out easy chairs, and a coffee table covered in beer cans. Three scrawny cats hunched over a plate eating what looked to be old cat food or fresh Spam. They stopped long enough to look at me, then calmly return to their mystery meal.

Stooping over, I moved down the path to the next window. It was a dining room in the same condition as the front room, but with more beer cans and fewer cats.

The silent house gave me that mausoleum feeling again. I wondered why Mather wasn't moving around inside getting a beer, fixing dinner, or assembling mail bombs.

The next window had to be the kitchen. I crawled down the path and stopped directly underneath. The old-fashioned wood frame window, screenless, with pulleys and a half-moon latch, was all the way open. I decided Mather left it that way to make it easier for the cats, rodents, and flies to come and go. Slowly, I raised up a few inches, then immediately dropped to the ground. A man was sitting just inside the window, his shirt collar soaked from the rainwater that dripped in off the sill.

Afraid to even breath, I hugged the ground, feeling trapped while I waited for the man to get up. Another thunder shower started with the same quickness as the earlier one. At the height of the storm, I stood up a second time. The man hadn't moved, and for good reason.

There was a huge hole in the back of his head.

# Chapter 26

The maid cleared away the dinner plates while Proctor Scofield watched his wife refill her wine glass. He passed on dessert, but asked for coffee. Margaret declined dessert as well, but asked for the crystal decanter of cognac.

"Red wine with a cognac chaser," Scofield said. "Must be something you picked up in France."

She gave him a faint smile, but didn't reply. The table's flowery centerpiece that filled the space between them made it easy for her to avoid his gaze.

He remembered the exact moment when Margaret gave up social drinking for a more enthusiastic approach to alcohol. They had attended the wedding two years earlier of the daughter of one of his vice presidents. The bride was young, not yet twenty, with a frail alabaster complexion and short red hair that bounced when she walked. He took his eyes off the girl long enough to notice that Margaret had remained quiet during the wedding and sullen when it concluded. After an obligatory appearance at the extravagant reception, she wanted to go home. Once there, she quietly and elegantly drank herself into a stupor. Scofield had left the next day on business. When he returned three days later, the maid came to him in tears saying that Margaret had spent the entire time in bed and none of it sober.

He let it pass, blaming it on the fact that she would turn fifty-five in a few months, but kept an eye on her just the same. The problem became clear several weeks later when he found her drinking and crying with an old photo album open on her lap.

Scofield realized later that the bride had resembled their daughter, who was not yet twenty when she died. Thoughts of the little girl that came into his life when he married Margaret almost drove Scofield to join his wife inside the bottle of cognac. Instead, he took her to Europe for a month. They stayed in remote villas in Tuscany and expensive hotels in Paris, Rome, and Vienna. Margaret's drinking slowed, but never stopped. Eventually, Scofield gave up altogether. Each time he tried to help Margaret, it brought back is own painful memories of their daughter.

"I'm still going to the beach house this weekend," he said after the coffee arrived. " Have you given some thought to going with me?"

"I have some letters to write and the charity auction is Saturday, but feel free to go without me."

She smiled, stood up and straightened her dress before carefully going up the stairs to her bedroom where, he assumed, she would continue drinking until she fell asleep.

"There's a call for you, Mr. Scofield," the maid said, as Margaret disappeared into the darkness at the top of the stairs.

"I'll take it in my study, Annie," Scofield said and pushed back his chair.

The tap of his footsteps produced a lonely echo as he retreated across the tiled floors to the only room in the house where he felt at home. The deep-pile silence of the carpet in the study made him feel less like he lived alone in a museum.

"The situation has been taken care of," Mitch Penroy said when Scofield picked up the line.

"Excellent. Can we expect any repercussions?"

"There's always that chance, but I'm confident everything will work out in our favor."

Scofield marveled at Penroy's new habit of never totally committing himself. He had started using weasel words that left just enough wiggle room in case things went bad.

His relationship with Mitch Penroy had been a long, but strange one. They had met when Penroy was a sophomore at the University of Oregon, a born organizer who shared Scofield's aversion to limelight and notoriety. Penroy approached him, said he knew about Scofield's fascination with politics, and presented a scheme too intriguing to ignore. Penroy's idea came with a high price, but one Scofield willingly paid to hide other secrets. As things turned out, they were a perfect match that had endured for more than twenty years. Scofield had come to place great trust in Penroy's advice and actions on behalf of Scofield and the company. Until recently.

Penroy was tiring of the game. Salaries, bonuses, stock options, and insider trading had made Penroy a millionaire several times over. The money seemed to dull his competitive edge. The killer instinct that Scofield so admired in the young Penroy had been lost as his protege passed his fortieth birthday. Scofield would have to find a way to reinvigorate Penroy or find someone else to do the corporation's dirty work.

"So, you have the manuscript?" Scofield asked.

"Yes," Mitch Penroy said.

"Have you read it?"

"I'm just getting started, but at first glance, I don't think it will be the problem we thought it would."

"I'll be the judge of that," Scofield growled. "I'll have the chauffeur come over in the morning to get it. Don't make any copies. Now, you're sure there weren't any problems at Mather's house?"

"I don't believe so. That matter should be taken care of."

Scofield bristled again at more weasel words such as "believe so" and "should be," but he didn't want to discuss details over the phone.

"What about our writer friend," he asked.

"That's being taking care of as we speak."

"You better keep tabs on things through the night."

"Definitely. I should know more within a couple of hours."

"What about the police? Did they copy the files from Krychek's computer?"

"It doesn't appear so. The man in charge of the investigation is just as incompetent as we were told. My guess is that he deleted them by mistake or they were never there in the first place. It's not unreasonable to think that Krychek deleted them himself. In any event, I'm confident we have the only copy."

Scofield hung up with an uneasy feeling. Something didn't add up. Patience, he told himself, then reached for the aspirin and the scotch.

After several hours of responding to e-mails and reviewing financial reports on the computer in the corner of the study, Scofield yawned and climbed the stairs to his bedroom. On the way, he stopped to check on Margaret. She lay asleep on the bed, but still dressed as she had been at dinner. The snifter of cognac had fallen from her hand, the brown liquid still pooled in the wrinkles of the down comforter. The photo album on her lap lay open to a picture of their daughter on her first day at the University of Oregon.

Scofield stared at the photo for a long time, then left Margaret as he found her to go back to his study and to the liquor cabinet in the corner.

# Chapter 27

I entered Mather's house through the small porch. A stack of firewood lined one wall under a shelf packed with canned goods, toilet paper, and bottled water. A plastic garbage can filled with empty beer cans had a place of honor in the corner near the back door. Through the porch was a small kitchen with washed-out Formica counters. Cupboards covered with years of spattered cooking oil and greasy fingerprints lined two walls. A sink filled with dirty dishes sat adjacent to a squat, fifties-style refrigerator smeared with more fingerprints. Flies buzzed around a long-handled pot on the gas range.

Buck Mather's body was held upright by the low arms of a chair that looked like it once belonged to a cheap dining room set. The cigarette in his left hand had burned down close to the knuckle and produced a faint odor of burned flesh. The other arm, encased in a cast, stretched out in front of him on the table, the hand wrapped around a can of beer. A series of butterfly bandages covered stitches under his left eye. The bullet hole in the middle of his forehead looked clean, surgical, and the size of a dime. If not for the larger, more vivid exit wound in the back of Mather's head, I might have mistaken it for some kind of gag, like fake vomit on a carpet.

I sagged into the chair across the table from Mather and stared at the hulking security guard's flaccid face. I wanted to feel sorry for Mather, but couldn't.

"It looks like the Buck stops here," I said.

I looked at my watch. Quarter to ten. According to Anna Krychek's instructions, I wasn't suppose to arrive for another fifteen minutes. Perfect timing to find Mather's body and further establish my reputation as a murder suspect.

I had to laugh. I wondered what Butcher would think if he knew Mather's killer drove a car owned by the lobbyist for one of the wealthiest and most reclusive men in the world.


"I'm not talking to that asshole."

I pointed at Butcher over the shoulder of Alfie Gitchell, who stood between the two of us like a referee.

"Calm down, John," Gitchell said, then dragged me out the door into the driveway. Butcher followed, but turned and went back inside when Gitchell waved him away.

I figured that Anna's plan called for having the police show up at precisely ten o'clock to find me standing over Mather's body. Instead, I had used Mather's phone to make the call myself. Then, I took a seat on a stool inside the back porch listening to the rain fall gently on the roof and waiting for the first black and white to roar up the driveway.

I had successfully fought the urge to look around Mather's house. Somewhere in the mess that had been Buck Mather's life were clues to whose dirty work he'd been doing. But the risk of leaving behind some tell-tale evidence of a search was too great. I chose instead to wait to greet the cops like the host at Christmas dinner.

When the police showed up, they hustled me into the barn, and waited for Harry Butcher. Within a few minutes, the pasture and trees surrounding Mather's house were filled with flashing red-and-white lights. It was the scene outside Jasmine's house all over again. Intermittent pops from the police photographer's strobe lit up the house's streaked windows. The lights and sirens attracted a half dozen gawking neighbors, who stood at the end of the driveway under striped golf umbrellas.

Gitchell arrived just as Butcher took the swizzle stick out of his mouth and accused me of making Mather victim number three.

"He's just doing his job," Gitchell said after dragging me out of earshot.

"Christ, Alfie, where do you find people like him? The guy eats peas with a knife." I was growing tired of flash bulbs and yellow tape. "Now, am I under arrest or not?"

The little detective used one Camel straight to light another, then broke into a coughing spasm. I took the pack from the helpless Gitchell and lit one for myself.

"You're not under arrest," Gitchell said, his voice choked and his face red, "but you've been popping up in some embarrassing places lately. You're making it hard for us not to charge you with something."

Two technicians from the medical examiner's office wheeled Mather's body out the door to the ambulance. Butcher followed along behind the body bag, carrying a brown paper sack. He talked briefly with the ambulance driver, then joined Gitchell and me in the barn.

"We found this in the corner next to the refrigerator," Butcher said. He handed the paper sack to Gitchell, who opened the top and peered inside. "It looks like piano wire. We still have to test it, but my guess is it's the same wire we found on the other two bodies."

Butcher turned to glare at me. The disappointment in his voice came straight from the heart.

My thoughts turned to Jasmine Grant, then to the night in the stairwell at Delaney College. I felt both disappointment and relief that I hadn't done more damage to Mather that night when I had the chance. Either way, Mather got everything he deserved.

"Anything else?" Gitchell asked.

"Not so far, but we're still looking." He gestured toward me. "You're not out of the woods yet, word man. You could've planted all this before we got here."

We were glaring at each other when a uniformed cop walked up carrying a plastic bag that he handed to Gitchell. Inside was the torn corner of a piece of typing paper. Gitchell turned it over in his hands a few times. In the faint light, I could just make out what it said:

1/Krychek/Thesis/Right v

Butcher walked away without looking at it. Gitchell folded the bag in half and slipped it into the pocket of his raincoat.

"If you didn't kill Mather, then who did?" Gitchell asked.

"Beats me," I said. "My guess is that the piano wire proves that Mather killed Krychek and Grant. Then someone killed Mather."

"Makes sense, but why are you here?"

"Just trying to make a living. Krychek worked for Mather. I just wanted to ask him a few questions. When I got here, he was dead and I called you."

"I though you already talked to Mather."

"I did, but I had some more questions," I said, hoping that Gitchell wouldn't push the issue too far. "Besides, you got me into this, remember?"

"Don't remind me. It looked like Mather was planning to leave when he was killed. We found a suitcase in the van along with a couple of duffel bags filled with automatic weapons. You probably don't know anything about that either, right?"

I shrugged.

"Get your ass out of here and don't be showing up at any more murder scenes," Gitchell said. "I've done all I can to keep Butcher off your ass, but I'm running out of excuses."

I left with stern reminders from both Gitchell and Butcher to be at the Salem Police Department first thing in the morning to sign a statement. Twenty minutes later, I was headed north on Interstate 5, doing my best to blend into traffic and keep my mind on driving rather than on another night of finding a dead body.

At the apartment, I chained smoked while nursing the last two beers in the refrigerator. When Vanessa came home, she put on a shorter show than usual, skipping her nightly shower and going to bed looking the way I felt. With the beer gone, I hooked down two fingers of cheap bourbon and fell asleep thinking about murdered security guards, dark Lincolns, and sun-tanned lobbyists with Blues Brothers glasses and large handguns.

# Chapter 28

Proctor Scofield sat on a footstool in front to the fireplace in the study carefully reading each page of Ivan Krychek's manuscript before burning it. By the time the pages were nothing more than gray ashes under the fireplace grate, he was convinced that Krychek had known very little about what actually went on twenty years ago at the University of Oregon.

Stirring the ashes with the poker, he wondered how much more Krychek would've learned had he been allowed to live. There had been nothing in the manuscript to indicate that he was anything more than a student with too much spare time, an overactive imagination, and a view of the future of American politics that mimicked his own. Still, Krychek had found out more than anyone else had, which meant it was possible that he could have learned the rest.

Scofield made a second Bloody Mary, slowly stirring the reddish-brown liquid with a celery stalk. The computer in the corner beeped with the daily message telling him the European markets were closed and asking for any special instructions. He ignored it in favor of the leather chair in front of the small, smoldering fire.

What would it be like to never leave this room, he wondered, to run his vast empire with nothing more than a computer. A modern-day Howard Hughes without the fingernails. With e-mail, attachments, and video-conferences, he wouldn't need a telephone or a fax. The staff could put food outside the door. Margaret probably wouldn't mind.

The fire was nearly out, the ashes of the manuscript indistinguishable from the others left by earlier fires. That the manuscript was no longer a threat made Scofield breathe a little easier. Too bad it never had really been a threat.

But he had to be sure. The deaths of Ivan Krychek and Jasmine Grant were part of the certainty. Now, Buck Mather had joined the list.

# Chapter 29

I left the apartment around eight-thirty the next morning after a night of intermittent dreams that left a lingering sense of doom that followed me up the street to where I'd parked the Jeep. Between images, I had come up with a plan that made me eager to get a start on the day and leave the night behind.

After putting gas in the Jeep at a station on SW Jefferson, I headed west out of the city on Highway 26 toward Beaverton. Even though most of the traffic was inbound, the number of cars heading out of town toward the high-tech plants of the Silicon Forest was getting greater all the time. Still, it took less than thirty minutes to get where I was going.

The streets of Ivan Krychek's neighborhood were in full suburban bustle, alive with children on roller blades and skateboards. Teams of Hispanics armed with lawn mowers, rakes, and hedge trimmers descended on the more expensive homes, leaving the less affluent to fend for themselves in an effort to keep their lawns the same bright green.

I pulled into Anna Krychek's driveway, hoping to have a frank conversation over steaming cups of freshly brewed espresso about why she tried to frame me for Buck Mather's murder and maybe her husband's and Jasmine's as well. An added bonus would be finding out who helped her. I had a pretty good idea, but I wanted her to tell me who pulled Mather's strings.

When no one answered the door after three rings, I followed the brick path around the side of the house to peek in the French doors on the brick patio. The leather furniture, oak tables, and everything else were gone. There weren't even indentations in the carpet where the table, chairs, and sofa had been. The door was locked, so I considered kicking it in or at least breaking a window to get inside and look around for some clue to where she might have gone. Instead, I walked up the street, stopping at several houses to talk to housewives, teenagers, and kids on tricycles. I learned nothing more than I already knew. No one had met the Krycheks, talked to them, or done anything other than wave occasionally at the two people who lived in the house at 2852 Baltusrol Way. More surprising, no one had seen a moving van.

I left, drove out to Highway 217 and then south to Interstate 5. I drove slowly toward Salem, spending most of the next forty-five-minutes wondering what happened to the widow Krychek. It didn't seem her style to abandon a nice house because she found it too painful to live there without her beloved Ee-von.

I got off the freeway at the exit at the north end of Salem and followed the Parkway into the center of town. At city hall, just south of the downtown business district, I found a covered parking spot in the garage and headed for the police department. When the clerk at the front desk told me Butcher wasn't in yet, I asked for Alfie Gitchell and she pointed toward a glass cubicle in the far corner .

Gitchell sat at his desk with one cigarette between his fingers and another burning on the edge of the large, butt-filled glass ashtray. The detective's red eyes were surrounded by dark circles set in an off-white face. The spittle on his chin told me I'd walked in on the tail end of another of Gitchell's coughing fits.

"You and Butcher make quite a pair," I said. "If I had to choose, I'd stick with the donuts and give up the smokes."

Too winded to speak, Gitchell handed me a typed version of my previous night's statement. I read slowly to make sure Gitchell had enough time to get his lungs working again.

"You were supposed to be here first thing this morning," Gitchell said.

The cop's hoarse and faint voice sounded like a French horn.

"Sorry. My alarm didn't go off," I said. "I take it Butcher didn't write this. There are no misspelled words, and it's not written in crayon."

"If that statement is an accurate and true reflection of what you told Sergeant Butcher and myself following the death of Buck Mather, please sign your full name in the appropriate places."

I took a pen from the desk, signed, and tossed the statement back on Gitchell's cluttered desk.

"Butcher still thinks you're involved in all of this," Gitchell said as I got up to leave.

"And what do you think?"

"I'm still not sure. It doesn't look like you killed Mather, but there are still two other unsolved homicides."

"Thanks for the vote of confidence."

"Don't thank me. This is still Butcher's case. I've already interfered enough as it is. He thinks I'm protecting you because you put me in that arson story. The only advice I can give you is tell the truth. Butcher equates lying with guilt. If he thinks you're shining him on, he'll chase you into hell."

Remaining a target of the single-minded Butcher made me think again about leveling with Gitchell. I didn't, but I wasn't sure why. It probably had something to do with wanting to believe the world could still be a safe place for people like Jasmine Grant. Simply letting the police take over, while I sat on the sidelines watching wasn't good enough. The revenge and redemption thing still gnawed at me. There would be other times to tell Gitchell everything.

"You know, Alfie, you really should do something about Butcher."

"Don't start with me. You know as well as I do that cops are no different than everyone else. There's good ones and bad ones, happy and sad, smart and dumb."

"Honest and corrupt."

Gitchell stuck out a tobacco-stained lower lip and shrugged.

"When you live in shit all day, it's hard not to smell bad."

"Be sure to put that on your tombstone," I said.

Gitchell fought back a smile, then turned serious.

"You know what's unusual about these killings? They were committed by a real criminal. I know that sounds odd, but think about it. There are no real criminals anymore, Standard, just punks who think rebellion means ignoring the crosswalk signs; little assholes who rage against the establishment by spray painting their names on the sides of buildings in the middle of the night. When that doesn't work, they beat up somebody who's different from them. Maybe they go to school and gun down some students because they can't get a blow job from some girl who doesn't know the difference between sex and breakfast at Denny's. Then they can't believe it when they're sent to prison for the rest of their miserable lives. They act tough in court like it means nothing to them, then cry for their mommies when the doors are locked behind them. The whole thing stinks."

The speech was as close as Gitchell ever got to eloquence.

"I think I smell burnout," I said.

"I'm not dead yet, but you could be if you're not putting all your cards on the table. I've got a twinge in my gut that tells me you haven't forgotten about that Grant woman, so if you're on some kind of vendetta against her killer, I'd suggest forgetting the whole thing. One night in the rack with her or any other woman ain't worth a hole in the ground."

"She was more than that," I shot back, then held my breath long enough to calm down. "Anyway, I'm no hero, just a guy trying to earn a buck. No one has any reason to kill me."

Gitchell dumped the ash tray into the waste basket and lit a cigarette to begin the process of refilling it.

"Make sure you don't give them one. I don't need a fourth murder on my hands."

# Chapter 30

The twenty-something woman at the registrar's office at Delaney College had blue fingernail polish, streaks of green in her red hair, and a Bela Lugosi complexion. She popped gum while I told her what I needed.

"Ivan Krychek is the dead guy, right?" she asked.

I slowly nodded.

"I don't remember anyone enrolled here named Anna Krychek," she said.

I told her that Anna and Ivan Krychek had been married late in the previous school year and that she might've been registered under her maiden name.

"Which is?" she said.

When I said I didn't know, she produced a patient smile that looked like a mouse sticking its head out of a hole.

"I'll see what I can do," she said.

She abandoned the counter for the computer terminal on a desk near the back of the room, while I found a chair in the waiting area and thumbed through year-old copies of *Smithsonian*.

The meeting with Gitchell had left me uneasy. That someone might want to kill me because of the manuscript didn't make sense. First off, I was pretty sure no one knew I had it. Second, if Penroy, Roark or Landis wanted me dead, why try to frame me for Mather's murder? Why not just put a bullet in my head the way they did Mather and call it good? Still, hearing Gitchell say it made the possibility real. So did raising the question of whether I wanted vengeance for Jasmine's death. Vengeance seemed like a strong word, but technically Gitchell was right.

"We had eleven students named Anna registered here last spring," the student with the Bela Lugosi complexion said when she returned to the counter twenty minutes later and motioned toward me. "All of them have already re-registered for fall term under the same names. My guess is that your Anna was never a student here."

I thanked her and walked over to the Political Science Department, following the same path across the grass and down the stairs where a few nights earlier I'd unmasked Mather. The broken window had been replaced with a piece of plywood, but bits of glass glistened in the dirt at the bottom of the steps. Inside, harsh overhead lights lit up the drab hallway. The office of the acting department head was two doors down from Krychek's. The little white card on the door identified him as Professor Gerald Miller.

I introduced myself to Miller, who puffed on a huge pipe while peering suspiciously at me over to the top of tortoise-shell reading glasses. After a stilted conversation about how the faculty was coping with the two murders, I got to the point.

"Anna Krychek told me she met Ivan during a political science seminar earlier in the year. She's a very beautiful woman. Hard to miss. I just wondered if perhaps you'd seen her?"

Miller answered with an almost imperceptible nod that I took as a yes.

"You wouldn't happen to know anything about her, would you? Like her maiden name?"

"No," he muttered, "but I'm sure she wasn't a student here. There was something different about her. She just showed up one day. The next thing I knew, she and Ivan were married."

"You never saw her attend a class or a seminar?"

"Not only didn't she attend any classes, we never had a seminar on post-communist eastern Europe," he said.

I left with little more than I came with.

From Delaney, it was only a couple of blocks to the county courthouse and the Office of the County Clerk. It took awhile, but I finally learned that the house on Baltusrol Way had been purchased the previous May by Anna Marie Carlisle for a quarter of a million dollars from Trask Properties, a local development company. I called the registrar's office at Delaney just to confirm that an Anna Carlisle had not been a student there. I got the same clerk and the answer I expected: no one by the name of Anna Carlisle had been registered at Delaney in the last five years.

I went to the bank of pay telephones inside the courthouse's main entrance and leafed through the tattered directory. Trask Properties was listed in the Realtor section of the Yellow Pages with an address in a downtown office building that was just two blocks away. I dialed the number, explained to the receptionist that I had an unusual request, and she passed me off to a salesman who had the idea that I wanted to buy a house. I played along by expressing an interest in 2852 Baltusrol Way.

"We don't have a listing for that particular piece of property anymore, but we have the same floor plan on a house just three blocks away. What say we get together, run some numbers, do a little noodling?"

I sounded interested in order to keep the man on the phone, then asked who owned the house. The sound of shuffling papers came over the phone.

"Sold it to a woman named Anna Carlisle. Closed that deal myself. Two-hundred-fifty thousand cash. That's why I remember it. Don't get that many cash deals. Anyway, I can get you into this same house for about that same price. With a good down payment, maybe a little extra, we could get you in there for a reasonable monthly payment of around . . ."

"I'll get back to you," I said, hanging up just as the salesman asked for a name and telephone number.

There were a half-dozen moving companies listed in the Yellow Pages. I called each one. None of them would admit to being at 2852 Baltusrol Way, and that was only Salem. There would be ten times that many in the Portland Yellow Pages.

Directory assistance had no listing for an Anna Carlisle and the number for Ivan Krychek had been disconnected. There was no new number. I tried directory assistance in every major city in Oregon without luck. The story was the same at the state Department of Motor Vehicles. I bluffed my way past the public affairs person at the Department of Revenue to learn that no one by that name had filed a tax return in Oregon in the last five years.

Anna Carlisle Krychek, or whatever her name was, had disappeared.

# Chapter 31

Tired of the freeway and needing time to think, I headed west out of Salem. It was the same route I'd taken the night Jasmine died, but instead of continuing on toward the coast, I picked up Highway 99W at Rickreall. Cruising south through Monmouth and Corvallis, I became comfortably lost amid the truck farms and grass seed fields that flanked the two-lane highway.

I knew I was getting closer to why Jasmine Grant and Ivan Krychek were killed. The feeling wasn't based on anything concrete, just a sense that who I am and what I was doing was making someone nervous. Tempting as it may sound, there was no other choice but to keep going. Jasmine expected it of me. I expected it of myself.

During our one lunch together, Jasmine had asked why I didn't leave Oregon, go someplace where I wasn't known and start over again. I didn't tell her, but I'd given a lot of thought to outdistancing my reputation, finding a quiet job somewhere writing thumbsucking features about county fair princesses or record-breaking pumpkins. Move to a town with guys named Garth and Earl, who married their high school sweethearts and had kids named Little Garth and Little Earl. Maybe buy a house in the woods and learn to grow organic vegetables. Maybe take up golf.

The last thought brought me quickly back to reality.

By the time I reached Eugene, I had come to the conclusion that instead of missing something, Krychek's thesis was missing somebody. But who? Penroy's car was involved some way, but was Penroy? If he was, did that mean Proctor Scofield was connected as well? Roark and Landis had the most to lose. The connection between them and Amanda Bishop was titillating and great fodder for a story about two rising political stars. But was it really a motive for three murders? It could be that what happened twenty years ago really did cause Roark and Landis to turn their lives around. If that was the case, then what was the problem? It sounded more like a tragic story with a happy ending for everyone.

Except for Amanda Bishop.

Maybe the man I was going to see had some answers.

I drove along the north side of the campus on Franklin Boulevard, turned right on Agate Street, then left onto Thirteenth Street. After plugging quarters in a two-hour meter, I walked up the hill into the heart of the campus of the

University of Oregon. It was summer term, which meant the student population was a fraction of what it was the rest of the year. Those who were there moved at a slow pace along the sidewalks or sat cross-legged in the shade of old elms and Douglas firs. The moss-roofed kiosk at the intersection of Thirteenth and University was covered with several generations of staples that once held handbills announcing concerts by the Grateful Dead and speeches by Abbie Hoffman. Now, the most prominent flyer announced a weekend seminar on how to improve LSAT scores.

The journalism school was housed in Eric W. Allen Hall, which was at the end of a cul de sac not far from the ancient kiosk. My footsteps echoed on the empty stairwell as I climbed three floors then walked along the equally barren hallway.

I had met Professor Marcus Towne ten years earlier when we shared the podium at a weekend conference on journalistic ethics. I considered the phrase an oxymoron and argued that all ethics went out the window as soon as one news organization gained an edge over another by breaching the unwritten rules of conduct. Privately Towne agreed, but publicly espoused restraint and responsibility by both television and newspaper reporters. Our friendship grew over dinner, drinks, and an animated conversation about the future of journalism that lasted long into the night. Afterwards, I had been a frequent visitor to Towne's show-and-tell days for freshmen eager to be the next Bob Woodward.

When I walked into Towne's office, I thought the old professor was asleep. An unlit pipe jutted out from under a gray, walrus mustache stained a dim yellow from years of tobacco smoke. Thin gray hair lay like whisps of cotton candy across a shiny pate, pink as a carnival balloon. His typical dress of white shirt, bow tie, suspenders, and baggy slacks was complimented by a clothespin dangling from one ear lobe.

"John Standard," the old man said when he finally looked up.

He let the name roll off his tongue as if remembering the contents of an expensive bottle of wine.

"Don't tell me you want to come back to school?"

Towne came around the desk to shake my hand and offer a seat at the small conference table wedged into the corner of the office.

"Care to fill me in on the clothespin, Marcus?" I said.

"Oh, that." Towne pulled it off and laid it on the table. "I've had this toothache and no time to get to the dentist. The pain from the clothespin takes my mind off the pain of my tooth. But never mind that. It's been too long.

Tried to call you when I heard what happened. Maybe you didn't get the message, what with everything that was going on."

I had gotten the message, but felt too embarrassed and ashamed to return it. Towne would've offered advice on how to handle the aftermath of the accident, when all I wanted was to crawl in a hole and pretend to be someone else.

I looked up to Towne as someone who still viewed journalism as a noble profession rooted in the First Amendment and John Peter Zenger. Feeling as if I'd tarnished that image and let down my old friend, I had chosen to avoid Towne, until now.

"It was my fault, Marcus," I said. "Some day we'll talk about it. Right now, I need to tell you a few things."

In the next half-hour I laid out the entire story, starting with Ivan Krychek in the portable toilet on the state fairgrounds and ending with the disappearance of Anna Krychek. Towne's eyes narrowed with concern and surprise when I described finding the body of Jasmine Grant. He frowned intensely when I told him about how withholding information from the police had contributed to my standing as a murder suspect. The description of the previous night at Mather's farm house turned Towne's already pale complexion another shade of white.

Sharing the whole story with someone for the first time made me feel twenty pounds lighter.

"This Jasmine Grant," he said. "You obviously had feelings for her. From the way you describe her, I can't blame you. I'm sorry."

"So am I, Marcus. So am I."

"I think maybe finding this killer will close a lot of doors for you. Am I right?"

I only nodded and even that told the professor more than I wanted him to know.

Towne pulled his wiry frame out of the chair, opened the bottom drawer of his oak desk, and produced a bottle of Teachers and two smudged glasses.

"That's quite a tale, my boy. Quite a tale," he said, pouring whiskey for each of us. "You probably don't know Professor Ansbacher. He teaches ethics. He could have a field day with some of the things you've done."

Towne finished off the shot of Teachers with the effortless motion of someone who wasted no time with beer, wine, or mixers.

I hooked down the whiskey with a less practiced but still proficient move, then reached across the desk to pour each of us a second shot.

"I take it you came to me to learn more about Roark, Landis, and Amanda Bishop," Towne said.

"You knew them, then?"

Towne nodded thoughtfully, sipping his drink this time and staring past my shoulder out the small, grimy window behind his desk. Huge fir trees blocked the light and kept the little office in perpetual gloom. The old man's eyes sank back in his head as he reeled in the years to bring long-forgotten images back into focus.

"I've been on this campus more than fifty years," he said, still gazing out the window. "I came here as a freshman. I'll retire next year when I turn seventy. That's right, John. Seventy. I don't know how many students have been through here during those years. Several hundred thousand for sure. Maybe even a million. Most of them I never knew, or even saw for that matter. But I've heard all the stories, good, bad, and otherwise. Everything that has gone on in this country since the 1940s. Think about that, John. The end of a war, the GI bill, the dawn of the nuclear age, assassinations, the first man on the moon, Vietnam, the computer, September Eleventh. They've all been acted out on this campus in one way or another. Sometimes in joy. Sometimes anger."

Towne stopped long enough to look straight into my eyes.

"In all those years, all those students, and all those stories, I have never seen anything like what happened with those two boys."

I got the feeling that Towne had been practicing that speech for years. Finally, someone walked into his office and asked just the right question.

Marcus Towne didn't engage in overstatements. Years of beating news writing into the heads of aspiring reporters left him with an acute ability to say what he meant. What he had said about Roark and Landis left no room for doubt. The two students from two decades ago had left a profound and indelible mark on him.

"It was like night and day." The old man's voice turned into a heavy whisper, like air leaking from a tire. "One week the two of them were worthless scum taking up space that rightfully belonged to someone less fortunate, but with a greater desire to learn. The next week, they were model students. The kind every professor yearns for, eager to learn, to advance, to make something of themselves and of the world around them."

"And you weren't suspicious?"

"Of course I was," he said. "Who wouldn't be? But everyone gave them the benefit of the doubt. We lived in a less cynical and more forgiving world then, my boy. After a few months, it was clear they were serious about turning their lives around."

"And all this happened after Amanda Bishop died?"

Towne nodded.

"All the energy they devoted to drunkenness and debauchery suddenly rechanneled into education and politics. I know it sounds silly today, but you had to be there. It was a different era."

"Sounds more like genetic realignment to me. People just don't change that much that fast."

Towne appeared not to hear.

"Did you know Amanda Bishop?"

"Not really," Towne said. "She introduced herself to me during a freshmen orientation session. I remember her as very shy and vulnerable. Almost doll-like: porcelain skin with little pink circles of rouge on her cheeks and tiny red lips. She made you want to put your arm around her and protect her from the world."

"And you know what happened to her?"

"Oh, yes."

Towne's eyes grew dark under the wiry brows.

"She killed herself. Jumped off a freeway overpass and was hit by a truck. Tragic is the only word for it. Someone so young. When I heard how she died, I went to the president and demanded that he expel Landis and Roark. It was no use. Their parents were generous supporters of the athletic department. I found that out later, but I should've known it was something like that. Then, when I heard later that no charges were filed, well, you know how it goes..."

His voice trailed off.

"Why were the charges against Roark and Landis dropped?"

"I don't know."

"Then why the change? They were off the hook."

Towne stared past me out the window again. When he finally spoke there was awe in his voice of someone reliving a mystical event.

"I know this sounds odd, but I can't explain it any other way. It was as if Amanda Bishop had been reborn in them. They became what she would've been."

Towne poured himself another drink and tossed it down.

"It was as if three people died, and two completely different people lived on."

We stared at each other. The secret of one had been passed on to the other

133

like a sacred chant of some long-forgotten religious order. Towne appeared spent and relieved at ridding himself of what he'd held inside for so long. I, on the other hand, felt burdened. I came seeking answers, but found more questions.

After a short silence, the old professor looked at me with pleading eyes. He placed a gnarled hand on my knee and squeezed.

"Roark and Landis. It was as if they had to change. As if . . ." Towne paused to search for the right words. ". . . their lives depended on it."

# Chapter 32

I wandered around the campus for an hour before heading toward the library. Marcus Towne's words echoed in my head, the leg where the old man touched me itching like poison oak. I walked passed Deady Hall. The granite building, with its tall, church-like spire, reminded me of Mayfield Hall at Delaney College and of Jasmine.

As I neared the library, I tried to imagine Amanda Bishop walking along the same paths that crisscrossed the block-long lawn known as The Walks. She would've been wearing a bright yellow slicker with the pointed hood pulled over her head to keep the rain off. The University of Oregon Fighting Ducks might have had a home game at Autzen Stadium that weekend, so there'd be a large "Go Ducks" button on her rain coat. An army surplus backpack would be slung over one shoulder. Inside would be the *History of Western Civilization* or *The Norton Anthology of English Literature*. She would've been young and eager to learn. Instead, it had all been taken away from her.

What would Amanda think if she knew that one of the two men who raped her, humiliated her, and drove her to suicide would be Oregon's next governor? Fortunate for Roark and Landis, I would never know the answer.

Too fortunate, I thought.

The words "Ye shall know the truth" are carved over the entrance to the Knight Library. I passed underneath them then wandered around for several minutes before asking the woman at the front desk where to find old University of Oregon yearbooks. She thought for a moment, then produced a map of the campus and gave me directions to the school archives in Fenton Hall. I retraced my steps back along the quadrangle to Thirteenth Street.

Fenton Hall could've been higher education's equivalent of Benny Orlando's apartment house. The sign on the white door on the west end of old block building said "Archives." A crude sign inside the cramped entry directed visitors up a narrow flight of dusty, metal stairs.

"Hello," I called when I reached the second floor.

"Yes." It was a sing-song voice that seemed to come from nowhere.

I peeked around the corner. A plump, pleasant-looking woman with red-hair and glasses hanging on a beaded string around her neck sat at a cluttered desk amid rows of metal shelves covered with books and files. Posters depicting a century of university life adorned the walls around her.

"Can I help you?" she said with an eagerness that said she didn't get many visitors.

"I'd like to see some yearbooks," I said, then rattled off the years I needed. The request seemed to confuse her.

"I'm sorry," I said, "perhaps they're by academic year rather than calendar year."

"No. It's not that," she said. "It's just that there was a period in there when the school didn't publish any yearbooks. They sort of fell out of favor for a while. Campus politics, that sort of thing."

"Could I see whatever you have?"

"Of course."

She vanished into the rows of metal shelves and returned a few minutes later with two large, dusty copies of *Oregana*, the University of Oregon yearbook.

"This seems to be all we have," she said, dropping them on the table. "It must have been the earlier ones that were discontinued."

The books appeared indistinguishable from the thousands of others produced each year by colleges and high schools everywhere. The rough-grained pages of black-and-white photos showed school officials, sports teams, and something called the Panhellenic Council. I flipped pages to the section titled ASUO: Associated Students of the University of Oregon, otherwise known as student government.

The large photo dominating the top half of the left hand page showed a group of students sitting on the stairs in front of Johnson Hall, the school's administration building. The entire group looked like some kind of disco band, their attire a mish-mash of white belts, short sweaters, and plaid pants. The men had either long hair, beards, mustaches, or sideburns of different lengths, colors, and thickness. The women wore short skirts or dresses, their faces framed by long hair. At the center of the photo stood a youthful Brad Roark wearing a Levi jacket, faded bell-bottom jeans, and sneakers. His hair and sideburns short by the standards of the day. To his left stood Kingsley Landis, his blond hair long and cut in bangs. He wore a dark, three-piece, corduroy suit with a wide, paisley tie, and a striped dress shirt.

Roark, Landis and the others wore the same serious looks required of those who assumed they represented the next generation of national leaders. With one exception. The figure at the far right hand side of the photo was shorter than the others. His expression more intent and defiant. Jet black hair matched his shirt, pants, and shoes. A drooping mustache curled around a down-turned mouth. Dark glasses with small, round lenses hid his eyes.

I ran a finger along the caption beneath the photo. It identified Roark as president and Landis as secretary-treasurer. I skipped the others and went to the name that corresponded with the somber, darkly dressed student at the far right.

Mitchell James Penroy.

"Jesus. Where does this stop?"

I closed the book and reached for the next one. There were Roark and Landis again in a photo of student body officers. Once again, Penroy stood at the far end, the same defiant look on his face. He carried the same title of administrative assistant, but with longer hair. A full beard had been added to the droopy mustache. The clothes were still dark, as was the demeanor and the glasses with the small, round lenses.

I tried not to jump to conclusions. Oregon's population is small, so there was nothing unusual about three people involved in campus politics showing up years later involved in state politics. Nevertheless, coincidences bothered me as much as small, purposeful-looking people with vague titles like administrative assistant, who grew up to drive dark Lincolns, represent large corporations, and perhaps kill people.

I made copies of the photos before retracing my steps back down the hill to the Office of the Registrar on the second floor of Oregon Hall. There were no lines for Academic Records and Graduation. I told the work-study student behind the counter that I wrote for *Inside Oregon*. She acted unimpressed, but appeared eager to help.

"I'm looking for any information about someone who was a student here about twenty or so years ago. Her name was Amanda Bishop."

She gave him a blank look.

"Yeah? And?"

"Would it be possible to look at her records?"

"Do you have her permission?"

"No," I said. "She's dead. I'm doing some research on her death."

I got that blank stare again.

"If this is a problem, perhaps I could talk to your supervisor."

"My supervisor's not here, but it doesn't matter anyway," she said. "We can't give out information about students to just anyone."

"All I need to know is who she put down to notify in case of an emergency."

"A little late for that, isn't it?"

"I know it's an odd request, but work with me here. Okay?"

With a sigh, she handed me an information request card. I filled it out, pushed it back across the counter, and watched her disappear behind a computer on the other side of the room.

The computer printout on Amanda Bishop was short, as expected for someone who committed suicide two weeks after enrolling. It contained the usual information about height, weight and home address.

At least it appeared usual, until I got to the line about who to notify in the case of emergency.

Proctor Scofield.

# Chapter 33

There was no room left to think about driving or about the miles of farmland along the interstate as I drove north to Portland. I raced by a couple of dozen slower cars and let an equal number of faster ones pass. Either way, they were little more than colorful blurs against the gray pavement. With each overpass came the vision of a body flying down into my windshield.

The same names ran through my head over and over again. Roark. Landis. Penroy. Bishop. Then there was the new name that closed the circle and connected all the dots. It seemed too good to be true. Politics, money, sex, and violence all wrapped up in one tidy package starring the reclusive billionaire Proctor Scofield who hadn't been seen in public in over a decade.

In Portland, I parked two blocks from the apartment and sat in the car watching the rush-hour cars go by. The last few people on the street dressed in suits scurried into car parks and emerged minutes later in their BMWs and sport utility vehicles. Slowly, the homeless came out, pushing shopping carts and checking the trash cans and pay phones along the sidewalk. I found myself not caring that I existed somewhere in between.

I walked home feeling excited and afraid. They were feelings I'd had before, but never at the same time.

That night I drifted in and out of sleep, marking each hour by glancing at the clock next to the bed. When it reached six a.m. I couldn't stand it any more. Showered and dressed, I walked across the Park Blocks to become the first customer at the neighborhood espresso bar. With a latte' and a cranberry-cinnamon muffin, I sat at a table outside reading the paper while NW Columbia Street filled with morning commuters.

At seven-thirty, I knocked on Benny's door. A sleepy-eyed Ivy answered.

"Benny's in Seattle on business," she said. "I'm sort of apartment sitting."

I apologized for waking her and turned to leave.

"You're welcome to come in," she said, opening the door wider.

She wore bikini panties and a short T-shirt that revealed the kind of breasts I hadn't seen since high school.

"No, thanks, but I appreciate the offer," I said. "Tell Benny I stopped by. I'll call him when he gets back."

I went back to my apartment, watched Katie Couric do a cooking segment with Martha Stewart, then called the office of State Senator Brad Roark right after eight o'clock.

"Senator Roark's office," the friendly female voice said after two rings. "How may I help you?"

I identified myself as a freelance writer for *Inside Oregon.*

"Is Senator Roark there?"

"One moment please."

I expected to be transferred to Roark. Instead I got a nasally press aide with the inflated sense of importance that comes with getting involved in politics at too early an age.

"Who did you say you were with?" the aide asked.

If I wanted to talk to Roark, pissing off some low-life staffer wasn't going to get it done. I took a deep breath, controlled the urge to tell the little asshole to fuck off, and asked again to speak to Roark.

"I'm sorry, but the senator is out of the office at the moment. Perhaps I can help you."

I wondered how the aide would react if I said I wanted to talk to the senator about drugging and raping the stepdaughter of one of the richest men in America.

"No, you probably can't," I said. "I'm working on a story, and I need to talk to him right away. What are the chances of having him call me?"

"Well, they'd be a lot better if you would tell me what it's about it."

"Just tell Roark that John Standard would like to talk to him immediately."

The aide took the number and I hung up.

I turned my attention to Kingsley Landis, making a few calls to sources around town. What I found out was that Landis really didn't work at the law offices of Morgan, Grodin and Dean, as it said in his legislative biography. He merely maintained an office there so his name could appear as one of several associates who handled the firm's corporate clients. Landis's real profession was politician and any success he had in that field was supposed to rub off on the entire firm.

So would his shortcomings, I thought, imagining the reaction of the stodgy firm's wrinkled partners when they learned that Landis was a college rapist and party monster. It might even mean something as drastic as another martini at the club.

I called the law offices, identifying myself to the overly polite receptionist as a freelance writer.

"I'd like to talk to Landis as soon as possible."

"Have you tried his legislative office," the receptionist asked.

"No, but I'm sure you could do that for me. I seem to be having trouble getting by staff members."

"Can I tell Mr. Landis what this is regarding?"

"Tell him it concerns Amanda Bishop."

I spent the rest of day in the apartment waiting for the phone to ring. After a wrong number and two attempts to get him to change my long distance carrier, I was ready to start chewing on the wallpaper when Roark called.

"What can I do for you, Mr. Standard?" His tone came off cold and impatient.

"I have some questions regarding an incident several years ago that might be related to a story I'm working on."

"What kind of story?"

"It would be better if we talked about it face to face."

Roark remained silent for a moment, then sighed into the receiver.

"I suppose I could make some time next week, but it would be extremely helpful if you'd tell me what this is all about."

"I'm afraid next week won't work. I'd like to see you as soon as possible. This afternoon or tonight."

"That's impossible. I'm tied up in hearings until six. Then I have a commitment tonight that can't be broken, a party fund-raiser. You'll have to wait until next week. I'll instruct my office to put it on my calendar. If you'll call on Monday, my press aide will give you the day and time."

After Roark hung up, I called the Democratic Party of Oregon.

"I was planning to attend the fund-raiser tonight, but I've misplaced my invitation," I told the volunteer who answered the phone. "Can you tell me where it is again?"

"Of course," she said. "The Woolen Mill Museum in Salem. It starts at seven."

I looked at the clock. Three hours. Plenty of time.

# Chapter 34

Proctor Scofield and Mitch Penroy stared at the speaker phone. The disembodied voice of Brad Roark sounded panicked as he told them about John Standard's request for an interview. The tinny sound of the speaker added a new dimension to the politician's whiny voice.

"I have no intention of talking to him, Mr. Scofield," Roark said. "I told him to call my office next week to arrange something. When he does -- if he does -- I'll make sure there's no time available. We'll just stonewall him."

Scofield and Penroy looked at each other. The billionaire businessman smiled at his protege', who shook his head in silent exasperation.

"Do you know what he wants?" Penroy asked.

"Not for sure, but what else could it be? You're the one who told me he's been nosing around about those murders. I don't know anything about them. Why should I have to talk to him?"

"What if it's something else?" Scofield interjected.

"Like what, Mr. Scofield?"

"Like Amanda."

A few seconds of silence followed the low groan that crawled out of the speaker.

"Relax, Brad," Scofield said. He reminded himself to be stern with Roark. "Now listen closely. We've been rehearsing this moment for years. We all knew it would happen. The timing is perfect. Now, just do what we told you, and everything will be all right."

Penroy looked concerned, but Scofield relished what came next. He'd seen the future, prepared for it, and now all that preparation was going to pay off. This was why he played the game. Moments like this were his Super Bowl. Let the others wring their hands and pull their hair. Let them be afraid to succeed, to cower at the moments when life became most worth living. What were they afraid of? Just follow instructions. A few days or even weeks of discomfort meant nothing compared to what they had done so far and what they would reap in the end.

"If Standard calls back, Brad, you talk to him," Scofield said. "You tell him exactly what we told you to say. Do you understand?"

"Yes, sir."

"Now, go to your fundraiser and do your job." Scofield disconnected the call and turned to Penroy. "What a dumb shit. Has Standard contacted Landis?"

"He's left a message and used Amanda's name," Penroy said. "Kingsley is glued together a little better than Roark. He'll handle Standard and do what we told him."

"They'll figure it out," Scofield said. "We can't do everything for them."

Scofield looked across the desk at Penroy. "And how are you doing, Mitch?" he asked.

The lobbyist smiled and gave a thumbs up.

"Nervous, especially about Roark, but I think we'll get through this. "

"It's happening just the way you and I predicted years ago." Scofield said. "If we weather this, we're home free."

Penroy nodded, but not with the conviction Scofield had come to expect from him.

"There's something wrong, isn't there, Mitch?" Scofield said. "Let's get it on the table."

The lobbyist shifted in his seat and straightened his Jerry Garcia tie before answering.

"We always figured that someone in the mainstream media would find out about this. A political reporter, maybe, who didn't have the instincts or resourcefulness of an investigative reporter. We even hoped it would be a television reporter. Standard is a wild card. He may be in disrepute, but there was a time when he was someone to reckon with. I guess I don't like it that things aren't turning out exactly like we planned."

"So what. Remember, we didn't plan on someone like Krychek coming along, either. We've had to improvise there. You've done a hell of a job keeping things on track. We're almost where we should be. Whether it's a freelancer like Standard or someone from *The Oregonian* or a television station really doesn't matter. The story will get out and every reporter in the state will be on it. After that, we stick to our game plan."

"There's something else we need to consider," Penroy said. "Standard must have a copy of Krychek's manuscript. How else would he have known to call Roark or Landis?"

Scofield pondered that for a minute. Another copy of the manuscript had always been a concern. Even though there was nothing in it that was particularly incriminating, he didn't like the idea that it was in the hands of someone he couldn't control.

"Then Mather lied to us."

"Could be, or maybe he just didn't know."

Scofield's head starting to pound again. He'd done his best to hide his concerns about Standard in order to keep Penroy and the others focused and upbeat. He hated when last-minute details came up during an important business deal. This was no different. It was an eventuality that had to be handled.

"It doesn't matter. We've both read the manuscript. There's nothing in there that can hurt us. Everything Krychek learned we knew would come out eventually anyway."

"So those deaths . . .?" Penroy asked.

"Don't ponder those too long, Mitch. There was no other way. Accept it and move on."

Penroy responded with an unconvincing nod.

# Chapter 35

The Thomas Kay Woolen Mill provided the perfect setting for a Democratic Party fundraiser. The museum, dedicated to the history of an old textile mill, stood as a symbol of the working-class heroes who slaved for long hours in the difficult conditions that existed prior to the dawn of the Labor Movement. The entire place had been refurbished and turned over to the Marion County Historical Society, which conducted tours and operated a gift shop and small restaurant. The barn-like buildings were popular places for wedding receptions, conferences, big band concerts, and political functions.

I arrived about seven-thirty and fell in behind a group of men dressed in Dockers, Rockports, and well-worn tweed sport coats. I followed them across the parking lot, through the gate in the black wrought-iron fence, and down the asphalt drive that led to the mill itself. Small groups gathered on the brick-and-concrete patio drinking donated beer out of white plastic cups.

Not seeing Roark, I went inside and took the elevator up to the party on the third floor. The doors opened on to a long, wide room with open rafters and floor-to-ceiling windows along each side. A display outside the elevator door included grainy, black-and-white photographs of tired-looking young women standing next to huge looms. They wore long dresses, wire-rimmed glasses and piled their hair Gibson Girl style.

Several hundred people stood gathered in groups around the room. They talked and laughed above the din created by a band playing music by Jim Croce and Credence Clearwater Revival. I hoped to find Roark before the band broke into a medley of Three Dog Night tunes.

I asked some people near the buffet if Brad Roark had arrived yet. No, they said, but he was expected any minute.

I grabbed a plate of celery sticks, a scoop of ranch dressing, and half-a-dozen meatballs from the buffet. After pouring a beer from the keg in the corner, I rode the elevator back to the ground floor and walked back toward the front gate. An empty picnic table near the information kiosk provided an unobstructed view of the entrance and a place to eat the bland finger food.

By eight o'clock, I eaten the food. A cool breeze came up, making me wish I'd worn a coat. I glanced around for a warmer place to wait. The sign on the large building adjacent to the wrought-iron gate identified it as the Wool

Warehouse. It looked warm, but closed. The wooden walkway across the front led to shops and a restaurant with the unlikely name of Karma's Cafe. The neon "Deli" sign in the window sat above a small, plastic sign that read, "Closed."

I turned around. Behind me, the mill race rumbled down a spillway and under a wooden footbridge, eventually disappearing under the main mill building itself. To the right, three refurbished, white clapboard buildings circled a small lawn. The buildings dated back to the mid-1800s, when they served as homes and, in the case of the two-story building with the balcony, a Methodist parsonage.

More people arrived in groups of three and four. Most ignored me, but some came over to shake hands and introduce themselves. They all treated me like an old friend from long-forgotten political battles. I played along, while keeping an eye on the entrance.

Roark arrived a little before eight-thirty followed by two young aides who wore indelible self-absorbed looks. Predictably, one of them whipped out a cell phone and began talking. I got up from the picnic table and moved quickly across the asphalt to fall into step beside Roark.

"I'm John Standard. We talked this afternoon."

Roark frowned.

"I thought we were going to talk next week," he said, anger just behind his blue eyes. "I really don't have time for an interview right now. Perhaps if you could tell me what you want, we might have a position paper that will answer your questions."

Roark was slick, I thought, even for a Democrat.

I walked faster until I was ahead of Roark, then turned to face him. Roark stopped. The aide with the cell phone ceased talking and moved toward me.

"Don't even think about it," I said to the aide. When he stopped in his tracks, I turned to Roark.

"I'm not a political reporter. I'm a freelance writer. I want to talk to you about Amanda Bishop."

We stared at each other, then Roark motioned for the aides to go ahead. He would be there in a few minutes, he said, then looked around.

"This way," he said.

We walked up a narrow path past the information kiosk and along the spillway to a small, one-story building huddled under a gnarled oak tree. It had a porch with a set of stairs at each end. The weathered sign stuck in the middle of a flower bed identified it as "The Pleasant Grove Presbyterian

Church, 1858."

Roark tried one of the double doors. The first was locked, but the second opened. We slipped inside where a dozen wooden pews faced a simple altar that favored no particular religion. I found a switch inside next to the door that turned on two dim lamps which sat on antique tables set along the back wall. Roark pointed to one of the pews at the rear of the chapel.

He took a deep breath and rubbed the bridge of his nose with thumb and forefinger.

Nice touch, I thought.

"I knew that sooner or later the story of Amanda Bishop would come up," he said.

He was sitting with his back against the end of the pew. The anger gone, his tone seemed suddenly equal portions of sadness, contrition, and resignation appropriate to the setting.

"It's too much to ask these days not to have events of that nature enter into political debate."

I stood in the aisle, staring down the length of the pew at Roark.

"I'm not sure I know of any time in the history of journalism or politics where this would not be a story," I said. "I think that the two major candidates for governor gang raping a coed falls within most definitions of news. Add the fact that the girl was Proctor Scofield's stepdaughter and that she committed suicide by jumping off a bridge in front of moving truck and I'd say we'd moved beyond the usual 'dog-bites-man' stuff."

Roark held up both hands in submission.

"I know. I know. I don't suppose it's going to do any good to tell you or anyone else that I am not the same person I was then. Neither is Kingsley, for that matter. But at some point, the sins of the past must become part of the past."

"That's pretty convenient for you."

"All I can tell you is that we knew the story of Amanda Bishop would come out eventually. King and I talked about it before we ever got into politics. I can't speak for him, but I can tell you that I have no intention of denying it happened or downplaying its significance in any way."

"Save it for the editorial boards," I said. "I could care less whether this helps or hurts your or anyone else's chances of becoming governor, senator or King of Norway."

"Then why are you here?" Roark said, looking confused.

I leaned forward, resting my hands on the end of the pew.

"I think what happened twenty years ago is somehow related to three murders that occurred over the last few days. I think you and Landis know something about those murders. You may or may not be involved, but there's a pretty good chance you know who is, and why those people were killed."

Roark lit a cigarette, then looked around for a place to throw the match, seeming surprised that there were no ashtrays in a church.

"I'm afraid I don't know what you're talking about," he said, blowing smoke out his nose. "Murders? What murders?"

"Have you ever heard of Ivan Krychek?"

He shook his head.

"Who?"

"Jasmine Grant?"

Another shake.

"Buck Mather?"

"Mather I know. Security guy at the capitol. Terrible what happened to him, but I don't understand what you're driving at. You can't possibly think that I'm in anyway involved in Mather's death or that what happened to him is in some way related to Amanda Bishop."

"That's exactly what I think. The murders are connected in some way to a doctoral thesis on politics that Ivan Krychek was working on before he was murdered, probably by Mather. That thesis contains all the information about you, Landis, and Amanda Bishop. It seems that anyone who comes in contact with it ends up dead. I think you know why."

"I really don't know what you're talking about," Roark said, pleading. "Honest to God. I don't know about any thesis. What happened to Amanda Bishop was a tragedy, a life-changing tragedy, as far as I'm concerned. I think King would tell you the same thing. The reputation he and I had in those days has no doubt been exaggerated by whoever told you about these murders. All I can say is that taking responsibility for what happened to Amanda helped both of us become better people."

"Protecting your image is a pretty good motive for killing Krychek and Jasmine Grant."

"That doesn't make sense. If I or anyone else murdered those people to keep what happened to Amanda Bishop a secret, it obviously didn't work because you're here now asking me about it."

Roark's answers were too pat, too rehearsed. The kind of transformation Marcus Towne described didn't sound the same coming from Roark. Towne made it sound miraculous. Roark made it sound like he'd gotten a flu shot.

"What about Penroy and Scofield?" I said. "Where do they fit into all of this?"

"Mitch and I met in college. He went to work for Scofield right after graduation. We've stayed in touch and he's been a friend and adviser for years. Same thing with King. We all go way back."

"And Scofield knows what you did to his daughter?"

Roark looked toward the back of the church, away from the altar.

"Of course he does. He also knows that I've changed. I apologized to him long ago for what happened and he's accepted it. We haven't talked about it in years."

"And he has no hold over you now?"

"We agree on some issues and disagree on others," Roark said. "He's given money to my campaign and he let's me know where he stands on issues before the legislature."

Roark crushed his cigarette on the bottom of his penny loafers and held the butt cupped in his hand.

"I take it you'll be publishing this story soon?"

"You can bet on it."

"And the other murders you mentioned? I hope you're not planning to implicate me in those. My involvement in this ended twenty years ago when Amanda Bishop jumped off that bridge. I accept responsibility for that. To suggest anything else would be a reckless disregard for the truth."

Lawsuit, I thought. Anytime someone, especially a lawyer, uses the phrase "reckless disregard for the truth," it meant, "Print it and I'll sue your ass."

"Thanks for your time," I said and left Roark sitting in the pew, gazing at the small altar. In the dim light, I was pretty sure I saw Roark's lips move as if in prayer.


Landis called the next morning just as I was fixing instant coffee and munching on what could either be a fresh bagel or a week-old doughnut.

"Brad phoned last night to tell me the two of you had talked."

Landis's tone sounded casual and collegial for someone whose dirty laundry was about to become part of the public domain.

"I'd like to talk to you about the same incident," I said.

"I'm sure you would, but in all honesty I have nothing to add beyond what Brad told you. I knew the story of Amanda Bishop would come out eventually. I have no intention of denying it happened or downplaying its significance in any way. It was a tragic occurrence that changed my life forever."

"Sounds like you and Roark have your stories down pretty well."

"We don't need to corroborate our stories." His tone came off indignant. "The truth doesn't need corroboration. We made a mistake, and we've dedicated our lives to rectifying that mistake. End of story."

"What does Proctor Scofield think of all this?"

"That question is best directed to Mr. Scofield. I will tell you, however, that he and I have not discussed his stepdaughter nor my future political plans."

"Roark said he apologized to Scofield. How about you?"

"That's none of your business," Landis said.

"Do you want to talk about the murders or did Roark fill you in on that as well?

"You're on a snipe hunt, Mr. Standard. You've got no business even suggesting any relationship between Roark and myself and any murders. Now, I've told you all I'm going to about the Amanda Bishop incident. Print what you need to print wherever it is you publish such material. If there's nothing else . . ."

"So you know nothing about Ivan Krychek, his doctoral thesis or Jasmine Grant?"

"Mr. Standard, please. This sounds fascinating and typical of the kind of journalism those of us in public life have come to expect. My advice to you is to be very careful about what you print beyond what happened twenty years ago. Am I making myself clear?"

Another threat of legal action.

"You can be sure, Mr. Landis, that anything I write regarding events twenty years ago or three days ago will be accurate."

"See that it is," Landis said and hung up.

# Chapter 36

I didn't leave the apartment for the next two days, other than to dart across the street to the deli for an occasional sandwich and a carton of potato salad. The rest of the time was spent hunched over the computer or on the telephone, lost in a search to piece together the story of Amanda Bishop, Brad Roark and Kingsley Landis.

Reluctantly, a clerk at the Eugene Police Department agreed to find the original report filed the night of the attack on Amanda Bishop and fax it to Benny Orlando's apartment. I had less luck with officials at Lane County, which had gone through five district attorneys since then, so no one had any idea why the charges against Roark and Landis were dropped.

I finally tracked down Charles Moorhead, who was the chief of police at the time and had retired a year earlier to the sun and cheap golf of Thousand Palms, California. Moorhead was gruff and direct.

"The girl's father came in and said they'd like to drop the charges," Moorhead said over the telephone. "He said he wanted to save the girl the embarrassment of having to testify against those two assholes. It seemed a little odd to me. Most parents would come in demanding that we cut the nuts off guys like that. This Scofield character was cool and collected. Laid it all out, plain and simple. I told him to go talk to the DA. The next thing I knew, the whole thing just sort of went away."

"What did the DA say?"

"Just what I told you. The father came in, made his case, and left. End of story. End of case. I just wrote the whole thing off as some emotional co-ed distraught over losing her cherry to the wrong guy. It wouldn't be the first time."

"Did you interview Amanda Bishop?"

"No, but I read the transcript and talked to the female investigator who did interview her. I've got to say that she seemed to handle the whole thing pretty well. It's not that uncommon for girls to be hysterical after something like that. She was anything but. I guess she just kept it all inside. At least that's the way it appears given what she did two weeks later."

A cooperative clerk at the Oregon State Police had little trouble locating the report on the suicide. It included the name of the driver of the truck that killed Amanda Bishop. His name was Barney Alweather and he lived in

Medford at the time of the accident. I found him through directory assistance still living at the same address.

"I was twenty-nine when that happened. Been driving truck about four years," Alweather said, when I reached him at home. "I'm almost fifty now and still doing the same damn thing. Probably driven over a million miles in all these years. Probably gone under a couple of hundred thousand overpasses. Never passed a one that I didn't think about that little girl. I can still see her like it was yesterday. All twisted around the grill of that truck. Her arm up on the hood like it was reaching for me. All those overpasses, and every time I thought somebody was going to jump off in front of me, just like that night. Hell of a thing to live with."

It took several more calls to the Eugene Police Department and the University of Oregon Registrar's Office before I tracked down a witness from the condominium complex. While reluctant to talk on the record, she seemed willing to verify everything contained in the police report.

"I got there just about the same time as the police, so I don't know who called them," said Leslie Post, a nurse in Seattle. "But there must've been fifty people standing on the balconies throwing things. It was disgusting. She was curled up in a ball on the ground with her hands over her head. It was humiliating."

"No one tried to help her?" I asked.

"Apparently not. Like I said, I got there about the same time as the police, so it's hard to know how long things had been going on. Eventually someone - the manager, I think - came out and started yelling. By then the police were there."

"Did you get a close look at her?"

"Pretty close. I remember thinking that it was odd that she wasn't crying. She just had this blank look on her face, like it wasn't real. I know that sounds odd, but that was just the impression I got."

"Do you remember the names Brad Roark or Kingsley Landis?"

"No, but that was a long time ago. I transferred to the University of Washington at the end of that semester, so I never heard what really happened. I didn't know about the rape or any of that. She was young, and I just figured it was another case of a freshman who had too much to drink. It happens. Maybe not that way, but it happens."

With more help from the registrar's office, I located Mary Franco, Amanda's roommate from the dormitory. She was a school teacher in Oakland, California.

"It was the strangest thing," she said. "Amanda acted like nothing ever happened. She was never very outgoing or demonstrative, but after that night it was like her mind just erased the entire event. I never saw her cry and she never mentioned it. I tried to bring it up once or twice, you know, just to see how she was dealing with it. But she looked like *she* felt sorry for *me*. She said everything would be okay. That she didn't remember enough of what happened to have it affect her and that I shouldn't worry about her. After that, I never brought it up again. I told the other girls in the dorm to do the same."

"What was she like before that?"

"Amanda was a hard one to get to know. On the outside, she looked so fragile, like a ceramic angel that would break if you handled it too much. On the inside, though, she was different. I don't know how to explain it, but it was a kind of inner strength, like she knew more than you did or had seen things you hadn't."

"Like what?"

"I don't know. It wasn't anything she said, but more the way she acted. Amanda had deep blue eyes that could almost look through you. Once you got past the little-girl appearance and focused on those eyes, it was like there was another person inside her. That's why her suicide surprised me. She seemed too strong and in control, despite what happened to her."

"Any boyfriends?"

"No one I saw more than once," Mary Franco said. "Remember, I didn't know her very long before she died, but Amanda seemed uninterested in boys or dating. When the rest of us talked about dating or sex, Amanda would sort of sink into the back of the room and wait for the subject to change. That's why what happened to her seemed so odd. For her to go off with two guys like that, it just didn't fit."

I wrote furiously, taking notes with the telephone receiver squeezed between my ear and shoulder.

"What about the night she died?" I said.

"When I came back to the room that night, she was gone. No one saw her leave, but that wasn't unusual. She had this new Mustang that she'd take out at night by herself. Sometimes she wouldn't come back until morning. When she wasn't in the room, I just figured she'd gone on another road trip. I didn't know what happened until a woman from the president's office showed up early the next morning to tell us. It was quite a shock. A few days later some men showed up and packed up all her things."

"Did you ever meet her parents?"

"Her father showed up quite a few times to take Amanda to dinner. I saw her mother once, maybe twice."

"What was she like around her father?"

"They seemed close, always laughing, sometimes holding hands," she said. "It was sort of cute."

"I don't suppose Amanda said anything about why the two boys weren't charged?"

"Not a thing. Like I said, we didn't talk about it."

I had less success with the parents of Roark and Landis. James and Barbara Roark refused to discuss the incident. Wilbert Landis had died two years earlier and his widow, Carol, burst into tears over the telephone at the mention of Amanda's name.

I had no luck talking to Proctor Scofield, coming away with nothing more than a tersely worded statement issued by the Public Affairs Department of Scofield Industries: "Mr. Scofield declines the opportunity to comment in any way regarding his stepdaughter and the events leading up to her death."

When I finished writing the story, I called Eldon Mock at *Inside Oregon*.

"Remember that murder story I talked to you about a few days ago? It just got a hell of lot better."

# Chapter 37

In the hours before *Inside Oregon*'s deadline, Eldon Mock and the paper's lawyer went over the story line by line.

"They're politicians, for Christ's sake," Mock yelled when the lawyer raised concerns about something in the story or expressed doubts about the wisdom of publishing it all. "They're the lowest form of life on earth. I can say anything I want about them. Hell, they probably don't care as long as I spell their names right. Why the hell should you?"

Mock was in his early forties, a wiry New Yorker with an attitude and a booming voice. Thick hair pulled back into a tight pony tail made his hooked nose and ears look too large for his small head. He wore a plaid shirt, striped tie, and baggy khakis. When he yelled, he had to take out his upper plate of false teeth so he wouldn't spit them out into someone's face.

The lawyer was a Stanford graduate named Clausen, who was a junior associate in a large firm that specialized in libel law. He was two years out of law school and wore a heavily starched shirt with gold cuff links and a dark double-breasted suit. The electric beach tan went well with his tall, trim body and blond hair carefully combed and blow dried to hide an expanding bald spot. A tightly knotted tie made him look like he was choking on something other than Eldon Mock's stubbornness.

"All I'm saying is ...." Clausen stuttered.

"I know what your saying," Mock said, pointing at the lawyer with his denture. "You just want to be able to say 'I told you so' when one of these sons of bitches sues me. Well let 'em sue."

I sat on an ancient leather couch in the corner of Mock's cluttered office watching the two men argue, a disinterested observer in the fate of my own words. I'd been in this kind of meeting before with better editors than Mock and better lawyers than Clausen. They all came out the same. Sooner or later Mock would brush aside the lawyer's concerns by declaring, "Fuck 'em. I'll print what I want. You'll figure out later how to defend it. That's what I pay you for."

"You're going to be famous, John," Mock said when Clausen left. "Its going to be good to see back on top again. This is one hell of a story. Great copy."

I held up my hand.

"Wait a minute, Eldon. Putting my name on that story will only dredge up a lot of old stuff that I'd just as soon forget. Roark and Landis are the story here, not me. I don't want to give them or anyone else the opportunity to discredit the story because of my past. Put your name on it or leave the byline off all together."

We wasted half an hour arguing back and forth before Mock agreed to leave my name off the story and run it with no byline.

"I don't understand why you don't want your name on it," Mock said, finally. "This will make your old employer sit up and take notice. Maybe get your old job back."

I conceded the point with a shrug, but in the end stuck with my demand. I had no intention of writing anything more about Roark and Landis. I was through with this story. It was time to focus on the personal business I had with Proctor Scofield, business that had to do with Jasmine Grant.

# Chapter 38

Proctor Scofield knew it was a mistake not to take his wife's feelings into account.

There'd been a part of him that hoped, at least for her sake, that the whole sordid story would remain hidden forever. It was an unrealistic expectation, but plausible enough to give him the excuse he needed to avoid dealing with how Margaret would react when Amanda's name and what happened to her starting showing up the evening news.

At four in the morning on the day the story appeared, Scofield had Edward drive him downtown to the east-side offices of *Inside Oregon* to buy the paper as soon as it came out. The trip wasn't really necessary, but the solitude of a pre-dawn cruise through downtown Portland gave Scofield time to enjoy the way his scheme was playing out. Anxiety became a drug that made him more euphoric.

The trip also gave him time to contemplate what to do about Margaret. A weekend at the beach house was a possibility but he knew that in the end, nothing he did could keep her away from the news stories.

He wasn't sure how much Margaret knew about the events in Eugene that led to Amanda's death. Scofield had done his best to insulate her from what happened before and after, but it still hung between them like a thick fog. The unspoken truce dictated that she didn't ask and he didn't tell. He knew she trusted his decision not to prosecute them, but what else went on behind the cultured exterior of his Sphinx-like wife remained a mystery to everyone but her. He did know that Amanda's death had slowly eaten at Margaret, the memory becoming a poison turned to acid by alcohol. The story and the frenzy it would generate might be a sport for him, but it could be the last straw for his wife. Too bad, he thought, that she never took time to see the pain Amanda's death had caused *him*. Then again, he never showed it to her.

The limousine pulled into a convenience store a few blocks from the newspaper's offices on Holgate Street on Portland's east side. Edward got out, shoved fifty cents into the box, and returned with a copy of the paper. The headline said it all:

"THE NIGHTMARE PAST OF THE DREAM CANDIDATES."

"Cute," he muttered.

The subhead read: "The stepdaughter of billionaire Proctor Scofield committed suicide twenty years ago after being raped by Brad Roark and Kingsley Landis."

Scofield noticed there was no byline.

"Nice try, Mr. Standard," he said as he began reading.

The story was accurate, as far as it went. What it didn't include, Scofield noticed, was any implication that what happened to Amanda had led to three unsolved murders years later. For some reason, Standard had kept that information to himself.

Scofield settled into the soft leather seat and tried to figure out John Standard's motive as the limo rolled silently through the early morning traffic. Whatever game Standard was playing, Scofield thought, it would have to wait until Margaret finished blubbering over the news that her long-dead daughter had become the center of a political scandal.

# Chapter 39

The *Inside Oregon* story on Roark and Landis generated a predictable response. The media frenzy produced by television, newspaper, and radio reporters trying to play catch up was in journalism's best tradition. Mock had released the story to Associated Press right after the late-night news. By the time the paper hit the streets the next morning, the story was already a major topic on local television and radio stations, all of them carefully citing *Inside Oregon* as the source. The morning dailies, including my former employer, would have to wait until the next day. Talk radio hosts were practically lactating.

Reactions from the Roark and Landis camps had all the markings of a public relations strategy two decades in the making. In a packed joint news conference called to get their spin on the story as soon as possible, the pair admitted everything. They called the rape and death of Amanda Bishop a "tragic event that changed our lives forever." Their responses were candid and contrite. They came off genuinely regretful for what had happened "long ago when both of us were different people."

What happened to Amanda Bishop, they said, was "the catalyst that redirected our lives into a commitment to public service." On cue, the two politicians' aides handed reporters separate fact sheets describing the accomplishments both men had achieved since Amanda's death.

"In many ways, what we've done with our lives over the last twenty years is dedicated to the memory of Amanda Bishop." Kingsley Landis delivered the line directly into the television cameras with emotion in his voice and tears in his eyes. It became the sound bite used that night by every local television station and nationally on CNN.

From the news conference, the two men made separate rounds of key editorial boards. They eagerly accepted requests for interviews from TV news anchors and radio talk show hosts. By the end of the day, they were off to shore up relations with key constituents and well-heeled interests groups.

The strategy was clear: admit everything and ask forgiveness.

It didn't take long for the political reporters to take over the story. Soon, what happened to Amanda Bishop became lost amid speculation about what would happen to Roark and Landis. Were they damaged goods? Could they still win the respect of voters? Were they electable? The political handicappers, partisan pollsters, and spinmeisters stepped in with speed sufficient to suck the political press in behind them. The temptation to treat political campaigns like horse races prevailed.

The evening news became little more than a parade of dull analysts, usually political scientists from obscure colleges, who offered conflicting opinions about the effect on each of the candidates, but always careful to hedge their bets. The pollsters were the worst, gleaning deep insights into the minds and attitudes of voters by analyzing endless tables of mind-numbing numbers that more often than not would change completely within a week. Finally came the press secretaries, public relations experts, and party hacks eager to put the best face possible on the rape and suicide of a young, long-forgotten co-ed. Try as they might, they were hamstrung by the fact that since both men admitted to doing the same thing, it made it hard for one camp to criticize the other without tarring their own candidate with the same brush.

Those who expressed outrage that one of two rapists might become governor were shunted onto the fringes of the debate. Those who carried signs reading "Remember Amanda" were treated as sideshows and given short shrift by the political press. Within a few days after the story broke, the conventional wisdom had been established: Voters had short attention spans, and the whole thing would be forgotten by primary election season next spring.


The story was two days old when my lawyer called to say the papers officially ending my marriage to Christine were ready to sign.

I found it oddly satisfying to sit in the plush, high-rise office, thumb through the documents, and put my signature on pages fixed with little red stickers in the shape of arrows that read: "Sign here." The decree gave me half the proceeds of the sale of our house, which, whenever it sold, would cover the rest of the legal bills and still leave me enough to find a better place to live. Everything else went to Christine. Unfair as it was, I really didn't care. It was over. Nothing else mattered.

After signing the papers, I thanked the lawyer, then rode the elevator down from the offices on the fifteenth floor of the KOIN Tower promising myself to never get married again.

The late afternoon sky was a hazy blue, the temperature hovering in the high eighties again. My shirt stuck to my back as I walked up SW Columbia Street toward home. The sudden sense of freedom left me oblivious to both the heat and the long walk. One by one, the bonds of my old life were cut, leaving me to float away and forget what had been.

It also left me free to find out what role Proctor Scofield played in the death of Jasmine Grant.

No arrest had been made in the murder of Buck Mather, which meant Harry Butcher would be dropping by periodically to make sure I didn't forget that I remained on his list of suspects. Butcher had called once, asking about why my fingerprints were all over Jasmine's bedroom. My explanation that I was looking for the telephone to call the police didn't wash with Butcher, but then nothing I said was going to make any difference to him anyway. I considered once again telling Butcher about the dark Lincoln I'd seen leaving Mather's house that night, but cringed at the thought of having to explain why I didn't tell him about it in the first place.

Krychek's murder had set off a series of events that, like a small chip in a car windshield, soon grew into an intricate spider's web of criss-cross lines that hid everything. Through the cracks, I could see three things: Ivan Krychek sitting in a portable toilet, Jasmine Grant tied her bed and a dark Lincoln racing down Packer Lane.

Even if Mitch Penroy wasn't driving the Lincoln that night, the lobbyist must know something about the murder. If Penroy knew, then it followed that Scofield did as well. There were too many coincidences not to think that somehow Scofield Industries wasn't involved right up to its hard drives in trying to keep secret the contents of Krychek's thesis.

The night before, I sat in the leather chair scribbling notes and questions about the motives and actions behind the murders. Vanessa was across the way fine tuning a new act. It had a military theme that involved a camouflage costume, a combat helmet, and a field rifle.

"Tell me, Vanessa," I whispered to myself as I watched her rehearse in front of the bedroom mirror, "why would the rich and powerful hang out with the scum of the earth? What is it that ties two ends of the evolutionary scale -- Proctor Scofield and Buck Mather -- together? Is Penroy the missing link? Someone in your profession must have gained some insight into what motivates men to do what they do. Or are you too removed? Do you shut your mind off, do your routine, and go home no wiser for the experience?"

The questions kept coming, some of them lingering like a bad jingle until another came along to replace it.

Now, walking up the hill toward my apartment, my curiosity about Scofield crowded out any remorse over a failed marriage. If there was one down side to this fascination with Scofield, it was that he kept reminding me that Jasmine Grant was dead.

Rather than go home, I walked down Fifth Avenue into the heart of the city, then up Burnside past Powell's Books, the Ringside restaurant, and Civic Stadium. It took more than an hour to reach NW 23rd Street and Papa Haydn's. I sat at the same table where I'd had lunch with Jasmine, ordered the same food and drank the same wine. When I finished, I walked up to the Knob Hill Bar and Grill, found the table we'd shared, and ordered a Black Butte Porter.

Nothing about my five years with Christine crossed my mind. All I could think about was the few hours I'd spent with Jasmine.

After two more beers, I caught a bus back downtown, then walked up Park Avenue to the apartment. Back in the leather chair, staring at Vanessa's apartment, I ran the names through my head again trying to find a way to get to Proctor Scofield. I sat there until after nine that night, when the heat and growing frustration with what to do next drove me out of the stifling apartment and into the streets.

The outdoor tables in front of the Virginia Cafe and the Brasserie Montmarte were full of people with the same desire to escape the heat, so I walked around the corner to the Pizzacato on Alder Street just off Broadway. I sipped a lemonade and read the early edition of *The Oregonian*. It had been three days since the revelations in *Inside Oregon* and already the stories about Roark, Landis, and Amanda Bishop had been shunted off the front page and relegated to the Metro section. The strategy of admit everything and ask forgiveness appeared to be paying off – for now. The story would come up again during the primary next spring, but for now it was slowly dissipating.

I gave up the table at around ten-thirty, but still didn't feeling like going home. To kill time, I walked down Broadway and into Old Town. The homeless bums and winos were eating up the night by sleeping, smoking, or urinating in the doorways along NW Davis. Tombs with a view, I thought.

I caught the MAX at First and Davis and headed back into downtown. After getting off at Pioneer Square, I trudged up Broadway past the Heathman Hotel, the Arlene Schnitzer Concert Hall, and the Oregon History Center before cutting over on Jefferson Street to the South Park Blocks. The key was almost in the door of the apartment building when the man appeared on the sidewalk behind me.

He was tall and thin with a pale complexion and a round head. The neatly trimmed, black mustache looked like a caterpillar crawling across a ghost pumpkin. Despite the heat, he wore a dark suit, white shirt, bow tie, and expensive leather gloves. The cap on his head resembled a Greek sailor's hat.

"Excuse me, are you John Standard?"

I slowly nodded.

"Would you mind coming with me for a moment? My employer would like to speak to you."

"And who would that be?"

"She's waiting in the car. I promise you, it will only take a moment."

When I hesitated, the man took a business card from the breast pocket of his coat.

"You're not in danger, Mr. Standard," he said.

I glanced at the card, then followed him around the corner and up a block to the parking lot of the Safeway store at Tenth and Jefferson. In a dark corner of the lot, away from the street lights, lurked a black limousine with its parking lights on. The man walked ahead of me, opened the back door, and stood at attention while I peered inside.

"Please come in and sit down, Mr. Standard." The woman's voice had a slight Southern accent, the tone both gentle and direct. It was the voice of someone comfortable with giving orders and having them obeyed without challenge or clarification.

The inside of the limo was done in red leather, polished mahogany, and luxurious red carpet. A crystal decanter with four matching glasses sat in special holders on a console above the small television set built into the side panel. The interior lights were turned low so I could barely see the woman sitting on the far side of the rear seat.

The man, who I now realized was the woman's chauffeur, closed the door, leaving me to ramble around inside until I sat down at the far end of a J-shaped seat, my back to the front of the car. I faced an elegant woman who looked to be in her mid fifties. Her hair was white and thick, elegantly cut to curl softly behind small ears with large diamond studs. Glasses with dark red frames rested on high cheek bones with the perfect amount of make up. Under her full-length coat was a short, clingy dress cut low with large white buttons and a hem line that resembled an inverted tulip. The style was newer than the body it covered, but she made it work.

"Thank you for taking time to see me, Mr. Standard," she said. The hint of Georgia in her voice made me think of an F. Scott Fitzgerald short story. "I'm Margaret Scofield."

I fingered the business card still in my hand.

"As in Proctor Scofield?"

She nodded.

Of all the names I had rolled around in my head for the last few days, never once did I think of Margaret Scofield.

"Then you're Amanda Bishop's mother?"

Another nod. She pushed the hair on one side of her face back behind her ear with a long, graceful finger. Her eyes were like sapphires that had retained their luster when the rest of her had surrendered to age and pain.

The glass partition behind my head was closed, so I didn't know the chauffeur had slipped behind the wheel until the limo started to move. Margaret Scofield picked up the intercom telephone.

"Just drive around for a while, Edward," she said, then hung up.

She looked directly at me.

"I understand that you're the person responsible for the newspaper story about my daughter's death." Nothing in her tone suggested anger, sadness, or any other emotion. "You created quite a stir and brought back some painful memories for me. I thought we should talk."

"How did you find out it was me?"

"I could tell you that I'm the wife of a billionaire, and I'm not without resources, but the truth is that there are people who work for my husband who maintain a certain loyalty to me."

Her eyes darted quickly from my face to the front of the limo and back again.

I accepted the explanation with a nod.

"So, is there a problem?"

"Not a problem, really. An oversight perhaps. You see, Mr. Standard, contrary to what you wrote, I don't believe my daughter killed herself because of what Brad Roark and Kingsley Landis did to her."

The statement landed on the lush carpet between us like an anvil.

"That's not what Roark and Landis told me."

It was a weak comeback, but I was still trying to get my mind around the implications of what Margaret Scofield said.

"They took total responsibility."

"I know." She reached into a Louis Vitton purse, pulled out a wrinkled envelope, and handed it to me.

"Please read this. It's Amanda's suicide note."

I read the typewritten note to myself, while Margaret Scofield stared out the window at the passing street lights.

164

Dear Mom and Dad,

Please forgive me and don't blame yourselves. I love both of you more than you will ever know. I did this because I can't live with what happened to me. Those two boys took something from me that I can never get back. It's so unfair. I'm sorry.

Good-bye, and God bless you both.

There was no signature. Only a large, flowery A.

I returned the letter to the envelope and passed it to back to her. "Seems pretty clear," I said.

"That was my reaction when I first read it twenty years ago. Now read this." She pulled a second envelope from her purse and handed it to me. "I found it among Amanda's things right after she died."

The envelope was blank and the letter undated. The flowery handwriting on the torn notebook paper matched the signature on the suicide note. I read it to myself.

Dear Mom,

I must have started this letter a thousand times in the last three years. Each time, I tear it up and try again. I just can't seem to find the words to tell you that there are things that have happened that can never be changed or made right again. I have lost something that I can never regain. More important, I have betrayed someone I love very much, you. We are the lucky ones to have escaped a life of misery for one of comfort. After what you went through with my biological father, you deserve the kind of love you've found with Proctor. What I'm afraid of is that I'll be responsible for the loss of that love. I have come to think of Proctor as my real father. He gave me everything a girl could want. We made mistakes, but I think he has been a better father to me than I have been a daughter to him. I hope that after I tell you everything, you'll forgive me and not hate me.

The letter stopped there, obviously unfinished. I read it a second time, then folded it up and put it back in the envelope.

"Do you know when this was written?" I said.

"Not exactly. I found it in a box of belongings we removed from her

.ormitory after her death," Margaret Scofield said. "It was in with some other letters and papers that were dated after she was raped, but it could have been written anytime."

The choke in her voice made her stop. I stayed silent, watching her stare out the window and struggle to regain her composure.

"I've carried both of these notes with me ever since and read them thousands of times."

Her voice was under control again, but I could hear the strain behind it. Margaret Scofield had all the appearances of a cable ready to snap after too many years of tension.

"To understand these notes, you would have to understand Amanda. I *did* understand her, and that's why I don't believe Roark and Landis had anything to do with her death. There was something she wanted to tell me, but before she could, she was attacked, then she was . . . gone."

Edward the chauffeur had navigated the limo over to Taylor Street and west to Interstate 405. Through the smoked glass, I could see we were headed south and then east toward Interstate 5.

"Are you saying Amanda didn't kill herself?"

"I'm saying that, if she killed herself, it wasn't because of what those two did to her."

"Why, then?"

"I don't know."

"There's something you're not telling me."

The graceful finger pushed the hair back behind one ear again.

"I guess I need to explain the situation. Amanda's real father was a cruel man incapable of demonstrating any emotion that didn't involve profanity and violence. I won't try to explain why I married him, but I left him shortly after Amanda was born. I did it for my protection and for hers. We moved from Georgia to Portland and changed our names. I struggled for seven years to give her a normal life. I waited tables and did secretarial work. I earned a real estate license. When Amanda was six, I was hired as an associate for a large real estate firm here in the city. One of my first clients was Proctor Scofield. We were married two years later."

She took one of the crystal glasses out of its holder and opened the mahogany console. With silver tongs, she lifted three ice cubes from a bucket and dropped them in the glass.

"Scotch?" she asked, holding up the decanter.

"Nothing for me, thanks."

She filled the glass half full with the smooth, brown liquid, then leaned back into the corner of the seat.

"That was thirty years ago. Proctor had money then, but nowhere near what he has today."

"That must have made it pretty nice for you and Amanda."

"Proctor gave me everything I ever wanted, and he doted on Amanda. There was nothing in the world he wouldn't do for her. She wore the best clothes, went to the best schools, had all the best things. We started out spending summers at the beach house. Later, we'd spend them in Europe or Asia. Proctor would fly over every couple of weeks to be with us. When Amanda was in high school, he'd take her on overseas business trips. She had seen most of the world by the time she left for college."

"How did she feel about your husband?"

The question seemed to surprise her.

"No one ever asked me that before." She held the glass of scotch against her lower lip. "They weren't like father and daughter. Not being her real father seemed to make Proctor treat Amanda differently. It was more like they were . . . I don't know. I can't describe it."

Her voice trailed off, taking her thoughts with it.

"Friends?" I asked.

"Yes," she said quickly. "Friends."

The limo passed the Highway 217 exit, then settled into the far right-hand lane before turning off onto Interstate 205, which circled through the east side of Portland. The big car moved effortlessly through the late-night traffic. Other cars seemed to move out of its way, the drivers gawking at the dark windows. Margaret Scofield poured another drink as the limo crossed the Willamette River at Oregon City.

"Anyway," she said, "Amanda grew up with everything a child could want. She had the choice of any school in the world, but decided to go to the University of Oregon. She said she liked Oregon. What few friends she had were going there, and she wanted to be close to home. I was ambivalent about it, but Proctor was thrilled. It was his alma mater."

I wanted to know where the story was heading, but felt no need to prod her along. The car and the story were her's. I just had to ride along and listen.

"It happened less than a week after she got there. She was so excited and eager to make new friends and learn. The week classes started, she was invited to a party at one of the sororities. Amanda never drank in high school - at least not that I know of. But at this party there was a keg of beer and loud music. She met one of the boys or both and left with them. The next thing she remembered she was lying naked in a parking lot with people throwing things at her. The police showed up and took her to the hospital. An examination determined that she had been raped multiple times."

She poured another drink. I didn't blame her.

"The school called to tell us what happened. We left for Eugene immediately. All the way down there, I kept thinking that Amanda would be hysterical. She didn't date much in high school and never talked much about boys. There was no way she was sexually active, so I couldn't imagine anything more horrifying for her than to be assaulted like that. But when we got there, she seemed oddly calm. I assumed she was in shock and that sooner or later her emotions would take over. I stayed with her while Proctor talked to the police. He told me later that the matter would be taken care of and that there was no need to file charges. I was too worried about Amanda to pay much attention. I trusted Proctor to take care of everything."

"Did you think it was odd that charges weren't filed?"

"I didn't really think about it at the time, but later - years later, actually - it bothered me. Her death seemed incomplete without those two boys paying a price for what they did to her."

"What did your husband say about why charges weren't filed?"

"He said we needed to keep it a private matter. He said he had the resources to take care of it personally, and there was no need for Amanda to go through the trauma of a trial."

"But he didn't tell you what those resources were?"

"I didn't ask. Proctor is a very strong person and a very private one. When he says something is taken care of, you can believe that it is. There's no need to know anymore than that."

"Did you know what happened to Roark and Landis?"

Her laugh came across as an ironic snort.

"I didn't even know who they were until your story in the paper."

I found it hard to believe that for all those years Margaret Scofield didn't know the names of the men who raped her daughter. If it was true, then it was a tribute to Proctor Scofield's power over his family and her subservience to it. It also spoke volumes about the depth of Margaret Scofield's grief.

"Didn't you want to know?" I asked.

"I did at first. Then Amanda was gone, and I didn't care anymore. Right after the funeral, Proctor took me to Europe for several months. It was a wonderful thing for him to do, and he made sure I had everything I wanted.

He did his best to keep me occupied, so I wouldn't dwell on Amanda's death. In all the years we've been married, we were never closer than on that trip. I never felt more fortunate for having him as a husband. By the time we got back, I had stopped caring about who they were."

"And now?"

"I still don't care. The only thing that's different is that now I know who they are."

"Thanks to me, you mean."

She nodded.

The limo took the Interstate 84 exit and headed west back into the city. She offered me another chance at the scotch. This time I took her up on it.

"You still haven't told me why you think Roark and Landis weren't responsible for Amanda's death."

She pulled the hand-written note from the envelope.

"Amanda wrote, 'What I'm afraid of is that I'll be responsible for the loss of that love.' What could Amanda have possibly done that would come between Proctor and me? Every time I read that, I ask myself the same question. The life the three of us had together was near perfection. I can't imagine what would destroy that except her death. Not even what those boys did to her."

I reached out and took the note from her.

"This part where she wrote about your husband, 'We made mistakes, but he was a better father to me than I was a daughter to him.' Do you know what mistakes she's taking about?"

"Proctor was nearly forty-years old when we were married. It was his first marriage, and his first experience with raising a child. There were some difficult times where things got a little tense. I initially thought she was talking about that adjustment period."

"And now you're not sure?"

She answered only after a long pause.

"I'm not sure of anything. I've read those notes so many times I could probably give you dozens of different meanings for each word and phrase. That's what time and loneliness do to you, Mr. Standard. They make you think, make you lose your perspective. Make you see things that probably aren't there."

Her voice trailed off again.

"What did your husband say about the unfinished letter?"

She finished the last of the scotch in one smooth, practiced motion.

"He doesn't know about it. I never showed it to him. Don't ask me why, because I don't know."

"You must not trust him."

She stared at me for a moment as if choosing her words carefully before answering.

"Proctor started selling typewriter ribbons out of a store front in southeast Portland. I don't have to tell you where he is today. I don't know what it took him to get from one place to another. To tell the truth, I don't *want* to know. All I can say is there is nothing in thirty years of marriage that would give me the slightest reason to think he is anything other than a good husband and an honest business man."

"You didn't answer my question."

Margaret Scofield's eyes begged me not to press the issue.

"Before all else, Proctor is a man," she said, "and like any man he is capable of doing anything, given the right set of circumstances."

She still hadn't answered the question, but I had read the message in her eyes and let the issue drop.

"What can you tell me about Mitch Penroy?"

"Very little, actually. I don't get involved in my husband's business or with his business associates. The few times I've met Mr. Penroy, I've found him to be polite and fiercely loyal to Proctor."

"Is he capable of murder?"

"I haven't the slightest idea. Why do you ask?"

"Just a shot in the dark."

The limo crossed the Willamette on the Morrison Street Bridge and drove up Washington Street to Ninth. It squeezed along the narrow street for eight blocks and stopped in front of my apartment building.

"What do you want me to do, Mrs. Scofield?" I asked.

She reached into her purse for another envelope and handed it to me. I looked inside long enough to see the hundred dollar bills.

"You were a reporter once, Mr. Standard, and from what I understand you were good at it. I guess in someways you still are. Your article about my daughter and those two men would confirm that. I'm telling you that Amanda did not kill herself because of what those two men did to her. Find out why, Mr. Standard. Find out for Amanda. And for me."

"This is a little outside my area," I said. "Why not go to the police?"

"We have a saying down in Georgia. Never play checkers with a possum. They're too stupid to win and all you're doing is wasting your time."

"There are good cops or you could go to a private detective?"

"That envelope contains fifteen-thousand dollars, Mr. Standard. I'll take it back if you don't need the money."

I pulled the money from the envelope and fanned the bills out like a deck of cards. Each one represented hours of work writing articles for airline magazines and grant proposals for school districts. With a silent sigh, I returned the money in the envelope and handed it back to her.

"Keep your money," I said.

When she began to protest, I held up a hand.

"I have my own reasons for wanting to find out things about your family."

"Such as?"

Telling Margaret Scofield about two dead Hispanic girls and a murdered lover seemed a waste of time.

"Let's just say it's a long story. I don't know how it ends. I'll let you know when I do."

"Please do," she said, sounding confused, and put the money back in her purse. "I'm leaving for New York tonight. I'll be back Friday, then Proctor and I will be out of town over the weekend. May I call you after that?"

I said yes and she reached out to gently lay her hand on my sleeve. It felt like a small bird seeking help.

"Do you have a photo of Amanda?" I said.

She took her hand away and reached in her purse for a thick leather wallet. The photo she handed me showed a girl with perky blonde hair, soft-white complexion, and doll-like eyelashes that looked like they'd blink if I tilted the picture. Her mouth was a thin smile that produced perfect dimples. Freckles dotted the bridge of her nose and both cheeks. She looked to be about fourteen years old.

"That's her high school graduation picture," Margaret Scofield said. "It was taken four months before she died."

"She was very pretty," I said, handing the photo back.

"All I ask is that you not forget Amanda." She was staring at the photo. "Don't let Roark and Landis use her death to hide some greater secret," she said and pressed the two notes from Amanda into my hand.

I stood in front of my apartment building, watching the tail lights of the limo disappear into traffic. No amount of culture and refinement could protect Margaret Scofield from the damage of two decades of grief. Losing a daughter wasn't made any easier by a fat bank account. I knew that, and so did she.

People die for all kinds of reasons, I thought. Most can be understood, dealt with, then forgotten, given enough time. The memories of the dead appear rich and textured to those left behind because death has a way of sifting out the bad and leaving behind a concentrated image for others to enjoy and relish. The Margaret Scofields of the world are the product of people dying for the wrong reasons and leaving behind too many unanswered questions.

"Careful," I said to myself, not wanting to scratch too deeply and find myself falling into the same trap as the haunted woman riding away in the black limo.

I pulled Amanda Bishop's notes from my pocket and stared at them. She wrote in riddles and unfinished ideas. Her secret, if she had one, lay buried between the lines for someone else to understand. But who?

The lights were still on in apartment above the front door, which meant Benny was watching television instead of locked in his computer room. I thought about the fifteen-thousand dollars that just drove away, sighed, then took the stairs to the second floor and knocked on Benny's door.

Benny was watching *Nightline*, sucking on a cold Corona, and eating salsa and chips. I passed on the food, but eagerly drank the beer brought to me by a wilted-looking Ivy.

"You look like you just lost your best friend," Benny said.

"Something like that."

I wondered what Benny would say about turning down Margaret Scofield's money.

"I need your help with something."

"Business or personal?" Benny asked.

"Both, actually. It's Proctor Scofield. I need to know as much about him as possible. There's probably not much, but what there is should be available on the internet. I also need to know more about his personal life. You know a lot of people in ... unusual lines of work. You mind taking a look for me?"

Benny smiled and gave me an evil wink.

"Sure," he said, handing his empty bottle to Ivy with silent instructions to get him another one. I marveled at how quickly Benny had turned Ivy from untamed street urchin into house cat. "Give me a day or two."

# Chapter 40

The party started at eight o'clock, but Proctor Scofield didn't plan to arrive until a little after nine. He hated stand-up social events, so he'd stayed in his study waiting for Penroy to come and get him.

He unlocked the door to the small room just off the study, went inside, and turned on the small goose-neck lamp in the corner. The computer terminal, television set, telephone and other equipment made the room an inner sanctum where Scofield could be totally alone with the things he knew best. He read several e-mails and scanned the reports attached to them. The more he read, the less important they seemed. Why did he bother with expense ratios, short-term liquid assets or cost-based pricing? What had once been his passion had become so many words on a computer screen. He knew it would either have to rededicate himself to his business or get out of it all together. But what then?

He was still searching for an answer when Penroy arrived.

"A couple of hours," Penroy said as Scofield emerged from the small office, locking the door behind him, "then I'll make an excuse to get you out of there. This event really is important."

"I know. I know," Scofield sighed, secretly wishing he'd flown to New York with Margaret. Her plane would be somewhere over eastern Oregon right now. She'd be having cocktails with the two friends who accompanied her. They'd arrive at JFK before dawn, settle into the Manhattan apartment, and get some rest before shopping. It sounded exciting compared to what waited for him downstairs. To his own surprise, he found himself looking forward to Margaret's return Friday night.

"Mitch, is everything arranged for this weekend?" Scofield asked. They were walking down the curved staircase to the living room. "I want you and the boys there. We need to begin making plans for getting them back into the public eye. Things appear to be quieting down and I think they'll stay that way. So, I want to start planning now for the months ahead."

Maybe when this thing with Amanda has blown over, Scofield thought, he'd turn the whole thing over to Penroy. Maybe with more authority, Penroy would regain his enthusiasm.

"Roark, Landis and their families are on vacation in Mexico. I sent them there to get them away from the cameras for a few days. They'll be back in plenty of time. The plan is to meet the helicopter at McNary Field in Salem at six in the morning on Sunday," Penroy said as they reached the bottom of the stairs. "I'll make sure both of them are with me."

"What about security?" Scofield asked. No one had ever bothered him at the beach house, but he still tried to limit the number of people who knew about the place or its exact location.

"The usual man," Penroy said. "He's been extremely helpful to us during the last few weeks. He'll do a good job, but I really don't think we'll have a problem."

"Let's hope not," Scofield said as they walked across the living room toward the small group gathered outside.

A buffet had been set up on the vast marble-floored veranda. City lights glimmered through the towering fir trees that fronted the property. The twenty or so guests stood in small groups, balancing plates in one hand and drinks in the other. The men were all short, middle-aged Japanese. The women were all tall, beautiful, young Americans.

Scofield had little use for the Japanese, except as a means of making money. He hated their cheap cigarettes, expensive suits, and Buddy Holly glasses. Tonight they'd eat his food, drink his liquor, and fawn over the women from the escort service. Tomorrow they'd sit at the bargaining table and quibble over the price of mouse pads.

When Scofield walked onto the veranda, the conversation and eating stopped. The plates and drinks were quickly set aside, so that the ritual of introductions to each of the Japanese businessmen could begin. He exchanged bows and handshakes with each, then began a less formal round of hugs and handshakes with the women. He'd met most of them before at similar events, always when Margaret was out of town.

Tina Davenport was his favorite. Once a striking brunette, she was now a blonde. Her sequined cocktail dress fit as well as her reputation on two continents as an adoring and friendly companion to men.

"Good to see you again, Tina," he said, as he calmly accepted her kiss on the cheek. "Thanks for taking my secretary shopping today. It was very kind of you. By the way, you look wonderful. You make a great blonde." Tina kissed him again. "I hope you have an opportunity to spend some time with Mr. Kobayashi. He's a very intense negotiator and may be in the need of some relaxation before we start again in the morning."

Tina nodded, took another glass of champagne from a passing waiter, and obediently went off in search of her prey.

Scofield moved gracefully through the crowd, doing his best to exchange a few words with each of the Japanese and their respective escorts. A little before eleven, Penroy interrupted a conversation about the changes in Hong Kong under Communist Chinese rule.

"You have an important call," Penroy said.

Scofield excused himself, after inviting his guests to stay as long as they liked.

"Get the little bastards and their girlfriends out of here by midnight," Scofield told Penroy when they were out of earshot.

Entering the study, he moved quickly to the bar where a bottle of champagne rested comfortably in a silver ice bucket. He filled two glasses and carried them across the room to his secretary, who stared in awe at the long lines of leather-bound volumes on the bookshelves.

"You look very nice tonight," he said. "I hope you know how much I appreciate you coming over at this time of night."

She giggled and did a curtsy to show off her patent leather shoes with white anklets and the short powder blue dress.

"I went shopping with your friend Tina today. She told me what you liked and helped me pick things out."

Scofield stood close to her, gazing down into her doll-like face framed by ringlets of red hair. He ran his hand up under her petticoats to find that she'd followed his instructions to not wear panties.

That produced another giggle.

"Champagne?" he asked, holding up the bottle.

"Okey dokey," she said and giggled again.

# Chapter 41

I left for Salem at eight the next morning after spending the night staring at the ceiling and going over the list of questions I'd written down while watching Vanessa rehearse. I didn't even waste time thinking how to get to Scofield directly. The only option was to attack the snake's head from the tail. That meant going back to the beginning.

A wreck on the Terwilliger curves in south Portland that brought traffic to a standstill put me on slow simmer. By the time I arrived at the state capitol building, I had to remind myself that boiling over into a rage wasn't going to get me what I wanted. With a forced smile, I slowly worked my way through a half-dozen legislators and an equal number of hide-bound bureaucrats before learning the answer to one of my questions: How did a low-life like Buck Mather get the contract to provide security at the state capitol?

It took three hours of work to learn that the contract went up for bid a year earlier. Prestige Security was one of four bidders and came in with the lowest price. After reviewing each bid, a recommendation went to the legislative committee charged with making the final decision. Senator Brad Roark chaired the committee. One of the other six members was Senator Kingsley Landis.

I found the committee administrator, Ellen Tillman, in an office that was part of a partitioned area of a large room on the third floor. She was young and serious with wash-and-go hair, sensible shoes, and a mail-order suit that looked stiff and scratchy. After a few moments of staring at me through oblong glasses with dark frames, she apparently decided there was no choice but to help me. She pulled a buff-colored file folder from the state-issued credenza behind her chair. After shuffling through the papers for a few minutes, she said, "The initial recommendation was to retain the services of Four Star Security, which I believe is located in Tigard."

"Was that your recommendation?" I asked.

"Yes. Four Star had the contract for the preceding five years. I felt they had performed well enough to retain the contract."

She politely reviewed the minutes of the committee meeting at which the contract was discussed. The debate centered around cost and some dissatisfaction with Four Star over a security issue the previous year.

"Would you like to listen to the tape of the meeting."

I declined.

"Who made the motion to hire Prestige?"

"Senator Landis," Tillman said, flipping though the pages.

"And who seconded it?"

"Senator Roark."

Ellen Tillman gave me the telephone number for Four Star Security and I headed for the public phones in the basement of the capitol. The owner of Four Star Security, John Shoemaker, was a talkative ex-policeman more than happy to vent his frustration over politics, politicians, and lost earnings.

"Slimiest thing I've ever seen. Landis cooked up some song and dance about how we botched a security problem at the Capitol. Botched, my Aunt Tillie's ass. There was nothing botched about it. Some anti-abortion nut went bat shit in the senate gallery, waving a gun and kicking out two glass doors before we could get him under control and out of the building. The guy was out of his mind. It's lucky he didn't kill someone. We probably saved some people from getting hurt, then lost the contract over a couple of stinking glass doors. Can you believe it? Landis said we treated him with disrespect because of his views on abortion. Jesus."

"The committee administrator said you never appeared before the committee to make a case for yourself. How come?"

"Politics," Shoemaker said, spitting out the word like someone who had just sucked poison out of a snake bite. "I was politely but firmly told not to raise a stink or I'd lose more than the security contract at the Capitol."

"Explain."

"My biggest contracts are two high-tech firms with big plants outside Portland. It was made very clear to me that if I did anything to protest the awarding of the capitol contract to Prestige, I would lose those contracts as well. It turned out I lost them anyway."

"Which high-tech firms?"

"Global Micro Systems and SI Circuit Boards."

"What are the chances they're owned by Proctor Scofield?"

"Dead solid perfect."

"And who delivered the message from Scofield?"

"A little weasel named Penroy."

I thanked Shoemaker, hung up, and walked down the hall to the capitol press room in the basement. I caught Maynard Argyle between naps and asked the dean of the state's political reporters what he knew about Mitch Penroy. Argyle had been around the capitol for four decades and seldom wasted time talking to any reporter who couldn't name Richard Nixon's press secretary. I was the one exception. For reasons known only to Argyle, the crusty old reporter had taken a liking to me during my two years as a capitol reporter.

"Penroy's the best there is," Argyle said, cramming an unlit stogie in the corner of his mouth, "if you like slime-ball influence peddlers who buy and sell legislators like baseball cards. Proctor Scofield is like God to these guys. Being God's right-hand man is as good as being God himself."

"Is it all campaign contributions?"

"Most of it, but not all. Scofield can do more than give money. He can prevent you from getting money. All it takes is a phone call or two. To these guys that's like not getting air to breathe. But that's only part of it. If a certain senator or representative votes the right way on a bill, Scofield might promise to build one of his factories in their district and give them credit for it. If they vote the wrong way, he'll say no way in hell and tell the local newspaper why."

"And Penroy is the messenger?"

"The voice of God, my boy. The voice of God."

Argyle walked the stogie from one side of his mouth to the other.

"Do you have Penroy's address? His home address?"

Five minutes and two phone calls later, the old reporter handed me a coffee-stained page from a reporter's notebook. On it was an address in a wealthy Portland suburb.

"You planning to tweak the cheek of the giant, John?" Argyle asked.

"I'm going to try."

Argyle lit the stub end of the cigar and blew a cloud of blue smoke.

"That a boy, John. That a boy."

# Chapter 42

An hour later, I was parked in front of Mitch Penroy's single-level condominium tucked away in a secluded corner of southeast Portland near Waverly Country Club. From the narrow cul-de-sac, there was little to see other than the garage door and a recessed front door. Facing the street were two narrow windows with vertical blinds turned shut.

There was little chance that Penroy was home at two in the afternoon, but it was worth a shot. I parked across the street, went to the door, and rang the bell a few times. When no one answered, I got back in the car and drove to a convenience store on McLoughlin Boulevard to call Penroy's office from a pay phone. After being danced around the may pole a few times by the Scofield Industries automated telephone system, I hung up and hit the convenience store for some rations.

With a paper sack filled with diet cola, several pieces of beef jerky, a small bag of trail mix, and a couple of peanut butter cups, I returned to the cul-de-sac. Backing the Jeep into a parking space across from Penroy's garage door, I pulled a can of cola out of the sack and waited.

Two hours later I was out of food and had seen nothing other than two guys walking a poodle and a couple in their sixties power walking with small weights in their hands. I was searching the radio dial for some local news when a blonde in a Honda Prelude pulled up in front of Penroy's garage door. Leaving the Honda's motor running, she went to the front door, unlocked it, and disappeared inside. Two minutes later she came out, talking into a cellphone, her large sunglasses pushed up on top of her hair. I watched her slide gracefully behind the wheel of her car and back out into the street. It wasn't who I was looking for, but she would do for the time being.

Heavy traffic made it easy to follow the Prelude up McLoughlin and across the Ross Island Bridge into downtown. I stayed three car-lengths behind as it moved slowly along Front Street at Waterfront Park and then west on Taylor. The car entered the parking structure on Fifth Street between Salmon and Taylor near Nike Town. When it parked, I pulled into a spot three spaces away.

The blonde took the elevator to the street level while I hoofed it down the stairs, arriving in time to see her disappear into Saks. I waited outside, smoking a cigarette, and trying to keep an eye on her through the mannequins in the window displays. When she came out and walked across Yamhill Street into Pioneer Place, I stayed fifty yards behind her.

I found an open bench near the brass-and-glass escalator. I hid behind a newspaper left on the bench, while she moved quickly through two of the more upscale stores. The ruse made me feel like a cheap detective, but I wanted to confront her on my own terms. When she took the stairs to the lower level, I jumped on the elevator and got off just as she entered an upscale lingerie shop. I waited a few minutes, then followed her inside.

"Is this where all the best-dressed widows shop?" I asked. "Or is it just for those who try to frame people for murder?"

The question interrupted Anna Krychek's well-practiced pawing at a carousel of skimpy bras and panties. She looked like she wanted to bolt when she recognized me, but I stood between her and the only exit.

"Leave me alone," she said in a harsh whisper, her eyes wide like those of a cornered cat. "I have nothing to say to you."

Short, blonde hair had replaced the long, dark hair that mesmerized me the day we met. Other than that, everything else seemed to be intact. The comfortable clothes and shoes told me that it was early drinks with a friend after an afternoon of shopping.

"Killing time before meeting Penroy?" I asked.

"None of your business." The words came out like a hiss. "How did you find me?"

"Luck. I was looking for Penroy, but you were too hard to pass up."

Her eyes turned from angry to vulnerable.

"Please. I didn't do anything wrong. What happened was terrible, but I didn't have anything to do with it. Honest."

A nice performance, I thought, but not up to the one she gave as Krychek's widow.

"We need to talk," I said. "Why don't the two of us find a place to sit down and chat for a while."

"Can't you leave me alone? I can't tell you anything. Please."

This time her voice attracted the attention of the clerk, who glared at us, while still trying to keep another customer's attention on a red satin teddy.

"Listen, Anna, or whatever you name is, I know where you live. I know the license number of your car. I also know a couple of homicide detectives who would love to hear the story about how you called me the night Buck Mather was murdered so I would find his body. It's your choice. Talk to me or talk to them."

I leaned on the carousel talking in a relaxed tone that I hoped would keep the clerk at bay for a few more minutes. Anna stared at me, then looked over her shoulder at the clerk. No help there. She gave a resigned nod.

We rode the escalator back to the main level and found a small table outside a coffee stand. Anna Krychek sat stiffly in the metal chair, while I got two small coffees in paper cups.

"You didn't waste any time getting out of the house on Baltusrol," I said.

"I didn't want to stay there after Ivan was gone." A tear rolled down one check. She looked away. "It was too painful."

"Nice try, but you didn't cry the day you learned he'd been murdered, so don't start now. I want to know why you married Krychek, and don't insult me with that Czechoslovakia crap."

"It's the truth."

The statement came attached to a pout.

"No it isn't. Now, either tell me what the hell was going on with you two, or you can tell it to the cops and I'll find out from them."

"No. No." The pout on her face turned to terror. "Please don't do this. Ivan was a nice man and I'm sorry he's dead, but I didn't have anything to do with it. I was only doing what I was told."

"Told by who?"

"I can't tell you. Please, just let me go."

"Was it Penroy? Did he tell you to get close to Krychek?"

Tears fought their way through the fear in her eyes. This time, they were real and spoke the truth.

"Yes."

"Why? What interest did Mitch Penroy have in a college student like Ivan Krychek?"

She sipped the coffee, leaving perfect lipstick marks on the edge.

"All Mitch told me was that he needed to know more about Ivan, so he paid me to meet him and go out with him a few times. Out of the blue, Ivan asked me to marry him. When I told Mitch, he said, 'Great.' I couldn't believe it."

Her eyes narrowed for a moment, the tears forgotten.

"Keep going."

"Mitch arranged for a quickie wedding in Nevada, a honeymoon in Mazatlan, and the new house when we got back," she said. "When Ivan was murdered, Mitch said to stand by the story and arranged for my alibi. He got me out of the house as soon as possible."

"You did more than leave town, you bolted in the middle of the night."

"I know. When you arrived, I was on the phone talking to Mitch. He told me some guys were coming that night to move everything out."

"And to keep quiet about it."

"I didn't care. I wanted out of there and Mitch was paying the bills. Murder was never part of the deal. Mitch said something about sending me to Europe for a month, but all I wanted to do was come back home."

"Why was Penroy so interested in Krychek?"

"He never told me exactly, but he always asked me about Ivan's research. What I told you about Ivan being secretive was true. He never talked to me about what he was working on. When I told Mitch that, he told me to keep pressing."

"And what about the thesis, the manuscript?"

"Mitch asked me about that, too, but I didn't know anything about it."

"Did Penroy ever tell you what was important about the research or the manuscript?"

"He didn't have to. Why would he pay me money, buy us a house, and make me marry Ivan, if it wasn't important?"

"I mean about *why* it was important?"

"No. I asked him, but he said it was none of my business. He told me my job was to keep tabs on Ivan, to learn as much as I could. We argued about it. I said I might be able to learn more if he'd tell me what was going on. Mitch refused. He told me all I needed to do was find the manuscript."

"What about Krychek's job with Prestige Security?"

"Ivan was working there before I met him. When I told Mitch about it he didn't even act surprised, so I figured he already knew. He told me to forget about it and concentrate on the manuscript."

Once again, I thought, all roads lead back to Mitch Penroy, and with Penroy you get Scofield.

"Was it Penroy's idea to have you call me and arrange to meet at Mather's house the night he was killed?"

"Yes."

"He was with you when you called, wasn't he? He coached you. Told you what to say."

The tears returned.

"I'm sorry for that. It was Mitch. He made me. The whole thing was his idea. I didn't know until later what he was trying to do to you."

"Did he tell you your little plan didn't work? Did he tell you that I found

Mather, all right, but that I got there early and called the police, instead of being found standing over the body?"

"Yes. He told me all that."

The tears increased.

"Did he tell you who murdered Mather? Do you think Penroy did it?"

Anna looked like she wanted to run and never stop.

"I don't know what to think. I just want all of this to stop. I want to be left out of it."

She lowered her voice when a couple at the next table turned to look at her.

"I never thought it was going to turn out this way, with all these ... dead people."

"Did Penroy order Mather to murder Ivan Krychek and Jasmine Grant?"

Anna took the question like a punch to the mid-section.

"Stop it, please! I don't know about any of this."

I moved my chair closer to the table, leaning forward until I could smell her perfume and see the red veins in her eyes.

"You tell Penroy for me that I saw his car leaving Mather's house that night. Tell him I saw the whole thing. Tell him I know who killed Buck Mather."

Anna Krychek picked nervously at her carefully lacquered nails.

"You think Mitch did it, don't you? You think he killed that guy?"

"Just tell him. He'll know."

An awkward silence fell between us. We sipped coffee and watched the shoppers scurry in and out of stores on the opposite side of the mall.

"So, now you're living in Penroy's condo," I said. "You and he an item?"

She looked away, as if hoping the coffee stand had suddenly started serving something more fortifying than caffeine.

"Yes," she said.

"So, what's your real name?"

"Tina. Tina Davenport. Can we go somewhere and get a drink?"


I hustled Tina Davenport out the door and down the street to the Red Star at the corner of Fifth and Alder. I asked the hostess for a table in the rear, sat the red-eyed Tina with her back to the sparse lunch crowd, and ordered her a glass of wine.

"Are you going to tell the police about me?" she asked.

"That depends on how much more you tell me."

"About what?"

"Let's start with why you did it. Why did you do everything Penroy told you to do?"

A blank stare appeared in her red eyes.

"You mean other than the money, right?" she said.

Her tone made me feel like some gomer who only came to town to buy new barn boots.

"Yeah," I said, smiling at her, "other than the money."

"What choice did I have? No skills. No education. That's me."

She held up her hand when I started to interrupt.

"Don't give me the secretarial school speech or the one about the opportunities for computer programmers. Mitch gives me everything. Money, clothes, security. Hell, he even paid for these boobs. If it wasn't for him, it would be someone just like him. Look at me. Do I look like I could live in the 'burbs with kids and a husband who sells insurance or something?"

I had to agree.

"I *like* the things I have. What I do for Mitch and Mr. Scofield is a small price to pay to keep them."

"So, playing house with guys like Krychek isn't the only thing you do for Scofield Industries?"

She answered with a pleading look while gulping down the rest of the wine. Catching the waitress's eye, I motioned for a refill.

"I sometimes entertain businessmen from out of town," she admitted.

"Define entertain."

"It's not what you think."

She sounded defensive and unconvincing.

"Yes it is," I said, "but I just want to know about Scofield."

The wine came. She waited until the waitress put it down and left with the empty glass. The tears had stopped altogether. The red that rimmed her dark eyes had faded to a pale pink. Persistent sniffles were tended to by an endless supply of tissues in her purse.

"You mean what is he like?" she asked.

I nodded.

"To tell you the truth, he gives me the creeps. I'm nice to him because I'm expected to be and he's Mitch's boss. I do what he tells me. That's kind of my job. But there's something about him that makes me want to wash my hands after each time I see him. Maybe it's because he's old."

A small shiver rolled through her body.

"If you want to know more, you really should talk to Mitch. They spend a lot of time together. I only see Mr. Scofield every couple of months."

She made Penroy out to be little more than a stylish gofer, the male version of herself, who stepped and fetched for the boss man in exchange for a big car, a nice home, and a trophy girlfriend.

"Tell me more about Scofield. I need details."

"Mitch doesn't talk much about him anymore," she said. "He's told me things in the past about his taste in women, but lately he hasn't said much. I think something's wrong."

"What about his taste in women?"

"Maybe not women."

She talked slowly, choosing words as carefully as the thong panties back at the lingerie shop.

"Girls would be more like it. The other day Mitch asked me to take Mr. Scofield's secretary shopping. He gave me a list of things to look for. It was mostly little girl clothes. You know, patent-leather shoes with little buckles. Dresses with lots of petticoats."

"Sounds like Scofield's some kind of freak."

"I don't know for sure, but he's never paid any attention to me or to the other girls who work the parties I've been to. He's always been a gentleman. Even steers us toward other men. It's kind of odd, since he could have any girl there."

"Any?"

She shivered again.

"God no. Not me! Just thinking about it makes my skin crawl."

I found myself starting to like her or at least the idea of what she was. As the dispassionate Anna Krychek, she had played a small part in a production too big for her to understand. I could overlook that, as well as her cameo appearance in the effort to frame me. After all, being told what do by men was how she made her living. But it was *how* she did what she was told that intrigued me. Tina Davenport was a beautiful hooker, a bedtime companion for the rich. What was there not to be curious about? But underneath was a sadness and discontent of someone resigned to their own fate. It was easy for me to be sympathetic.

"So, what does your boyfriend have to say about all this?"

"You mean about Mr. Scofield being a freak? Nothing. I don't think Mitch is very happy. I've peeked at his bank account and heard him on the telephone talking about investments and stuff, so I know he has a lot of money. I'm kind of hoping one of these days he'll quit, and we'll live somewhere together where its peaceful and warm."

I could picture Penroy hanging out in the South Pacific or the Mediterranean, but not with Tina Davenport. Penroy didn't come across as the type to hold hands and watch sunsets.

"You ever see Scofield with his wife?"

"No. She's a real mystery woman. Rumor has it they had a daughter who died. At least it was a rumor until all those stories in the newspaper and on television. Mrs. Scofield never got over the daughter's death, I guess. Now she spends most of her time in New York or Europe and the rest in bed drinking."

"I want to talk to Scofield," I said. "How do I get to him?"

She looked at me over the top of her wine glass.

"Why do you care about this? Are you going to write something about Scofield and Mitch, because if you are ...

"Let's just say it's personal. Now, how do I get to him."

Tina Davenport shrugged.

"You can't. No one can. Not without Mitch's help."

"Where is he now? Scofield, I mean?"

"Last night at eleven he was home, but I think they're going to Mr. Scofield's beach house this weekend. At least that's what I heard last night."

"Where's this beach house?"

"It's near Cape Perpetua, south of Newport," she said. "I've been there a couple of times, but always by helicopter. Mr. Scofield lets Mitch use it when he's out of town. I'm not sure I could find it if I had to drive."

I nodded, then leaned across the table toward her. I wasn't much on career counseling for professional party girls, but if she was going to help me, I could try to do something for her.

"Listen closely, Tina. Your boyfriend and his boss are involved in something very weird and very dangerous. I know some of it, but not all. Mysterious manuscripts and murders are part of it, but it's more than that. Your little fling with Ivan Krychek means you're involved. Right now, I'd say it's every man for himself. If you hang out with this crowd much longer, you'll be in just as deep as they are."

She stared at me in silence until the tears welled up in her eyes again, then reached for the purse and the tissues. She was on the gritty edge of panic.

"What should I do?"

"You need to figure that out for yourself. All I can do is warn you that something more is going to come out of all of this and to be careful."

I wrote my telephone number on the back of a Red Star coaster and for good measure added my address before sliding it across the table to her.

"I need to know exactly where that beach house is. Find out and call me."

"Can I come by your place? I'd be safe there, right?"

"Of course."

Our eyes met for a moment then we both looked away.

"For your own protection, you'd better tell Penroy that I found you and that we talked. Just don't tell him everything we talked about. Give him this message. Tell him I know everything. Tell him the price for my silence is a meeting with Scofield."

She nodded and slipped the coaster into her purse.

"That's the best I can do for you," I said. "The rest is up to you. Stay or go."

Tina Davenport excused herself and left for the bathroom. I ordered a scotch and was half way through it when she returned, looking good as new except for a few red lines in her eyes. Instead of sitting across from me, she slid into the booth on my side of the table and let her leg rest against my thigh.

"I'm sorry for what I tried to do to you. That thing with Mather."

Her perfume was fresh, her voice low.

"I know you won't tell the police about me. I don't think you're that kind of person."

I stared into my drink, convincing myself that she was sincere and not staging another one-woman performance to save herself from Butcher and Gitchell.

"I need to go, now," she said.

With a breathy kiss on my ear that made me remember how alone I was, she got up and left.

# Chapter 43

Mitch Penroy started to fidget about half way through his explanation of Tina Davenport's encounter with John Standard.

"My guess is that he wants to sell the story to someone, probably the same newspaper that published that other story," Penroy said.

After a long pause, Proctor Scofield finally asked, "Did you say Standard told Tina he knows *everything*. What exactly does that mean?"

"He only knows as much as what was in the manuscript. I think he's trying to bluff his way into an interview with you. He's a freelancer. Just proving you're alive is probably worth something to one of those tabloids he works for."

They were sitting in the leather comfort of Scofield's study, the muffled sound of a lawnmower creeping in through the closed windows to mix with the giggles of Scofield's secretary, who sat in front of the television eating ice cream and watching a rerun of *That Girl*.

"It doesn't make sense," Scofield said. "Why are we topic A with him? Why? He's not still a suspect anymore in the murder of that student and his teacher, is he? Despite your efforts, there's no evidence that he killed Mather. So, who got him all stirred up?"

Penroy shrugged.

"Has that cop been bothering him again?

"Could be. He still has an unsolved murder on his hands. I guess from his perspective, Standard is worth keeping an eye on."

"That still doesn't explain what he wants."

Penroy toyed with the crease in his slacks.

"It might be the Grant woman. There might have been something between them that keeps him going."

Scofield walked over to his secretary and stood behind her. The one-piece bathing suit hung loosely on her thin frame, the red nylon looked bright against her pale skin. The Shirley Temple curls, wet from swimming in the pool, dangled limply on her thin shoulders. He rested a hand on the back of her neck, then let it snake around to her chest and down the front of the bathing suit. As his fingers caressed her small nipples, he waited to feel something deep inside him. She didn't respond and neither did he.

Scofield glanced at Penroy, who looked embarrassed.

"All right, then" Scofield said, leaving his secretary to her television show and walking back to the couch. "Let's forget Mr. Standard for a while. If you're right and he's bluffing, then we have nothing to worry about. If he persists, then we may have to take some other action."

Penroy responded with a noncommittal nod that said he knew what Scofield meant by "other action."

"Is everything set for the weekend?" Scofield asked. "We're driving over in the morning. I want all of you there early Sunday."

"Not a problem," Penroy said. "They got back from Mexico last night."

"Good. It's time we gave the boys a glimpse of their future. The primary election is eleven months away. By the following November, one of them will be governor, and the other will be perfectly positioned to run for the United States Senate."

"The press isn't going let people forget about what happened," Penroy said. "Every profile of them will mention it."

"Fuck 'em. It's the voters I care about. If you do your job taking care of any challengers, then the voters won't have any other choice, no matter what the media says."

"It's going to take one hell of a lot of money."

"That we got," Scofield said with a smile. "That we got."

The secretary suddenly appeared at Scofield's side. She plopped down next to him and draped her milky white legs over his lap.

"How about another itsy-bitsy swim? Just you and me."

"You go ahead. I'll be right there." Scofield smiled.

He watched impassively as she ran out of the room, giggling.

"One more thing, Mitch," Scofield said, nodding after the girl. "Call the manager of that assembly plant in Bangkok and tell him I'm sending a new employee his way. You make the arrangements. I want her out of here right after we get back from the coast."

# Chapter 44

Benny Orlando dove into the beef with broccoli as if it was the last plate of food in China Town on a Saturday night. The chopsticks worked like extensions of his pudgy fingers as he shoveled the food down between swallows of Tsing Tao.

"You know who introduced beer to China?" he asked, then didn't bother waiting for my answer. "The Germans. Sometime in the late 1800s, the Chinese started giving away land to European countries. Don't ask me why. That's how the English got Hong Kong. The Portuguese got Macao. My ancestors, the Italians, showed up, and the Chinese told them to bug off. Poor Italians. Even the Chinese don't respect us. Anyway, when the Germans got some land, the first thing they did was build a brewery and start making beer out of rice. When the Chinese threw the Germans out, they kept the brewery."

"Italian?" I said. "I thought you were Hispanic."

"What difference does it make. Latin is Latin. We hang together when we're insulted by someone from another race."

"Whatever."

I poked at the noodles I'd ordered, but didn't feel like eating. The day had been spent waiting to hear from Tina Davenport about the location of Scofield's beach house. I sat in the oven-like apartment all day waiting for the telephone to ring. When Benny came by at six to suggest dinner at the House of Louie, I reluctantly agreed, but once there could think of nothing else but getting back to wait for her call.

"You going to eat those noodles?" Benny said, gesturing with his chop sticks.

I slid the bowl across the table.

"What did you find out about Scofield?" I asked as Benny began slurping up a mouthful of what had been my dinner.

"A rags to riches story," Benny said. "Started out selling typewriters in the late sixties. Now - according to *Forbes*, anyway - his personal wealth ranks somewhere between the Mars family that makes candy bars and the Quandt family that owns BMW. Scofield Industries itself ranks eighteenth on the *Fortune 500* and has its fingers into everything and anything that has to do with computers, and then some. In other words, he probably doesn't take out his own garbage."

Watching Benny scarf down the noodles made me reconsider eating, so I grabbed a serving a pork shu mei from a passing dim sum cart.

"What about Scofield himself?"

Benny polished off the last of the noodles, then plopped more broccoli and beef into a bowl of rice. He held the bowl up to his chin and started shoveling again. A little girl at the next table watched him with a horrified look.

"He hasn't been seen in public for several years," Benny mumbled. Grains of rice clung to his lips. "I found some people who'd actually seen his private jet land in places like New York, New Delhi, Jakarta, San Antonio. The plane apparently has this weird logo of two snakes. Anyway, they watched people get off the plane, but Scofield was never among them. The best anyone can tell, he does business right there on the plane, then flies away."

"What about here in town?"

"Ah, that's where things get kind of interesting. The word on the street is that Scofield's something of a freak, in the new vernacular."

"Tina Davenport described Scofield the same way," I said. "Seems he likes his women young."

Benny shrugged and drained the last of the beer.

"Young, old, fat, skinny, male, female. The rumors read like *Penthouse Forum*. One thing's certain, though: Whatever he does, he does it with the best Portland has to offer. Uptown, Rolex babes. The old adage is true: the rich are different. Silicone girls for silicon guys. It's the new millenium, John. Money rules. The economy going in the tank didn't seem to do much more than eliminate the competition. Guys like Scofield survive no matter what. So do their habits."

"So what else is new."

The waitress brought the check with two fortune cookies. I cracked one open. It read, "All that ever stays the same is change."

It was the same quotation from Lao Tse that Jasmine had left on my mirror after our night together. Without a word to Benny, I quickly slipped the small piece of paper into my shirt pocket.

Over the rest of the tea, I told Benny more about my conversation with Tina Davenport. At the part about taking Scofield's secretary on a shopping spree for little-girl clothes, Benny's thick eyebrows started bouncing up and down like trained poodles in a dog act.

"So, what's the problem?" Benny asked and gave me an inquisitive look.

I remembered Ivy and changed the subject.

"Anything about Scofield's wife?" I said.

"Nada."

"What about his stepdaughter, Amanda?"

"Nothing other than what you've already written."

"Is it that people don't know anything or they're afraid to talk?"

"A little of both, I think," Benny said. "Everyone I talked to, and that was quite a few, seemed to have a little piece of the puzzle, but no one had the whole picture. It's odd that in this day and age a man with that much money could be such a mystery, but that seems to be the case."

I looked around anxiously for the waitress. When I caught her eye I motioned for the bill. When it came, I tossed a twenty on the counter as we left

"Why the interest in Scofield, anyway?" Benny asked when we were on the sidewalk outside.

"I thought he'd make a nice feature story I could sell to one of the business magazines."

"Bullshit. No one's talked to Scofield in years. If he's going to break down and grant an interview, why would he give it to you?"

I scowled down at Benny as the little man waddled along beside me, trying to keep up on the short walk back to the Jeep.

"Don't be an asshole, Benny."

"Sorry, but I'm right. Scofield's no Bill Gates and you're not from the *New York Times*. He doesn't write books or appear on big-screen televisions to lecture to the CEOs of the world. The guy's a classic recluse. The Howard Hughes of high-tech. I'm not even sure all the stuff I found out for you is true. He could be dead or crazy for all anyone knows."

I knew Scofield didn't fit either category, but I wasn't in the mood to discuss it with Benny.

"You know what's odd about Scofield?" I said as we climbed in the Jeep. "I can't get a picture of him in my mind. Usually when you know something about a person, you get a sense of what they look like. The color of their hair, their eyes, their height, and weight. With Scofield, it's like he's invisible. He casts no shadow. A vampire in a mirror. His name evokes money and power, but no image."

"You got that right. All the material I looked through, the newspaper and magazine articles, none of them had pictures of him or even a description. They didn't even mention that it was impossible to find out what he looks like. It's like all these hot-shot reporters never thought to ask for a description of the man. Pretty weird."

We rode along in silence until we got to the traffic light at the intersection of Burnside and Broadway. Street people moved slowly along the sidewalks in the cool of the early evening. A hooker in tight, yellow shorts and a striped tube top stood in the doorway of a closed tattoo parlor munching suggestively on a corn dog. Benny rolled down the window and yelled at her.

"Nina, honey, where you at, darlin'?"

The hooker scowled then smiled.

"Hey, baby," she said, shaking her booty at Benny. "If business was good, this wouldn't be a corn dog, you know what I'm sayin'?"

Benny laughed and rolled up the window.

"Who's that?" I said.

"One of Joey the Freak's girls."

"Who?"

"Joey the Freak. Joseph Frecanado. He owns a tittie bar on the east side and runs a string of three or four girls, including Nina back there. Rumor is he's mobbed up, but it's doubtful. Nina calls him the Italian Scallion on account he smells like onions all the time."

I shook my head in amazement.

"Is there anyone is this town you don't know?"

"Yeah," Benny said. "You."

My glare demanded an explanation.

"This interest in Scofield is showing me a new side of you," Benny said. "I didn't know you when you were at the top of your game, but my guess is that what I'm seeing now is pretty close. It's also my guess that it has something to do with Jasmine Grant and getting yourself square with the world for those two little girls you killed. That's it, isn't it? You wouldn't be carrying a cross for some one-night stand unless there's more to it. Am I right?

I went silent, reluctant to tell Benny more than the little man needed to know.

I drove up Broadway, cut over to Ninth Street at Taylor, found a parking spot near the First Congregational Church, and walked across the park. Benny struggled along a few steps behind me.

A block from the apartment building I stopped and turned around. Benny caught up, then tilted his baseball hat back in order to look up at my face.

"This isn't the time to talk about it, but I need to do this myself, for my own reasons," I said. "I need to take some risks or nothing is going to be right again. Is there a story in this? You bet, but there's more. The night Jasmine died gave me an odd sense of recklessness, as if I really didn't care what happened to me because it couldn't be worse than what had already happened. I've never really lost that feeling and the closer I get to Scofield the stronger it becomes."

"So it is Jasmine."

"Yes, but not because we spent the night together. I lost her, but so did everyone else. The world is a lesser place when people like her die the way she did."

"You got a lot of reasons to find Scofield," Benny said. "I just hope they're all the right ones."

Silence was the only answer Benny got.

"You know," Benny said when we reached the apartment building, "it's too bad Amanda Bishop committed suicide. Just think about the things she could tell if she were here today. I guess we'll never know."

"I guess not," I said, watching Benny unlock the door.

"What if she didn't kill herself?" Benny said, the key half way in the lock. "What if someone, Scofield maybe, threw her off that bridge?"

"Even if that were true, she's still dead, which gets me nothing."

Benny turned the key and shoved open the door.

"Yeah, you're right, but it makes for a pretty story."

"The problem is proving it."

"Some day."

As we went inside, I had no idea how soon that day would come.

# Chapter 45

I was sitting in the chair, gently curling and uncurling the fortune with the words of Lao Tse when Tina Davenport called a few minutes before midnight with directions to Proctor Scofield's beach house.

"It's just south of that little town of Yachats. There's a turnout where the Highway 101 takes a hairpin turn."

"I'll find it. Is Penroy with him?"

"Not yet, but soon."

"Then Scofield is alone?"

"I don't know about alone, just that Mitch isn't there yet."

"Are you going to the coast with Penroy?

She hesitated.

"It's possible. Mr. Scofield occasionally invites others to the beach house, but not a lot. Security reasons, I guess. Are you going to try finding him tonight?"

"Now is as good a time as any," I said, then asked, "How are you doing? Given any more thought to your future with Penroy?"

A long silence gave me hope that she was at least considering leaving him.

"I don't know yet. He'll probably be with Mr. Scofield for a couple of days, which means he won't be back until Tuesday at the earliest. If he doesn't ask me to go, I could be packed and out of here in a few hours. I just don't know where to go."

I glanced around the apartment trying to imagine Tina Davenport living with me in a place that even I could barely stand. A few hours in the peeled paint and stained porcelain of my adopted world would send her scurrying back to Mitch Penroy wondering why she left in the first place. I felt stupid and confused. Instead of resenting her for trying to implicate me in a murder, I suddenly wanted to tell her that while I was no great catch, at least I cared enough not to peddle her to other men. Almost to the point of saying she could come and stay with me for awhile, I stopped. It wasn't her I wanted. It was anybody.

"Whatever you do, stay in touch," I said.

It was as much of a good by as I could muster.

She hung up after giving me a thank you thick with disappointment.

I went to the bedroom to put the fortune in the dresser next to the note Jasmine had left on my mirror after our night together, then out to the kitchen to rummage through the drawers for a crumpled road map of Oregon I'd thrown in there months before. I found it under a food-encrusted spatula and spread it out on the kitchen table, running my finger down the red line of Highway 101 from Tillamook to Lincoln City. South of Newport, the highway ran hard up against the beach all the way to Yachats. Scofield's beach house was somewhere between Yachats and Florence, the next town twenty-five miles farther south.

It was time to go, but I needed one more thing before leaving. I refolded the map and called Benny, then took the elevator to the second floor.

"You sure you know how to handle this?" Benny asked, holding out a sleek Beretta in a shiny, black leather holster. Ivy was at a concert at Civic Stadium, so we were alone in the computer room. The gun looked huge in Benny's small hand.

I took it, surprised at its weight and how comfortable it felt when I gripped the handle and pulled it out of the holster. The feeling of security and power was immediate, like the rush of a good drug.

"No," I said, "but I don't plan to use it."

"That's not how guns work," Benny said. "When you have one, they have a tendency to get used."

"Let's hope you're wrong."

"And if I'm not?"

"Then I'm no worse off that I am now."

I put the Beretta in my coat pocket, left Benny's apartment and walked across the park to my car. Driving out Barbur Boulevard to pick up the highway to the coast, I remembered the words of Maynard Argyle that day in the press room at the Capitol.

"You going to tweak the cheek of the giant, John?"

"Yes, Maynard, but it's a much bigger giant than either of us thought."

# Chapter 46

Proctor Scofield moved a step closer to the edge of the rocky point to let a gust of wind heavy with salt hit his face and blow away the memory of the one and only time he went out onto the ocean. It was fifteen years earlier on a tuna-fishing trip out of Depoe Bay. Sea sickness hit him when the forty-five-foot charter boat was five minutes outside the bay's narrow entrance and didn't stop until five minutes after it docked two days later. In between was an endless and embarrassing parade back and forth from his sweat-stained bunk to the boat's railing that left him feeling like he had turned himself inside out.

The constant nausea made him briefly ambivalent about living or dying, but it was the image of the vast, horizonless ocean that stayed with him. On a trip to the railing sometime in the middle of the night, he found himself alone on the back deck while everyone else slept except for the captain in the wheelhouse. He stood unnoticed while the boat rose and fell on waves and troughs, lost in a black-and-white world of high-beam lights hanging in the rigging and hellish darkness just a few feet away. Panic replaced the nausea as he came face to face for the first time with a force much greater than himself. Fear grabbed his throat and forced out a scream that was lost in the wind. He started crying, fell to his knees and crawled back to his bunk.

Scofield never told anyone about that night. Instead, he came away from the experience convinced that the ocean should be viewed rather than lived. Two weeks later he purchased the ten-acre parcel on a secluded cove between Yachats and Florence and commissioned an architect to design a house that would become part of the rugged landscape rather than stand out from it. He wanted to recapture that night on the fishing boat without having to relive the misery and panic that came with it. Over time, the house became more and more important to him, a sanctuary from work and then from Margaret. It was a place where he could do what he wanted with whomever he wanted. It was the only thing he loved any more, the last recipient of his warped affections.

Scofield stepped back from the edge of the cliff. It was a little after midnight and the ocean out beyond the end of the rocky point was the same as that night on the tuna trip, the sea and the sky merged into one huge impenetrable blanket. No beginning. No end. The only difference was he could now appreciate its power and size without feeling insignificant. It was a perfect compromise with something that could not be bought outright.

A noise made him turn around. The security guard stood ten feet away lighting a cigarette.

"Everything all right, Mr. Scofield?"

"Fine. Thank you."

The interruption had broken the moment. Just as well, Scofield thought, and turned his back to the sea.

A few dim lights shone down on the grass as he walked slowly back toward the silent house built against the cliff underneath the coast highway. He thought of the waves pounding into the huge crevasse next to the house as the uncontrolled power he could wield whenever he chose. The abandoned lighthouse on the other side of the crevasse stood for the composure he needed to avoid using his power foolishly. Power without composure was like an ocean without a lighthouse: whoever had it just wandered aimlessly until finally crashing into a reef.

He went inside through the glass doors on the lower level, then climbed the spiral staircase to the living room. Pouring a drink, he thought again about John Standard.

He had decided that there was only one option left in dealing with Standard. It had been used before, so once more wouldn't make that much difference.

This time, though, it wouldn't be so untidy.

Scofield took his drink into the small office at the end of the living room. It was the weekend, so the world's financial markets were closed. He stared at the computer screen and ignored the intermittent beep of in-coming e-mail.

The muted ring of the telephone next to the computer surprised him. Not that many people had the number and none of them would call this time of night. He said hello, then patiently listened to the familiar voice on the other end.

"Thanks for passing that on," he said. "We'll be waiting for him."

Yes, he thought after hanging up and heading outside to find the security guard. It was definitely time to deal with John Standard.

# Chapter 47

Twenty miles west of Portland, the traffic all but disappeared. The radio offered nothing more than the poison of conservative talk radio or rock 'n roll that was either too old or too new.

I finally found a jazz station that lasted as far as the wine country around McMinnville then faded into annoying static. After that, I turned the radio off and listened to the Jeep's engine ping its way toward the Coast Range. I passed the time reading the garish billboards advertising Indian casinos, motels, aquariums, and the other tourist traps found along coastlines everywhere.

Two hours after leaving Portland, I was once again cruising through the dim-lit streets of Lincoln City. After getting coffee to go at a twenty-four-hour convenience store, I scanned the highway map again, trying to pinpoint the exact location of Scofield's house. Based on what Tina had said, it was near where the highway takes a hairpin turn around a small cove. The gas-station map didn't have the necessary detail, but I could at least narrow it down to a couple of places.

Twenty-five miles farther south, Newport was as quiet as Lincoln City, so the drive through town and over the Yaquina Bay Bridge took less than ten minutes instead of the usual thirty. Around Seal Rock, the night sky clouded over and the temperature dropped. Five miles later it started to rain. The light mist which required little more than putting the wipers on intermittent, soon turned to a heavy drizzle.

I reached Yachats at three a.m. The correct pronunciation was yah-hots, but that didn't prevent all visitors and some Oregonians from calling it yeah-chits. I found an all-night diner with no waitress, just a cook sitting at the end of the bar, smoking cigarettes and doing a crossword puzzle. A stained T-shirt stretched across his enormous belly and the tattoos on his forearms proclaimed a life-long devotion to the US Navy and to someone named Delores.

"I'm lost," I said. "I was supposed to spend the weekend at a house near here. I got away a little late and left the directions at home."

The cook gave me a look that said, And?

"You might know the people. Scofield? Proctor Scofield? His house is supposed to be somewhere near an old lighthouse."

"It's probably that place three miles south on the highway," he said. "Look for the sign that says 'Lighthouse.' It's the first driveway around the next curve."

I went outside and sat in the Jeep for a few minutes. I was close, very close. Benny's Beretta lay on the passenger seat. I picked it up and let its weight and sleekness provide a little additional courage, then put it down and drove away.

Just south of Yachats, the highway narrowed and clung to the edge of a cliff as it followed the rugged outline of the coast around Cape Perpetua. Two turns later, the pavement turned sharply east, then swung around to head back toward the ocean again. I slowed down at the small, green State Highway Department sign that read "Lighthouse." The parking lot immediately off the highway was vacant, but open. I parked near the "Closed" sign that hung on a chain across the asphalt path that led into the darkness. The ocean sounded like distant cannon fire. I rummaged around in the Jeep's center console for a flashlight that came with a car kit Christine had given me for Christmas several years earlier. I flipped on the small, but adequate beam.

A path under ancient fir trees warped by countless winters of wind off the Pacific led from the parking lot about a hundred yards to the lighthouse. The trees dripped with the pre-dawn rain and salty mist. Huge ferns and low rhododendrons reached out from the dark, groping at the edges of the asphalt like hands from a grave. Large patches of emerald green moss clung to rocks so large the path had to wind around them. The air was thick with the smell of salt and seaweed.

The abandoned lighthouse at the end of the path had a short, stubby tower with a conical top and a rusted metal catwalk. Next to the tower was a smaller, octagon-shaped building that served as a storage shed for those who maintained the facility in its heyday. What the salt water hadn't destroyed, the graffiti artists and vandals had. All the windows were broken out and spray painted initials and symbols covered the curved base of the tower. Still, the forty-foot lighthouse stood its ground, a ghost beacon warning ghost ships.

I stopped at the end of the trail, hanging back under the limbs of an ancient fir. The lighthouse stood in the center of a triangle-shaped peninsula that jutted into the ocean. To the right, along the north side of the peninsula, a stand of fir trees extended behind the lighthouse into the darkness. To the left on the south side, a weathered, split-rail fence stretched maybe a hundred yards toward the ocean. The expanse of grass between the lighthouse and the fence looked well-groomed, but would be probably be patchy brown in daylight.

Moving across the grass toward the fence, I sensed danger before seeing it and aimed the flashlight's narrow beam at the ground. The grass ended three feet beyond the fence at the jagged edge of a cliff. I got close enough to peer over the edge. Eighty feet below, a churning punch bowl of angry waves gnawed at barnacle-encrusted rocks. The foam that shone with a dim luminescence against the dark water shifted constantly into a hundred different shapes. Water-soaked logs that looked like armless bodies bobbed up and down with each rise and fall of the waves. The chaotic movement of water and debris was contained in a long, narrow crevasse that could've been made by a giant finger poked into cooling lava millions of years ago. An eternity of waves pushed by the ocean threw themselves into it in a contest to see which could reach the farthest inland. At the end, the waves crashed in desperation against the steep rock cliff, then retreated, taking a little bit of the cliff with it.

I moved along the fence line toward the ocean, careful to keep the cliff on the left and the graffiti white walls of the lighthouse on the right. The wind had increased, but the rain had slowed to a thick mist. Low clouds to the west parted enough to allow the faint light of a half moon to escape. The crashing of the waves grew louder, announcing that I was nearing the ocean. My steps slowed.

The flashlight beam flickered and went out. It didn't matter. Even without the light, I knew I couldn't go much farther. The grass had disappeared and the ground underfoot turned sandy and dotted with large rocks. I'd reached the end of the peninsula. Beyond lay nothing but ocean. The combination of wind and waves was deafening.

I stopped and looked across to the other side of the crevasse at a peninsula that mirrored the one I stood on. On the other side stood a large, two-level house that looked like it had been carved out of the rocks by some ancient king. In the dim light, I could see a curved bank of windows on the upper level and a deck with no rails that wrapped around three sides of the house. The lower level consisted of a daylight basement with a stone patio that cascaded down onto a wedge-shaped lawn that came to a point at the cliff opposite where I stood. Light, blurred by the rain, shone along the deck and the patio.

A helicopter sat on a concrete pad a few yards beyond the house. The way its four blades were tied down gave the appearance of a giant insect caught in a few strands of a spider's web. The intertwined snakes of the Scofield

Industries logo on the door were just visible in the faint glow of the house lights.

I hunched down in an effort to get under the wind. A cigarette would taste perfect, but trying to light one would be useless. Instead, I studied the house. The crevasse prevented any access from the lighthouse side, which left me with little choice but to back track and find the driveway the cook at the diner had described. As I stood there trying to come up with a third alternative, a man moved along the deck of Scofield's house, disappeared around the far side, and then reappeared on the patio below. The man walked out onto the grass, lit up a cigarette that I wanted so badly, and stood watching the ocean.

The man pulled up the hood of his raincoat, turned away, and walked back to the shelter of the patio. I studied the figure for a few moments until absolutely certain who it was, then I slowly worked my way back toward the path to the parking lot. By the time I reached the Jeep, everything had fallen into place. Blind anger added to my resolve to confront Proctor Scofield on his own turf. The sense of recklessness that had never really gone away was suddenly stronger than ever.

# Chapter 48

Before walking the quarter-mile around the hairpin turn in the highway, I locked the car and put the holstered Beretta on my belt. The weight of the gun brought back the sense of security I felt after first holding it in my hand. I had brought the gun along as a precaution with no intention of using it. Now, with the Beretta nestled comfortably in the small of my back, I wasn't so sure. I was slowly gaining a greater appreciation for the seductive fascination of firearms.

I followed the shoulder of the road around the curve and up a slight incline to the point where the pavement turned south again. The tide was high. I fought back the feeling that the sea wanted to climb up on the cliffs to grab me. I walked at a steady pace, never even considering turning back. The anger that came with recognizing the guard on Scofield's front lawn added to what I already felt about freak accidents and dead lovers. It had gone on too long for too many different reasons. It would all end here, tonight.

Instead of following the highway as it curved south, I kept going straight ahead into a small turnout. It looked like a place where travel trailers and motor homes were supposed to pull over to let other cars pass, which explained why it looked so unused. At the southern end of the turnout, hidden from the view of cars driving along the highway, lay the start of an unmarked road that disappeared down into the trees toward the ocean. It was nothing more than two dirt tracks running through the rotting pine needles scattered on the ground, but it had to be the entrance to Scofield's house.

I started walking. The overhanging firs dripping with rain water and the healthy ferns and salal creeping onto the hard surface had the same crypt-like appearance as the path to the lighthouse. Thirty yards from where the driveway left the turnout, the rotting pine needles turned to smooth asphalt. Another hundred feet later, I found the driveway blocked by an electronic gate hung between two brick pillars. A sign on one pillar warned trespassers of certain prosecution. A plaque in the middle of the gate read, "Scofield."

I paused, then walked around the pillar, crawled over a five-foot rock wall, and back onto the driveway on the other side. My pants and shoes were soaked, but I ignored the cold that crept up my legs.

With each step came the greater possibility that men with guns and Rottweilers would leap out of the trees. People like Proctor Scofield didn't live without some kind of security. Even if it wasn't men and dogs, I decided that by now my every move was being watched on closed-circuit television screens inside a dark room by men like Buck Mather. I scanned the trees for cameras, but it was too dark to see them even if they were there.

No need to worry though, I thought, I had a contact on the inside who knows the owner.

A couple of minutes beyond the gate, I heard voices, followed by the high-pitched whine of a powerful engine and a slow thumping sound that quickly grew louder and faster.

It took a moment to remember the helicopter sitting on the dimly lit pad. I could both hear the noise and feel it. It came from directly ahead of me which meant I was just south of Scofield's house. I moved to the far side of the driveway and followed it down in a gradual turn to the north.

When the helicopter lifted off, I stepped off the asphalt and behind a large Douglas fir. The aircraft rose past me over the tops of the trees, the lights on its underside flashing through the trees and brush. Hovering above the dense foliage, it rotated gracefully in place, then darted out over the ocean before turning east to head inland.

I stepped back on to the pavement. I was twenty feet closer to my destination by the time the screaming of the helicopter engine and the heavy thumping of its rotors disappeared to allow the sound of the ocean to resume. I looked at my watch. It was a little after four a.m.

I had to be nearing the house. My hands were fists, teeth clenched until my jaws ached. I remained convinced that there had to be more security than the man on the front lawn. But where? The more I thought about it, the more I was ready to leap into the underbrush in the event someone chose a more conventional means of leaving the property.

Ten more yards down the driveway and Proctor Scofield's beach house rose from the mist and darkness. Approaching from the south, the first thing I saw was the three-car garage at the bottom of the driveway. On the upper level above the garage, I could see the profile of the deck and some of the wrap-around windows that looked west toward the ocean. The back of the house hugged a cliff so there was nothing that resembled a back door. Access to the front of the house was blocked by a rock wall that extended from the garage, past the helicopter pad, and ended at another cliff over the ocean. A wooden gate large enough for a car breached the wall halfway between the house and the helicopter pad. I trotted over to the gate and pushed on it. Locked.

I moved away from the house, past the gate to the wall and felt along the top for embedded glass. Finding none, I pulled myself up. I lay belly-down on top of the wall, ready to drop to the other side when I looked across the lawn toward the ocean. The flare of a lighter and the quick outline of a man's face just twenty feet away made my hug the wall and hold my breath.

The figure in the raincoat paused to take a deep drag, then headed toward the house. As the man neared the lower patio, I dropped silently to the ground and moved away from the house toward the ocean. If I wanted to see Proctor Scofield, dealing with the man smoking the cigarette would be the price of admission.

The lawn ended at a sandstone point littered with large rocks covered in a thin veneer of bird shit. I climbed up on top of one and yelled "Hey" as loud as I could, then dropped back behind the rock to wait. It wasn't a particularly innovative plan, but good enough, given the circumstances.

I pulled the Beretta from its holster and let it hang muzzle down along my leg as I leaned against the rock waiting. The gun felt good. Too good. I checked the safety to make sure it was off, then peered carefully around the rock toward the house.

The man with the cigarette was standing at the edge of the lawn, his own gun out and pointed straight ahead, Slowly, he began moving forward. I waited until he was on the other side of the rock, then moved around behind him. With one swift motion, I pressed the Beretta to the back of the man's head. It took all my self-control not to pull the trigger and leave the body to the seagulls and sand crabs.

"Doing a little moonlighting?" I asked.

The man hacked out a cough before turning his head just enough to see me.

"Fuck you," said Alfie Gitchell and dropped his gun without being asked.

"Let's go inside and say hello to your boss," I said. "I'm sure he'll be impressed with the job you're doing."

"You're going to die an ugly death," Gitchell said.

He spoke without turning his beefy head, the wind ripping the words from his lips.

"At least I'll go with a clean conscience."

I picked up Gitchell's gun, tossed it into the sand near one of the large rocks, then shoved Gitchell in the direction of the house.

"Let's go. Just remember I could blow your brains out right now and introduce *myself* to Scofield."

It was a cheap line, but Gitchell bought it and stiffened before turning back toward the house. He kept his head down like a bird dog coming home empty-mouthed. I stayed two paces behind to survey the front of the house for signs that the occupants were up and about. All I could see was a dim light at the south end of the upper level.

Gitchell led me across the patio and through the sliding glass doors. Inside, the detective snapped on a table lamp to reveal a room decorated with ship's wheels, colorful pennants, and framed prints of graceful wooden ships in full sail. As we started up a spiral staircase to the upper level, I felt like Ned Land on his way to see Captain Nemo.

We emerged into a large room that resembled the bridge of a cruise ship. In front of us were wrap-around windows looking out at the dark ocean. Two long, leather couches sat facing each other. They were perpendicular to the windows, creating a perfect place to watch the constantly changing sea. To my right in back of one of the couches was a hallway that looked like it led to the bedrooms. The kitchen was behind me through a large archway. A few steps inside the room Gitchell stopped.

"Where is he?" I asked.

The homicide detective motioned toward a small room to my left. It looked like an office just off the end of the living room. In the dim light I had seen from the yard, I could make out the thin figure of a man hunched over a computer keyboard.

"Call him," I said.

"Call him yourself," Gitchell shot back.

I kneed the little man in the crotch, sending him tumbling into a glass table that shattered under his weight. I suddenly felt better, the anger down a quarter tank. The little cop's betrayal meant he'd pay the price for everyone else who had done the same thing to me.

Gitchell lay curled up amid shards of thick glass clutching his groin and moaning between coughs, when the man appeared in the doorway of the small room. We stared at each other for a few moments, my gun pointed down at the fetal Gitchell.

"You must be John Standard," the man said. "I'm Proctor Scofield. I've been expecting you. Would you care for some coffee?"

# Chapter 49

Even with no image of Proctor Scofield, I was still surprised at the appearance of the small, gentle-looking old man with the chalky complexion and thick mane of gray hair. Large ears stuck straight out from a small, round head. Razor-sharp lines radiated from the corners of dark, deep-set eyes. The nose resembled a small beak perched over a down-turned mouth with thin, slightly chapped lips. The dark moles on his face looked like spatters of dried blood. An oversize, terry cloth bathrobe, which looked like it came from a Hilton on Maui, sagged on stooped shoulders. The hands that poked out of the robe's floppy sleeves had the swollen knuckles and twisted fingers of an advanced case of arthritis. Peeking out from the bottom of the robe were small feet encased in leather sandals that squeaked as he crossed the room in graceful, gliding steps.

What I had expected was someone vigorous and larger than life; a dapper, gracefully aging aristocrat. What I got was an old coot.

"Coffee would be great," I said, then pointed the gun at Gitchell. "What would you like me to do with your Rottweiler?"

Scofield shrugged.

"If you're going to shoot him, please do it outside. If not, leave him where he is."

Scofield waited until I returned the gun to the holster, then walked past me to stand over Alfie Gitchell.

"When you've sufficiently recovered, Mr. Gitchell, please check the grounds to see if our guest brought any friends with him. If he did, I hope you can manage to handle it in a more professional manner."

Gitchell could only manage a deep groan.

"Please, Mr. Standard," Scofield said. "Join me in the kitchen."

Closer now, I could see the skin on Scofield's face. It was pulled tight, like plastic wrap over a slice of melon. A smile revealed ill-fitted denture-white teeth that gave his reedy voice a slight lisp. The same thin skin stretched over his bony hands and feet. The smell of aftershave was too strong for that early in the day.

Scofield poured two cups of coffee and we sat at the table in the large country kitchen like a couple of old friends who had gotten up early to go fishing.

"May I call you John?" Scofield asked.

I nodded.

"May I call you Proctor?"

Scofield laughed.

"Of course. Now, tell me, did you come here to kill me, John?"

"I came for a lot of reasons. Answers mostly. Killing you crossed my mind."

"Because of the Jasmine Grant thing. Right?"

"You had her murdered. That's not a 'thing,' but let's get to that later. First, tell me how you knew I was coming."

"Tina Davenport was kind enough to let us know. She called several hours ago."

I tried to keep the disappointment off my face while wondering what there was about me that made people want to betray me.

"So much for the whore with a heart of gold."

"Indeed," Scofield said. "It's hard to find people you can trust. That's why I'm so disgusted with Mr. Gitchell. He was supposed to intercept you."

He blew into his coffee and then took a sip.

"In any event, you're here. Would you like something stronger in that coffee. I have an excellent selection of single-malt scotch and you look a little chilled."

I said no and Scofield walked to the counter for the sugar bowl, then fished a pair of spoons out of a drawer.

"Tina is quite a woman, don't you think. I can't imagine you didn't find yourself attracted to her. Most men are. Anyway, I'm reasonably sure that you have a fairly good understanding of her role in all of this."

I nodded, then gave Scofield a shy smile.

"Pretty slimy."

Scofield's agreement came with a nod and a sigh. When the old man sat down at the table, I could almost hear his bones creak.

"I know. It was Penroy's idea. I didn't like it, but she was his girlfriend, so . . ." His voice trailed off. "But we're not here to talk about Tina, are we? I've learned a lot about you in the last few hours. John Kennedy Standard, former reporter turned freelance writer after an unfortunate accident in which you killed two young Hispanic girls. It cost you your job, house, and marriage. Now you're living in a run-down apartment building managed by a former rodeo clown."

"Circus clown, actually, but close enough."

"Your divorce was final just a few days ago. Your former wife, Christine, is living in Scottsdale and about to remarry. The marriage produced no children. Your parents were relatively well off and active in the Democratic Party in the 1960s, which explains your name. They died in the crash of their small plane in the early eighties. A younger brother, Michael, died of AIDS three years ago in Miami. Your closest relative is a cousin in Iowa. I have video clips of the press coverage of the accident and your trial. It's in the VCR if you'd like to watch it later. In any event, it appears to me that you wouldn't be missed, if something unfortunate were to happen."

Scofield stared over the rim of the mug to gauge my reaction.

I did my best to give him nothing to gauge.

"It might also mean that I've got nothing to lose," I said.

"In other words, there's nothing of value I can offer to get you to turn your talents in another direction?"

Scofield asked the question like someone who already knew the answer.

"You're not going to tell me you could use a man like me on your team, are you, Proctor?"

A smile danced across Scofield's pale face.

"Touché. No, but only because you wouldn't accept, and I don't take rejection well. You realize, however, that by being here you've put yourself at enormous risk. Believe it or not, I do have resources beyond that thing on the floor in the living room."

"I would hope so, but a lot of people have been killed. I just want to know why. Let's say, it's hard for me to let certain things go."

"We're back to Jasmine Grant, aren't we? And Ivan Krychek?" Scofield asked, staring into his coffee cup.

"And Amanda Bishop."

Scofield squeezed his eyes shut and held them that way for a second or two.

"It will be light soon," he said. "Let's go in the front room. I love to watch the sea come alive this time of the morning. Have you ever been on the east coast, John, or some place where the sun rises over the ocean? I grew up in Oregon watching the sun go down in the west. I was twenty and visiting a college friend in Hawaii when I first saw the sun come up in the east. It was really quite remarkable."

I tried not to laugh. Where the hell did Scofield think the sun came up?

Alfie Gitchell was gone, but the outline of his fat, little body remained visible in the shattered glass on the expensive carpet. We stepped around the mess. Scofield sat on one of the long couches in front of the windows, his back to the hallway leading to the bedrooms, and propped his tiny, sandaled feet on the round coffee table. I sat opposite him on the other couch, watching the billionaire's small body melt back into the over-stuffed cushions.

Scofield stared at the dark sea and sky, while I waited for him to start talking.

"How much have you surmised?" Scofield asked.

"Mather killed Krychek and Jasmine Grant at your request. Then you ordered either Penroy or Gitchell to kill Mather."

Scofield's head bobbed like a cork as he stared at this feet.

"And why did we do all this killing?"

"Krychek died because his doctoral thesis threatened to expose what Roark and Landis did to Amanda. Jasmine died because she had the manuscript and you wanted it. Mather was next because he was probably shaking you down and couldn't be trusted anymore."

Scofield continued staring out to sea.

"You reporters amaze me. The way you get right to the heart of things is incredible. It really is a wonderful talent. Weeks of work and you narrow it down to a few short sentences. Anyway, you're right about everything so far. Keep going, please."

"I don't know how long Alfie Gitchell's been on your payroll, but it really doesn't matter. He must've been working for you the night Krychek was killed. What were his marching orders? To keep the heat off Mather until he found the manuscript? Gitchell decided the best way to do that was find a patsy, and then turn the investigation over to Harry Butcher."

A sly smile crawled across Scofield's face.

"That was very clever of Gitchell," he said. "Believe it or not, he thought that up on his own."

"I suppose he learned from some cops who attended the gun show that I'd been at the fairgrounds about the same time as the murder. That made me a convenient suspect. Given my past, it wasn't hard to convince Butcher that I was his man. On the night Jasmine Grant was killed, Mather was there in the house with her when she called me. I conveniently showed up to find body number two. Butcher was practically foaming at the mouth by then. Things were pretty much going your way."

Scofield shrugged.

"It really was clever," I said. "What better way to hide a couple of murders than to turn the case over to a guy who couldn't find hair on an ape. The harder

Butcher worked to pin the murders on me, the easier things were for the rest of you."

Scofield slowly clapped his hands and stood up.

"Congratulations. That's it in a nutshell. Now, I'm hungry. How about some eggs and bacon?"

Scofield led the way back into the kitchen, where he quickly produced a fry pan from a cupboard next to the stove, put it on one of the gas burners, then went to the refrigerator for a package of pepper bacon and a carton of eggs. He deftly peeled off a half-dozen slices, lined them up in the pan and poked at them with a fork until they started sizzling. I stood in the doorway as the smell of bacon and fresh-brewed coffee quickly filled the room.

"Now it's your turn," I said, walking to the counter to refill my coffee cup. "Tell me how you found out what Krychek was up to."

Scofield spoke without taking his eyes off the pan of bacon.

"We learned about his scheme when he was working security at the Capitol. Mather had hired him without knowing who he was. Then Roark found him snooping around his office late one night. When Mather asked him about it, Krychek told him he was a working on a doctorate in political science. It didn't take much to put two and two together. We tried to find that manuscript without killing him. That was when Penroy hatched the idea of using Tina as bait in a honey trap. All we wanted was the manuscript, but the poor bastard actually fell in love with her."

Imagine that, I said to himself.

"And that didn't work, either."

Scofield flipped the bacon over.

"I hope you like yours crispy. I love crispy bacon. It all seems kind of silly now, doesn't it? Killing people to protect a scheme that most people would find idiotic. You're probably saying to yourself right now, 'Why bother with any of it? No one cares about government and politics anymore.' Am I right?"

"Yeah."

"I can understand that, but you're taking it all out of context, and that's the problem with journalism. Isn't it? It's all facts without context."

"So, enlighten me."

Scofield moved the bacon to a paper towel, then cracked four eggs into the hot grease.

"You'll have to settle for basted. That's the only way I know how to do it. I never could master that flipping thing."

I said basted was fine.

"My ability to make money has been both a blessing and a curse," Scofield said.

His voice overflowed with eagerness. He was the professor; I was the student.

"A blessing in the sense that I can own anything I want, make other people do anything I ask. The curse is that what I have to do is not always to my liking. I am not a vicious or mean-spirited man, but there were times in my life when I have been nothing but that."

I sat back down at the table, feeling comfortable enough to let Scofield ramble.

"I knew years ago that politics and government were going to hell. Sooner or later either the Bible-thumpers or the fags were going to run the whole country. It may still happen, but I'll probably be dead by then. At least, I hope so. You see, I believe politics is the last refuge for the desperate and the uninspired; those who need the adulation to fill some inner need or don't have the talent to make money in the real world. That makes it the playground for men like me, mischievous men with too much money in their pockets and too much time on their hands. Everything Krychek wrote in that thesis was right. Liberals one year. Conservatives the next. Back and forth, year after year. Scandals, hearings, independent counsels, investigations, indictments. The rich versus the poor. Rather than accept the fact that voters rejected their ideas, the losers seek retribution in court by filing ridiculous charges. It's the criminalization of political debate. We've seen it ever since Clinton. It's sad, but inevitable. They even have a new name for it. It's a combination of the words chaos and order: chaordic."

He poked at the eggs, then continued.

"Don't you find it odd that people hold politicians in such contempt, yet keeping turning to them to run the nation? I think a benign dictatorship would be more productive, but that's just me. Anyway, what I saw, others ignored. While I took action, others sat and waited to see who'd win. It's really been nothing more than a game."

Scofield sipped coffee while flipping hot grease on the eggs with a long-handled spatula. I gazed across the living room toward the windows. The swells off the end of the point were visible. The ocean rose and fell like a giant beast breathing in and out.

"I gave money to a lot of candidates and causes, most of them losers. Then I decided that the only guaranteed way to win any kind of game is to own both teams. It's a simple concept that most people can't afford, but one that lets things take whatever course they may and you come out a winner either way. Imagine going to the Super Bowl as the owner of both teams. You can enjoy the game for what it is. Immerse yourself in the strategy, rather than anguish over your team's mistakes or root for your opponent to make some. It's one of the luxuries of being wealthy. What you don't own is what you don't want."

"I assume you're talking about Roark and Landis?"

Scofield slid two eggs each onto flowered plates and laid three strips of bacon along side.

"I forgot to do toast. I can make some if you like."

I shook my head no.

"Fine. Let's take this into the front room. The sun is coming up. Bacon. Eggs. The sea. Sunrise. It's hard not to be awed by the sheer beauty of it all."

We took the same seats and ate with plates on our laps.

"Anyway, Roark and Landis," Scofield said after two bites of egg. "They really have been quite wonderful to watch, you know. I made them what they are. Without me, they would've gone to jail for a few years, then wasted the rest of their lives squandering their fathers' meager fortunes. Instead, one of them stands on the brink of greatness. Maybe both. And you know what's nice about it? I really don't care which one. The natural forces of politics may well anoint one and discard the other. Who cares? Should the political winds shift, as they surely will, the other will be waiting to step in. Either way I win. Eventually I may own not only a governor, but possibly a senator and maybe even more than that."

"You really believe that, don't you?" I asked, cutting into the eggs. The yolks were perfect.

"With all my heart. That's the only way to be successful. You have to believe with all your heart. Look at it this way, I've given the public two men who have learned their craft, the craft of politics, trained in making laws and governing free of any ideological baggage. Oh sure, they espouse certain philosophies, but they don't really believe in them. They just do what I tell them. I'll admit that I was resistant to the idea at first, but turning adversity into opportunity is what made me wealthy. I could've turned the two of them over to the police, pressed charges, then sued their families into oblivion. To be honest, that was my first inclination. When I heard what they did, I wanted to strike them down, to use what wealth I had at the time to grind them into bits as fine as the sand on that beach over there."

He used a strip of bacon to point southward past the empty helicopter pad to a small cove with a half-moon beach awash in the morning tide.

"You never knew Amanda or the kind of child she was or the woman I knew she would become," Scofield said. His voice became faint, the food forgotten. "Nothing in my life hurt more than what happened to her, but blind revenge is useless. I wanted more. I wanted their souls. I wanted to own their every breath, their every heart beat. I wanted them to know that they walked the Earth because of my generous spirit. That I was the only one who could wash away the guilt of what they had done to her. I wanted to be their religion, their god."

I put my unfinished meal on the table and leaned back against the cushions until I felt the Beretta press against the small of my back. Two seagulls landed on the deck outside. They waddled up to the windows, tilting their heads as if trying to get a closer look at Scofield's insanity.

And that's what it was: complete and utter insanity.

"But how?" I asked. "Why would they or their families go along with you?"

"Simple. I had the power to destroy all of them. I could send Roark and Landis to prison and drive both families into poverty. I told them I was purchasing controlling interest in Roark's father's car dealership and that I had information about the billing records at the firm where Landis's father was a partner. If they rejected my offer, they would've been collecting cans along the highway within a year."

"And the offer was?"

"A straightforward business deal," Scofield said. Saying the words brought a thin smile to his brown face. "I get their sons, or I ruin both families."

When Scofield picked up the dishes and took them back to the kitchen, I looked out toward the ocean. The day was breaking to reveal thin, dark clouds the same color as the sea. It looked as if the ocean had risen up to become the sky and both would eventually crash down on the two of us.

"It's hard to believe their parents would agree to your offer," I said when Scofield returned with two cups of fresh coffee.

"What choice did they have?" Scofield settled back into the cushions. "The options were presented to them in a forthright, businesslike manner. There was no need for threats. I held all the cards. It was a simple matter of turning each one up at the right moment and waiting for the two families to fold. I've made deals with presidents, kings and shieks. A car dealer and a lawyer! A piece of cake. I have to give their fathers credit, though, for being pragmatic businessmen who knew how to lose and still survive. It was either give up two shiftless sons headed for jail, or face financial ruin. What would you do? They considered the offer for about five minutes before accepting. It was probably less than that, but I left the room to go to the bathroom."

"And you dropped the charges?"

Scofield proudly nodded.

"And arranged the rest of their lives. Law schools, law firms, congressional posts, legislative races. Everything."

Scofield nodded again, this time more vigorously.

"Incredible," I said, speaking more to myself than to Scofield. "What about the statute of limitations? Your hold on them was only as good as the possibility they'd be charged."

"Who cares? I told them I would have them killed if they reneged on the deal. They believed me, because there was nothing in my past that would make them think it was a lie. In fact, the way we handled Krychek and the woman served to reinforce my position with them. Always deal from strength. That's my motto."

"And now you're going to make them famous. How does that work?"

"Money, John. You know about money and politics."

"But they're rapists."

"Reformed rapists with loving families and solid records of public service."

"And the blessing and financial backing of the father of the woman they raped."

"Exactly," Scofield said.

"But why? Amanda killed herself anyway. What good does it all do?"

Scofield's eyes wandered across the panorama of coast and ocean before answering. When he spoke, it was slow and deliberate, as if every word had to be delivered in precisely the right way.

"What good it did was that every day of their lives, those two boys have remembered what they did. How her death cost them their freedom. And every day, the life that Amanda would've had took on greater meaning and importance. Don't you see? In many ways she's still alive. It was a perfect plan. If I had it to do over again, I would do everything exactly the same."

"And where does Mitch Penroy fit in?"

The question seemed to brighten Scofield's mood.

"Excellent question! You truly are amazing, John. In case you haven't noticed, Mitch Penroy is the perfect political operative. He has no conscience, no morals, and hates public attention. He's been my eyes and ears for twenty-some years. Without him, I could never have gotten this far."

I snorted in disgust.

"I hate to tell you this," I said, "but the guy's an earthworm."

Scofield turned, ready to defend his assistant, then stopped. A small smile became a big laugh.

"You're right. Penroy *is* an earthwork, but he's *my* earthworm."

Then, he left to refill our coffee cups.

I was standing at the windows when I felt a thumping in the air followed by the sound of a powerful engines. I looked north just as the helicopter with the Scofield Industries logo appeared in the sky above the lighthouse. It banked in over the ocean, moved slowly across the lawn in front of the house, and gently lowered itself onto the concrete pad.

"That will be my guests," Scofield said, emerging from the kitchen. "Excellent timing, don't you think?"

I watched as Roark and Landis popped out of the helicopter. They ran, hunched over, toward the house. The blast from the craft's rotors smashing their hair down and beating at their pant legs.

# Chapter 50

Roark and Landis didn't notice me at first. The two politicians came up the stairs and headed straight for the bar, after giving cold greetings to Scofield and bored glances at the shattered table.

As if on cue, Mitch Penroy emerged from hallway behind Scofield looking freshly showered and wearing jeans and a golf shirt. I wondered about Tina. Was she here? Was she asleep in one of the bedrooms down the hall? Penroy's bed? The hurt and anger over her betrayal lasted less than a second. It was Scofield I wanted.

Penroy nodded to Roark and Landis as he walked to the couch and whispered something to Scofield. In mid-sentence, he noticed me staring at the two of them.

"Where's Gitchell?" Penroy said angrily. "You shouldn't be alone with this man. He's a murderer."

Scofield stifled a laugh.

"Relax, Mitch. The play's over. We've been having breakfast," he said, without getting up from the couch. "There's fresh coffee in the kitchen. Why don't you join us? John has been entertaining me with his version of events. Maybe you can help fill in the details. We'd just finished discussing the origins of my two proteges over there and how fate made us such a close and loving family. Isn't that right, boys?"

Roark and Landis raised their glasses in a mock toast to their mentor and tormentor. They both looked like they'd rather be gassing puppies at the Humane Society.

"How'd he get in here?" Penroy asked.

"Our security isn't what it should be, I'm afraid," Scofield said.

"How much does he know?"

"Enough," Scofield said, winking at me as if we were old friends sharing an inside joke. "Things sort of fell into place when he saw Gitchell."

Scofield nodded toward me.

"For the benefit of the latecomers, John, why don't you fill them in on what we've been talking about?"

"I don't want to hear it," Penroy said. "So what if he knows everything. We've already decided what to do with him."

I looked around the room trying to find answers in the faces of the four men. Penroy and Scofield looked way. The two politicians remained at the bar, showing little interest in what was going on.

The silence lingered until Scofield propped his feet on the coffee table again.

"Brad, would mind running downstairs and getting Mr. Gitchell for me?"

Roark quickly obeyed, leaving with drink in hand.

"You made a terrible mistake coming here, Standard," Penroy said.

"Don't talk tough to me, you little weasel. Just shut the fuck up."

Penroy's eyes narrowed and he started to say something, but changed his mind.

Scofield grinned at me.

"Damn, I wish I had men like you around me, John - men with the intelligence to figure things out. With the courage to take the right action, call a spade a spade."

Penroy gave his boss a hurt look.

"I'm sorry, Mitch, but John's right: You are a weasel."

Roark returned with the sheepish and slightly pale Alfie Gitchell in tow. The old detective walked with a limp that said he was still feeling the effects of my knee in the crotch.

"Mr. Gitchell, I believe John has a pistol on him," Scofield said. "Please remove it."

Gitchell walked over to the couch, stood looking down at me, and pulled back his coat. The gun that I had thrown away earlier was back in Gitchell's shoulder holster.

"Let's have it," the detective said.

I pulled out the Beretta and handed it to him.

"Very good," Scofield said. "Now, Mitch, please take Mr. Gitchell and the boys downstairs for a while and tell the pilot that I'll be leaving soon for a short trip. But first, John and I need to have a word in private. Come back in about fifteen minutes."

"I don't think that's a good idea," Penroy said.

'I'm sure you don't, but humor me," Scofield said.

The dejected and angry Penroy left with Roark and Landis close behind.

Alone again, Scofield leaned forward so both elbows rested on his knees, the coffee cup clutched in both hands.

"Forgive me, but I can't say this in front of Landis and Roark. It's important that I keep them away from anything untidy. Plausible deniability, I think Richard Nixon called it."

"A little late for that."

"Perhaps, but it can't hurt. Anyway, I don't want them to know that you can't leave here alive."

The way Scofield delivered the threat made it sound like something from the florist.

"There's sufficient fuel in the helicopter to fly twenty miles out to sea and twenty miles back. You'll enjoy the trip. At least half of it."

Deep in my bowels, the eggs and bacon started doing battle with the coffee. I took a deep breath to force back the panic. Not leaving Scofield's house alive had always been in the back of my mind, but knowing how I would die made it more real. The more I thought about bobbing helplessly in the icy ocean waiting for the water to fill my lungs, the more reasons I found to stay alive. Recklessness had its limits.

"That would make five deaths, counting Amanda," I said. "That's a lot of bodies to indulge your fantasies about being a kingmaker."

"I know," Scofield said. "It's not something I planned or enjoyed. Hopefully, you'll be the last."

I focused all my attention on Scofield's chalky face. It was time to play another card, one given to me hours earlier by Benny Orlando. It was a high-risk play, but it wasn't like I had anything to lose.

"Before we leave," I said, "tell me why Amanda really killed herself, and don't give me any bullshit about being raped by your two poodles."

Scofield's face went another degree of white, the mask of composure shattered for a moment.

"I'm afraid I don't know what you mean."

"Sure you do."

I refused to take my eyes off him, telling myself that the next few minutes would be the difference between getting out alive and becoming crab bait.

Scofield ran his hand through his hair, buying time while the blood returned to his face.

"No, I don't," he said. "Amanda committed suicide because of what they did to her. She jumped off a freeway overpass exactly like you described it in that newspaper article."

"Not quite. She went off that overpass, all right, but I don't think she jumped. "

Scofield ran his tongue over his chapped lips and started cracking his knuckles. He refused to look at me, letting his eyes roam around the room instead.

"Why are you doing this?" he said to the ceiling. "You came here knowing

I couldn't let you leave. What part of this is worth your life? I don't get it."

"But you should. This is about commitments to the dead. About getting even for past wrongs. About good people who die too young for the wrong reasons."

"Jasmine Grant again," Scofield said.

"Her, and others."

"Others?"

Trying to explain two dead Hispanic girls or never having the chance to really fall in love with Jasmine Grant was a waste of the one thing I didn't have, time.

"You wouldn't understand, so let's get back to Amanda. You've concocted this charade about protecting her memory, about making Roark and Landis pay, about living her life through them. All along you've pretended this scheme was your way of extracting a pound of flesh from those bastards for what they did to your step-daughter. Their families made a deal with the devil, and you were the devil. That's what you'd like me to believe. But there's more to it than that, isn't there, Scofield?"

His eyes went dark and distant.

"You're absolutely right about the Grant woman," he said, his voice on the verge of stuttering. "I made the wrong decision. She didn't need to die. I know that now. Neither did Krychek for that matter. But that's hindsight. I had no way of knowing what was in that manuscript. I had no choice."

I refused to let up on him. Pressing the old man was the only chance I had.

"You ordered the murders of two people who didn't need to die. Fine, but let's get back to the real reason Amanda is dead."

I looked outside. A man walked across the grass toward the helicopter parked on the concrete pad, opened the aircraft's door and jumped into the pilot's seat. Time was running out.

I glanced quickly at the clock on the wall behind Scofield. I was watching the second hand, counting the seconds I had left, when I saw the faint shadow of someone standing back in the darkness of the hallway to the bedrooms. Someone else was in the house. A plan came together in my head. It might work.

Scofield didn't notice the shadow. Instead, he looked lost in his own thoughts.

"Penroy came to me with the whole idea," he said, his voice stronger, less defensive. "It was right after Roark and Landis attacked Amanda. He had this plan to use what they did to Amanda to control them, enslave them would probably be a better description. He was very persuasive. He said prosecuting them or suing them and their families didn't get me anything I didn't already have. 'Use them,' he said. 'Use them to win things you can't buy with your money.' I agreed. Penroy did everything. The rest is history."

"And then Amanda died," I said.

"Her suicide made me even more convinced that Penroy's plan was the right thing to do. Amanda was a beautiful girl. She would've grown into a beautiful woman. During the years before her death, I learned a great deal from her about how to enjoy life."

"And her mother?"

"I can tell you this because you're not going to live out the morning, but looking back on it, Amanda was the biggest reason I married Margaret. Amanda was the light that filled the dark hole in my life."

"Interesting metaphor, considering how many people you've killed."

The squeal of the helicopter's electric starter made me look toward the landing pad just as the rotors started to turn like the second hand on a huge clock. The faster they spun, the less time I had. If my plan was going to work, it had to start now.

"So, how long were you and Amanda lovers?"

Scofield stared down at the carpet, then out the window at the ocean. Tears welled up in his eyes.

"You really are amazing, John."

"Just answer the question," I said.

"Three years. They were the best and the worst years of my life. I took her on a business trip with me to Zurich when she was fifteen. Right before my eyes, she became a woman instead of a little girl. When she gave herself to me it was like the devil took my hand. I had waited so long for her to grow up, and when she did she was exactly like I wanted her to be. It was perfect."

"You like little girls, don't you, Proctor? You seduced Amanda because she had doll-like features and a cute little nursery mouth that said things that made you crazy. Was she all crinoline and patent leather? Sachets in her dresser and teddy bears on her bed? Did you tuck her in at night and maybe leave your hand under the covers a little too long? Did you accidentally walk in on her when she was taking a bath? Maybe you went into her room when she was gone. Feel things. Sniff things."

When Scofield looked away again, I quickly glanced at the shadow in the hallway. The slight movement of one arm, the glint of something shiny, and the shifting of weight from one foot to the other. The shadow had to be hearing everything being said.

"That's not romance," I said. "You're just a sick old man, who thinks seducing his stepdaughter doesn't make him a pervert. Well, it does! So does dressing up your secretary like Little Bo Peep."

Scofield's eyes narrowed.

"That's right," I said. "Tina told me all about it. She talks to everyone, I guess."

Scofield nodded in resignation that no one could be trusted anymore.

"But this goes beyond your personal problems." I said, "This is about murder. The murder of Amanda Bishop."

"No! What are you talking about? Amanda killed herself. It was because of what they did to her."

Scofield's voice was shrill, his arm pointing in the general direction of the front lawn.

"Then, why did she wait to kill herself? Why not do it right away? Time would've helped heal what happened that night, not made it worse. Why didn't anyone see it coming and do something to help her? Why did she use a typewriter to write her note when she wrote everything else in long hand? Because she didn't kill herself, that's why. You murdered her."

"How do you know about the note? It hasn't been out of our possession for twenty years. The only way you could've seen it is if Margaret . . . "

The air went out him, making his body shrink even more under the oversized bathrobe.

"Oh, I see now."

Outside, the screams of the powerful helicopter engine sent seagulls screeching into leaden skies. The sound beat against the windows like thunder. I saw Penroy and Gitchell standing on the grass, yelling at each other over the noise and gesturing toward the house.

"It's time, John," Scofield said, looking down on the lawn, his voice thick with sadness and disappointment. "Our conversation has been interesting and, may I say, painful. You're a very smart man, too smart perhaps. You know what comes next, don't you? You probably knew before you came here, which makes me admire you even more."

I had only a few moments left. I was cutting things close, but it could work. It had to work.

"There's one more thing. Something that never added up, never made sense," I said. "Her suicide was too convenient. What if Amanda had lived? She'd be nearly forty now, a grown woman fully capable of understanding what you did to her when she was fifteen and why Roark and Landis are where they are today. Do you think she would've let things get this far? I doubt it. You're a true visionary, Proctor. You looked twenty years into the future and saw what a pain in the ass Amanda would be, so you had her eliminated. Who did it. Did you do it yourself or did Penroy do it for you?"

Scofield sank farther back into the cushions, appearing to have aged ten years in the last hour.

"No one would be surprised if she killed herself after what happened to her," I said. "Only she wasn't despondent. Maybe she didn't care. Maybe she was too drunk to remember. Either way, no one who saw her after the attack described a girl on the verge of suicide."

Scofield started to speak, but I held up my hand. "Let me finish. You had Krychek and Grant killed because you thought the manuscript contained proof that *you* had Amanda killed. You didn't care if people knew that Roark and Landis had sex with her. That would have come out eventually anyway. Hell, you probably didn't care that much if people knew that you'd had sex with her. But, you couldn't let the true story of her death get out. Krychek might have pieced things together. You couldn't take that chance, so you had him killed."

"I had to get that manuscript to protect Margaret," Scofield said, his voice weak, his tone defensive. "She's very frail. If she ever found out, it would kill her."

"Fuck you, you sick son of a bitch." I said. "If you cared about your wife, you wouldn't have seduced and murdered her daughter."

Scofield rocked back and forth on the couch. His hands slapped wildly on his thighs, tears streaming, face distorted.

"No! No!" He was whimpering now. "You don't understand. She committed suicide. I would never have murdered her. I would never have hurt her. I loved her in a way neither you nor anyone else can understand. In a way Margaret could never understand. Amanda's death was the worst thing that every happened to me. I'd do anything to bring her back."

"Nice try, but it won't work," I said. "You killed her or you had her killed. She had to die or your plans for Roark and Landis would never work. You threw her off that overpass. You and you alone."

Outside on the lawn, Penroy and Gitchell were moving toward the front of the house. I knew they'd be too late. The fuse was lit. The figure emerged from the shadows of the hallway. I tensed, finally turned my gaze full on the figure standing directly behind Scofield, and waited for the explosion.

Margaret Scofield's scream filled the room. Her startled husband turned around long enough to see his wife and the barrel of the gun just before it went off point blank into his face. The last look Margaret Scofield got from her husband was a fleeting one of surprise and apology.

# Chapter 51

The first shot killed Proctor Scofield instantly. Blood splattered across the plate-glass window and quickly pooled around his head where he lay face up on the carpet.

I sat frozen in place, unsure what Margaret Scofield would do next. Still pointing the gun at the place where her husband had been sitting, she turned to look at me, her face cold and blank. Sleep-mussed hair hung across vacant eyes. The hand that held the gun quivered only slightly.

Without changing expressions, she pulled the trigger again. The second shot shattered one of the five-foot sections of the plate glass windows. Jagged pieces of glass hung for a moment in the casing before falling out onto the deck. The room filled suddenly with the deep thump of the helicopter rotors and the roar of the engines. Still staring at me, she kept pulling the trigger until the gun was empty and the hammer clicked uselessly against metal.

Margaret Scofield acted like she wanted to say something. Instead, she glanced at the gun as if she'd never seen it before, dropped it on the floor, then looked at her husband's body. I still hadn't moved, nor did I say anything to her; I doubted she would hear it. She was beyond my reach, shackled to the bottom of a well, the water rising.

Through the broken glass, I saw Penroy, Landis, and Roark standing on the lawn staring up at the house. Alfie Gitchell stood off to the side. While the others looked confused, Gitchell knew more than they did about guns and the noise they make. If anyone in the group knew someone had just died, it was the little detective.

I watched Gitchell move instinctively toward the house. The others hesitated, then looked at each other before slowly following him. When the men disappeared under the deck, I grabbed a vase from the coffee table and hurled it through the broken window to clear out the rest of the glass. An indifferent Margaret Scofield watched me pick up the empty gun at her feet and follow the vase through the empty window frame. I leapt the eight feet to the lawn below just as a panting Gitchell appeared behind me in the living room.

Expecting Gitchell to start firing, I ran low, ducking and weaving on rubber legs toward the gate in the stone wall. Sand blasted by the "whoomp, whoomp, whoomp" of the spinning helicopter blades stung my face and hands. I could see the pilot sitting at the controls flipping switches, oblivious to what had gone on in the house.

Veering toward the gate, I glanced back long enough to see Mitch Penroy on the deck next to Gitchell. The glimpse was short, but long enough to recognize the look of someone who'd gone from winner to loser in the time it takes to silence an old man's heart.

The gate opened easily, and I found myself back on the asphalt driveway. The back of my legs burned as I ran up the steep hill toward the highway. At the top of the grade I turned to see Alfie Gitchell emerge through the open gate and head up the hill after me. On short legs, Gitchell began to make his way up the hill clutching my Beretta in one hand

I watched for a moment, then ran farther up the driveway. Once out of sight around the curve, I stopped, and waited. The empty gun in my right hand made me feel a little less naked.

Seconds seemed like hours, but eventually Alfie Gitchell trudged around the curve, gasping for air. His head hung down, legs trembling, arms at his side. The Beretta pointed harmlessly at the ground. When he was six feet away, I stepped out of the brush and the detective stopped to look into the barrel of the gun that had killed Proctor Scofield.

"Lose the gun, Alfie," I said. "No sense dying for a dead master."

We stared at each other, then Gitchell handed over the Beretta, butt first. I took it and threw the empty gun in the bushes next to the driveway. It hit the ground at the same time Gitchell's knees hit the asphalt, his lungs sending out spasms of phlegm-filled protests.

I waited until the coughing stopped, then placed the muzzle of the Beretta in the middle of Gitchell's forehead and fought the urge to pull the trigger. The image of Jasmine Grant, naked and garroted on her own bed, wasn't helping. Neither was being framed for her murder.

"I'm not going to ask you to explain," I said, lowering the gun and taking a step back. The red circle on Gitchell's forehead slowly faded to match the purple of the rest of his face. "All I'd get is a lot of crap about low pay, shitty pensions, and no respect from the people you're sworn to serve. If that didn't work, then you could drag out those liberal judges, stupid legislators, and lazy voters."

Gitchell sat back on his haunches. He was too weak to talk, too wrong to argue. My disgust turned to pity.

"You know what'll happen now, don't you?" I said. "Your friends back at the house are going to cut you loose. You're going to end up with nothing. No money. No self-respect. You made a hell of a deal, Alfie. Was it worth it to betray your friends and yourself?"

Another graveyard cough wracked Gitchell's body. He leaned forward to put both hands on his knees until he caught his breath again.

"Let's cut the crap, John." Gitchell said between gasps. "Whatever truth you were looking for stops right here. What's left is between the two of us. You can shoot me, or I can go back and tell Penroy you got away. Then he'll take me up in that helicopter and throw my sorry ass in the ocean instead of yours."

I stood stone still, watching Alfie Gitchell get ready to beg for his life.

"There's one other option," Gitchell said, a pleading look distorting his face. "Take me with you. I'll tell everything. We'll blow these fuckers out of the water, myself included. You'll have one hell of a story. Maybe get your old job back."

I pointed the gun at Gitchell again just to watch him cringe.

"Please," Gitchell said.

He held up his hands and turned his face away.

I lowered the gun. Gitchell relaxed and stood up.

"You'll take me, then?"

"Did you kill Mather?"

"Yeah, but Penroy was with me. He drove the car, but I went inside, killed him, and came out with the manuscript. Penroy's just as guilty as I am. I can hang him. Just get me out of here."

"What about Jasmine Grant?"

"That was Scofield and Penroy. I knew about it, but they ran everything. Mather did the dirty work on her and on Krychek, but they ordered it. I can prove it, but you have to take me with you!"

I tried to piece together what the next few months would be like if I left with Gitchell. All I could see were reporters, lawyers, depositions, trials, and testimony. I would be back in the one place I didn't want to be. Knowing I had what I came for, I put my foot on Gitchell's chest.

"Sorry, Alfie. You chose your friends. They're down there at the house. You'd best be getting back to them."

I shoved as hard as I could, sending Gitchell rolling backwards down the driveway.

# Chapter 52

Scofield Industries made no attempt to hide the death of Proctor Scofield - only how he died. News accounts and the obituary in *The Oregonian* that appeared two days later mentioned natural causes. Rumors ranged from anorexia to obesity, but there was no mention of a bullet in the face. It was obvious that Scofield's money and power had been put to use dealing with local officials to keep the true cause of death a secret held closely by those who where there.

After reading the Portland papers, I called over to the weekly papers in Newport and Florence for copies of their stories on Scofield's death. It was all the same: The sudden demise of a visionary captain of industry who brought jobs and wealth to a region and a world.

At loose ends and not wanting to work, I decided to get out of the city with what little cash and credit limit I had. I drove north to Seattle, caught the ferry to Victoria, then up the east coast of Vancouver Island to Port Hardy. At a fishing resort that overlooked Queen Charlotte Strait, I rented a one-room cabin with a wood stove and a bed that squeaked. For two weeks, I fished for flounder, read trashy novels, and explored the local villages.

The idea of selling the story of how Scofield really died never left my mind. I considered writing it myself or taking the easy way out and contacting one of the print or television tabloids. Either way, it would mean money until the sale of the house I'd owned with Christine. There would be no more dingy apartment. No more Vanessa the Undresser. No more Benny Orlando and his calliope music. Maybe there would be enough money to buy my way back to respectability as the man who brought down the House of Scofield and exposed the Prince of Snakes for what he was.

Each time I made up my mind to take the money and run, I thought about Margaret Scofield. The memory of her face as she stood over her husband's body refused to fade. I wondered if I'd done the right thing by using her as the instrument of my revenge for the death of Jasmine Grant. Maybe Proctor Scofield didn't murder Amanda Bishop. Maybe he only seduced her. Maybe she did kill herself because of what Roark and Landis did. Either way, I had little choice but to taunt Scofield as Margaret moved farther out of the shadows behind the couch, the gun in her hand.

At night, I sat in the cabin listening to the water lap against the rocky beach, trying to put himself in Margaret Scofield's place. I tried to imagine what the rest of her life would be like, whether she would've been happier living out her years never knowing the truth about her husband and her daughter. What did she think of me and the way I chose to carry out her request not to forget Amanda? I'd walked into their house demanding answers and left ruins in my wake. She had every reason to hate me for what I'd done and the way I did it because there was no way for her to know why it had to be done.

In the end, I decided to keep the story to myself as long as Margaret Scofield was alive. Maybe after her death I'd tell what really happened. Maybe.

I remembered the conversation with Jasmine the day we had lunch -- the only day we had lunch. I told her that maybe fate would bring three people together and give me a chance to repay the debt I owed for two dead girls. Fate had held up its end and I had held up mine. The world was a much better place without Proctor Scofield. Knowing I had saved my own life and avenged the death of Jasmine Grant was all the comfort I needed.

I left Port Hardy with a stomach full of oysters and a Styrofoam cooler packed with frozen halibut fillets in dry ice. Instead of going back to Seattle, I took the ferry to Port Angeles, then followed Highway 101 around Olympic National Park to the Washington coast. I crossed into Oregon at Astoria and followed the Columbia River to Portland. It was early afternoon when I arrived and found an empty parking spot right in front of the apartment building. The good fortune added to my growing feeling that things were going to get better.

I picked up my mail before taking the elevator to the top floor. I unlocked the door to the apartment and immediately threw open the windows to make it easier for the mold to escape. After showering and digging clean clothes out of the dresser, I started going through the mail.

Crammed in among the two-weeks worth of catalogues and flyers was a letter from Tina Davenport. It was short and to the point. The death of Proctor Scofield had opened new opportunities for Mitch Penroy. He'd been named to oversee the relocation of Scofield Industries' holdings from Hong Kong to Singapore. She was going with him.

She wrote:

I know I let you down by telling Mr. Scofield you were coming, but don't hate me. I had to protect myself. I think things will be better for Mitch with a change of scenery, and with Mr. Scofield gone. If I'm wrong, I'll still have had the chance to live in another part of the world that's far, far away from this one.

I wasn't surprised. Tina would never stop wanting to be another man's unappreciated prize. Doing something with her life that didn't involve relying on others was never an option.

The last letter in the pile was a plain envelope with no return address. I tore it open. Inside was a check for fifteen thousand dollars made out to me and signed by Margaret Scofield.

I started it for a long time, thought about tearing it up and then slipped it into the top drawer of the desk. I needed the money, but not the memory of where it came from. I decided to deal with it later.

I cruised through the back issues of the newspapers that had piled up in front of my door, pausing over a story about Governor Martin Sloane announcing that his health had taken a turn for the better and he'd be seeking re-election after all. Five paragraphs down, the story speculated about the impact of the announcement on the possible candidacies of Brad Roark and Kingsley Landis. The story said both men were on vacation, and staff members refused to comment. I figured that after a respectful period of time, they'd issue separate news releases announcing they intended to "seek opportunities other than being governor of the great State of Oregon."

Around five, I walked down the back stairs to Benny Orlando's apartment. We drank Corona and lime served by a smiling Ivy, who seemed as much at home in Benny's apartment as one of his computers. We talked about Vancouver Island until coming up with the idea of cooking some of the halibut I'd brought back. We gave Ivy some money and sent her to the store, while Benny hauled an old Hibachi out of the basement storage room and up to the fire escape outside my kitchen window. Ivy returned with lettuce, tomatoes, bottled salad dressing, two bottles of chardonnay, and a bag of briquettes.

We sat on the fire escape drinking wine, talking, and waiting for the coals to get an even coating of gray ash before putting the fish on to cook. I did more listening than talking. Benny's stories of circus life were both interesting and funny. They contrasted with Ivy's poignant and chilling tales of life on the streets. For the first time in more than a year, I felt at ease with myself and at peace with my world and the people in it.

When Ivy went inside for more wine, Benny tried to get me to talk about what happened the night Proctor Scofield died. I brushed aside the questions, telling Benny that someday the whole story would come out.

"That's fine," Benny said, "but the real question is, are the demons gone?"

I had asked myself the same question a thousand times since that night at the coast. The answer eluded me until now.

"Yeah, Benny, they are."

"Good," he said. "Good."

The discussion turned back to Benny's days at the circus. He was half way through a story about performing with Ringling Bros. Barnum & Bailey in Madison Square Garden, when Ivy pointed to Vanessa's apartment.

"Who's that?" she asked.

"Her name is Valerie Michaels and she pays her rent on time," Benny said, interrupting his own story. "That's all I know."

"Maybe she'd like to join us," Ivy said. "There's plenty of food. I can run down and get some more wine."

They gazed at me as I looked across the air shaft just as Valerie, a.k.a. Vanessa, dropped her oversized gym bag on the couch and waved at us.

The narrow hallway outside my apartment was covered with a threadbare rug that came within a few inches of the scuffed moldings on each side. The music of tinny stereos crept through the cheap plywood doors to mix with the voices of equally cheap television sets. The smell of boiled cabbage and permanent-wave solution filled the air.

I followed the hallway around to the right until I was on the opposite side of the building. I knocked. She answered.

"Hi, Valerie. My name's John Standard. I live across the way. I was wondering if you'd like to have dinner tonight. I know a great place with fresh fish and outdoor seating."

She looked confused for a second, then turned to look out her window. Benny and Ivy waved at her from their perch on the fire escape.

"I'd love to," she said. The smile took years off her face. "Do I have to dress?"

"No," I said, doing my best to hide a wry smile. "It's a little late for that."

**The End.**

Printed in the United States
1187700002B/214